THE KILLING

"You got any money boy? Empty your pockets—now!"

"No way!" Terry replied. He knew with horrifying clarity what was coming and just exactly what he was going to do.

The man reached into his pocket, producing a pistol. "I'm going to kill you and just watch you bleed and holler."

Before the words had left his tongue, Terry was moving, running through the snow, darting and zig-zagging, heading for cover.

Ed followed him, and when they were two steps apart the man made his first move. But he was too anxious; it was the wrong move. He lunged at Terry, but Terry sidestepped him, then buried the blade of his knife in Ed's chest. He jerked it out and stabbed him again, this time in the belly. Ed was still standing when Terry pulled the knife out of his stomach. Ed slowly sank to his knees, blood staining his shirt and jacket. Pink froth formed in bubbles on his lips. Then he slowly collapsed on the snow, face down.

Terry walked up to him, but did not feel sick or numb or guilty. Ed had tried to rob him, beat him, and kill him. Terry had defended himself—that was that.

Terry was sixteen years old that day and he had just murdered a man. How did he feel? He wasn't sure. But somehow he knew the killing would not be his last . . .

WILLIAM W. JOHNSTONE
THE PREACHER SERIES

THE LAST OF THE OF THE DOG TEAM

William W. Johnstone

Pinnacle Books
Kensington Publishing Corp.

http://www.williamjohnstone.com

PINNACLE BOOKS are published by

Kensington Publishing Corp.
850 Third Avenue
New York, NY 10022

First Zebra Printing: March, 1981

First Pinnacle Printing: August, 1997
10   9   8   7   6   5   4

Printed in the United States of America

But what am I?
An infant crying in the night:
An infant crying for the light:
And with no language but a cry.

—Tennyson

Prologue

The white mercenary died hard, but he died bravely, enduring hours of torture. Not one scream passed his lips. Not when the skin was stripped from his arms and legs; not when he was castrated; not when his hands were cut off.

He suffered silently; alone. Asking no help from anyone. Just as he had lived for most of his life. Alone.

The Communist-backed black guerrillas left him under a tree on a flat plain. They hated the mercenary, what he stood for, fighting for a white minority government, but the guerrillas admired his bravery under torture.

The mercenary watched them go, waiting until the band of rebels had disappeared, then he croaked out his agony.

Above him, African vultures circled and waited.

Hard-driven Land Rovers kicked up dust, sliding to a halt in the veldt. "My God!" the Red Cross representative yelled. "This man's still alive."

The mercenary heard the voice, but could not reply. His bloody mouth held no tongue.

"Damn this war!" a medic cursed, virtually helpless to do anything for the dying mercenary.

The Red Cross representative looked down at the merc. "Dear God in Heaven," he sent a prayer to his Maker. "The man is trying to laugh!"

BOOK ONE

One

Terrance Samuel Kovak stalked the rabbit with all the patience of a born hunter—which he was. The boy imagined he was in Korea, stalking a North Korean soldier through the heavy snow. He held an M-1 in his hands instead of the seven-shot, clip-fed .22 caliber rifle. The North Korean soldier (the rabbit) jumped out of the snow a few yards in front of Terry and the boy let him run for a few seconds, following through the fixed iron sights. He took up slack on the trigger, let the rabbit run for a few more yards, then shot it, sending the animal tumbling and somersaulting, jerking out its life, staining the snow.

"Gotcha!" Terry whispered to the cold Georgia wind. The wind ruffled his blond hair and colored his Slavic features, tinting his cheeks a pale red. He picked up the rabbit, checked to make certain the animal was dead, then placed it in his homemade game bag. Five rabbits—enough. He would clean them when he got home and his mother would fry them up for supper, or maybe make a stew. If she fried them there would be biscuits and gravy and fried potatoes, too. Terry's stomach rumbled, reminding him he hadn't eaten since breakfast.

He looked up at the weak sun trying valiantly but unsuccessfully to shove its rays through the clouds. He guessed the time to be two-thirty. Best be heading home. It was a good five miles back to the house on the outskirts of Bishop, where his Poppa worked at the mill during the summer, spring, and early fall. Nobody hauled much timber during the winter—not in this part of Georgia—so Mr. Kovak took whatever jobs he could find during the slack time, with all the kids pitching in to help out in whatever way they could. Terry worked at many odd jobs, and hunted for food after school and on the weekends. During the winter months the Kovaks ate a lot of rabbit, squirrel, and sometimes venison. His Momma canned during the summer, out of their large garden, and they had a potato bin, so no one ever went hungry, but the menu didn't vary that much.

Terry's older brothers, Robert and Danny, were both in the service, in Korea. Robert was a retread, called back into the Marine Corps, and Danny was in the Army; both sent money home whenever they could. It wasn't much, but it helped. Their wives, Mavis and Vera, lived in the Kovak home, along with their two babies. It was a houseful, but it was, for the most part, a happy house, full of love and laughter and joking.

When one is poor, there are two choices: give up, or cope.

Mavis and Vera both worked as waitresses downtown, and they brought home (Vera did) packages of sugar and salt and things like that. Mother Kovak did fuss about it, saying it was sort of like stealing, but she never told Vera to quit it. Everything was put to some use around the Kovak home.

As Terry trudged along through the snow, conscious of the rifle slung over his shoulder and the game bag hanging by his side, bumping his hip with every step, he was suddenly saddened. The war in Korea was over, and he would never get there in time to shoot any Gooks, to fight with his brothers. But there would be another war, in another country—there always was—and Terry would join the Army and fight in that war.

Terry wanted to be a soldier. He imagined combat to be glamorous, adventurous; killing and dying to be clean and brave. The serving of one's country something to be proud of;

something the public would be only too glad to honor and never forget.

He'd been reading a lot lately—not school books, for he hated school—but adventure books, books about Soldiers of Fortune. Mercenaries. Men who fought for pay. To the boy, they sounded exciting. Maybe someday he'd do that. His mood lifted.

It was Saturday, and soon it would be Saturday night, and there would be Clarissa with the long brown hair and dark serious eyes and big boobs. He would take Clarissa to the movies and they would sit in the balcony. Thinking of Clarissa made him walk a little bit faster in the snow, and he stumbled when he hit a slick spot, coming to the gravel road that would take him to town. Terry flailed his arms, caught his balance, and looked around to see if anyone had seen him. He felt foolish.

Clarissa! She had allowed him to feel her breasts last Saturday night and it had almost driven him crazy, the way she kissed him and moaned and wiggled. He must have French-kissed her for an hour, fondling her breasts through her blouse, slip, and bra. He wanted to put his hand up her skirt, but just thinking about that scared him so badly he trembled. What was he supposed to do when he got his hand *Up There?* He couldn't screw her in the balcony of the Bishop Theater, although he was certain no one else would notice, there was so much moaning and groaning and panting and sighing among the other teenagers. Usually one or two guys would start bitching about the stone-aches, and having to go out-side to pick up the back end of a '40 Ford for relief. Terry had experienced the stone-aches, but damned if he'd ever pick up the back end of a car for relief.

But tonight, now, this was going to be something special. Vera had promised him he could use her car, a jazzy-looking '46 Ford. And Vera—who was only twenty herself—had winked at him and said to be careful in the back seat, don't get it all messy. Thinking of Vera made Terry feel a little messy— and guilty. Thinking of Vera made him feel all gooey inside. Thinking of his brother's wife got him a hard-on, too.

He knew Vera was stepping out on his brother, Danny, every now and then. Not regularly, just every now and then. But he supposed Danny was getting some Korean pussy, too, so that pretty well evened things up.

But not Robert's wife, Mavis. She was some kind of religious nut. She prayed all the time and wore clothes that were out of fashion and too big for her and took ice-cold baths two and three times a day. Mavis was weird!

But Vera, she knew what he was thinking when he looked at her. She had such a terrific body and such great-looking tits. Sometimes she got him to zip up her dress when she was going out and she would tell him off-color jokes and run her smooth, cool hand over his leg. Stuff like that got Terry so excited he felt he would blow up. Once, when everybody was asleep in the house, Vera had climbed the stairs to his room and stood in the doorway with the light behind her. She stood for a long time, looking at him in his bed, the light pushing through her thin gown, showing him everything she had. He could even see the outline of her Thing. Terry had pretended he was asleep, watching her through slitted eyes, but his heart was pounding so furiously he was certain she could hear it hammering. Finally, Vera had closed the door, leaving the boy with his palpitations, dry mouth, and rock-hard erection. But Terry knew what it was she wanted. He knew it was going to happen pretty soon, too— if Danny didn't come home.

Part of Terry wanted to see his brother; the other part wanted to see more of Vera.

Problem was, Terry had never been with a woman, sexually. He had seen pictures of men and women . . . doing it. There was a gas station across from the high school that sold dirty books and pictures from under the counter, but he had never done or seen or felt the real thing. But maybe tonight . . . ?

It was snowing again when he reached the huge old Kovak house. Two-and-a-half stories of run-down frame house, full of adults and kids and dreams and almost-but-not-quite poverty during the hard winter months. Terry cleaned and thoroughly bled the rabbits in the shed out back. He removed his boots on the porch of the house before entering the kitchen. He stored his rifle in the small room off the kitchen, carefully checking the weapon and removing the cartridges, putting them in a tin can.

"Momma," he said, kissing his mother on the cheek, all the while savoring the smells of home-baked bread. Saturday, Mother Kovak always baked bread to last the week. He put the cleaned rabbits in a dish.

"Fat rabbits, Terry," his mother smiled at him. "They'll cook good in a stew. We'll have them tomorrow for supper, maybe."

She covered the rabbits and put them in the ancient refrigerator.

Terry peeked into the living room and was surprised when he did not see his father listening to the huge old console radio. "Where's Poppa?"

"Working," she answered proudly. "Old Mr. Service down at the power plant twisted his ankle and your Poppa is taking his place for a week—started this morning. Forty-five dollars a week, and I can tell you the money will come in handily."

Terry laughed at her accent and speech. "Come in handy, Momma. That's the way to say it."

The old clock in the hall chimed its message. Terry poured a cup of coffee from the ever-present pot on the stove, sugared and creamed it, then sat down at the table, his back to the wall, warm and secure and comfortable in the kitchen, his Momma's favorite place in the house. He had walked fifteen or twenty miles this day, but he was young, and was not tired.

"Something special for supper, Momma?"

"A roast," she smiled, proud she was going to please her son and family. "With carrots and potatoes and onions and gravy."

"And biscuits, too, Momma?"

She left the sink to pat her son's cheek. "And biscuits, Terry. When you marry, Terry, be sure to marry a girl who can bake you biscuits." She clucked her tongue. "So many girls nowadays don't know from nothing about cooking. Popping open cans and stuff. It's not healthy."

Terry sat in silence, listening to his mother talk of this and that, busy all the while, peeling potatoes and scraping carrots. He sipped his coffee, thinking how much he loved his family—although Terry could never bring himself to say the words. He was not an emotional young man. He watched his mother fumble in the back of the pantry and bring out an old jar. She counted out a dollar and a half in dimes and nickels and put the change in front of her son.

"I know you got a little money, Terry, but it's Saturday and you got a date with Clarissa and your Poppa's working at the plant and he don't ever need to know I give you any money." She pushed the money toward him. "Take it, and have a good time at the movies."

It made Terry feel a little bit guilty, because he was thinking of Clarissa's boobs and body at just that moment. He pushed thoughts of her from him and smiled at his mother. "Thank you, Momma. We'll have a good time, I'm sure."

The front door slammed and the mood was broken. Terry was relieved it was. Clarissa slid smiling and wiggling back into his thoughts.

"It's me, Mother Kovak," Vera called from the stairs. "Let me change this stupid uniform and I'll be down to help you. I smell like fried potatoes and stale coffee." She was gone up the stairs in a run.

Clarissa slid out of Terry's thoughts and Vera slipped in. He thought of her changing clothes and hoped his sudden flush was not evident. Had he stood up at that moment, something else would have been most evident.

"A woman could smell worse," Mother Kovak muttered, not really unkindly. She knew her daughter-in-law was restless, getting more so as the months rolled by and Danny stayed away. "A man needs a woman and a woman needs a man," she mumbled under her breath.

"What's that, Momma?"

She flashed her son a broad smile. "Nothing, Terry-boy. I'm getting old, is all. Talking to myself. Pretty soon I'll be answering myself; then you got to worry."

"You're not getting old, Momma," Terry drained his coffee

cup and got up from the table. "You're the youngest one in this house."

She laughed, blushing at the unexpected compliment. "Get yourself out of here and out of my way. Get cleaned up. Save your sweet talk for your giggling girlfriend." But she was pleased. Terry could be so charming when he wanted to be.

But—she watched him leave the kitchen—there is a mean streak in him. He can be cruel when he wants to be. Poppa had said it the other night, lying in bed.

"The boy worries me, Momma. He's growing up too quick."

"Like you, Karl. Huh?"

"Not just like me. No. But some, yes."

"That don't make no sense, Karl."

"It does to me."

She had rolled over and gone to sleep. But he had tossed all night, Terry on his mind.

In the kitchen, Mother Kovak got down the flour, preparing to make her son's biscuits. He does have mean eyes, she thought, rolling up her sleeves.

Terry got clean underwear from his room and took his shower in the basement of the old house. A lukewarm shower, because the water heater was, as Poppa Kovak put it, "on the blink."

Terry shivered under the spray and thought: *On the blink, hell, it's just old. Like the house: old.*

Terry shaved, proud of his whiskers. Most young men his age had only peach fuzz. Terry's beard was stiff and heavy and blond.

He dressed in clean, peg-legged pants and a dark button-down-at-the-collar shirt, shoving his feet into polished Wellington boots that could use a half-soling. He combed his very blond hair. Not really handsome—his features were too Slavic—but he was a very nice-looking young man, just under six feet, with broad shoulders and heavily muscled arms. His mouth, when he frowned, turned into a cruel slit; and then transformed pleasantly when he smiled. Terry *could* be quite charming when he so desired.

But it was his eyes that both held attention and repelled. A cold, pale, almost icy blue. Even in the middle of his fifteenth year, his eyes could be warm and friendly, or menacingly dangerous. Slightly slanted, they were his most alarming feature.

Among his friends—and they were few—he was known to be very quick with his fists. While Terry did not seek out fights, he had never been known to back away from one.

An intelligent young man, always scoring high on IQ and aptitude tests, his grades at school were just slightly above average. School did not interest him. War interested him; guns interested him. Sports did not interest him, so he did not play sports. Because of his refusal to "go out" for sports, he was not well-liked by many in his peer group. By the boys. The girls, however—many of them—found Kovak to be . . . interesting. Odd, but interesting.

Robert and Danny had done well in high school, graduating with some honors. They had both played football and basketball. His older sister, Virginia, had been an outstanding student, and was now in college, studying to be a lawyer. His younger sister, Shirley, was also bright. At this point in her life, she wanted to be a doctor.

The Kovak family.

Upstairs, in the second level of the home, Terry knocked on Vera's door, waiting until she called out for him to come in. She sat at her dresser in a robe. Terry could see, all too plainly, that she wore nothing under it. His blood quickened, running hot.

She's your brother's wife, he cautioned. And you're just a kid. So what do you know about anything?

"Still gonna let me use the car, Vera?"

"I promised, didn't I?" she smiled at him. "Sure, you can use it. Just be careful, huh? It's not paid for."

She reached for her purse, digging in the bag, crossing her legs as she did so. The robe parted at mid-thigh, displaying a lovely view of skin. Terry almost groaned. Vera handed him the keys with a wink. "I also put in five gallons of gas for you. Have fun, Terry."

He knew he should leave, get out; but something in him told

him: stay. He met her level gaze. "What are you gonna do this evening?"

"Stay home and behave myself." Her eyes never left his.

He took the keys from her hand. For just a moment, her fingertips touched the back of his hand, lingering there two seconds longer than necessary. He looked around the room. They were alone. The baby, Daniel, was with his cousin, Edith, in the playroom Poppa Kovak had built downstairs, converting the old storage room. Shirley was looking after the kids, and she would never leave them alone. Not for a minute.

"What do you mean, you're going to behave yourself?" Terry asked, speaking around the sudden lump in his throat, very much aware of a thickening in his groin, the racing of his blood, and the pounding of his heart.

She winked at him again, soft brown hair framing her face. "Stay home, Terry-boy. Talk to Momma and Poppa Kovak." Her green eyes seemed larger than real. "Are you going to behave yourself?"

"I . . . hope not, Vera."

She smiled. "Got anything special planned?" Her eyes seemed to mock him.

"Well, you know," he shrugged, embarrassed.

She reached into her purse and removed a small square box. She looked at the box for a few seconds, then abruptly handed it to Terry. "These are prophylactics, Terry. Use them. I don't want you to knock the girl up."

Terry's face reddened and he was suddenly very flustered, the box of rubbers strangely alien in his palm. He didn't know what to say.

"You know how to use them, don't you?"

Terry nodded his head, afraid to speak. Somehow, he *knew* the moment he'd been longing for was here, but he didn't know how to handle it, what to do. He stood like a blond lump of stone, looking down at the box in his hand.

Downstairs, the front door banged, and Vera stood up, walking to the window, ever-so-slightly parting the curtains. Mother Kovak was talking with the next-door neighbor.

"Out of baking powder," she said.

The two of them, shopping bags swinging, trudged down the street toward the small family-owned grocery store. The women would shop and gossip for at least a half an hour. When Vera turned to Terry, her eyes were hot.

"You're Danny's wife," Terry managed to say, his words coming thick and strange on his tongue. And with absolutely no conviction. Vera moved on him, and Terry's arms circled the softness of her.

"Big deal," she spoke against his mouth, her hands busy against his groin. "I know he's gettin' some somewhere, so why not you and me?"

"We don't have time," Terry protested, suddenly afraid. Not physical fear, but fear he would be inadequate, disappointing to the woman.

"We have the time," Vera said. "It's your first time—I know that, so it won't take long."

His slacks were down around his ankles and he stepped out of them, wondering how it had happened so fast.

Dream-like, they were on the bed, and Terry didn't remember getting there. His shirt was off and all he had on were his socks and T-shirt. He felt kind of silly. Vera was putting one of those things on his jutting stiffness and then she was naked beside him. He touched a nipple, timidly, then cupped a round breast, feeling the nipple grow in his palm. Vera groaned, took his hand, and placed it between her legs. Right there! She was incredibly wet.

"You're . . . I'm . . . we're Catholic," Terry gasped, as she touched his rubber-covered hardness. "We're not supposed to use those things. Are we?"

Despite her heat, and her longing for a man, Vera chuckled. She moved under him, grasping him, guiding him. "Terry, don't be such a dumb-ass."

Suddenly, boyhood began the sexual march to manhood as he felt himself pulled into the vortex of life, sinking into the soul of woman, exploring all the heretofore subtle mysteries and much-talked-about and fantasized and masturbated dreams of "getting some."

"Oh, my God!" Terry said, pumping his hips frantically, toes digging in the sheets, seeking leverage.

"Not so fast, baby," Vera schooled him, calming his hunchings. "Do it slow. Measure it. There! Right there. Now . . . make it good for Vera."

Her hands and legs and arms were all over him, so it seemed to Terry, enveloping him. Her mouth kissed his face and lips and neck.

"God, you're all man," she said, pulling him closer to her, her breasts flattening on his chest. "Terry-boy, you are a stud! Now, do it harder and faster!" She was panting out her words, her phrases exciting the young man.

Holy shit! Terry thought. I'm really doing it.

"Slam it!" she panted in his ear. "Hard! All the way!" Her hips rose to meet his lunging and she shuddered beneath him, her hands tightening on his back.

"Did you come?" Terry asked. "Is it over?"

"Yes. No. Shut up."

Terry felt certain he was hurting her with the force of his thrusts, but if he was, she liked it. Her tongue licked him like a cat and her face was contorted. His eyes were wide with sexual excitement and fright. He wondered what would happen should his father suddenly come bursting into the room, hollering. He wondered how many bones could be broken from being thrown out the second-story window.

Time moved onward, and the young man began to experience a slight feeling of nausea. Then he was cold, and he began to shiver in anticipation of climax.

"Come, baby!" she urged him. "Come. We don't have much time."

He exploded against the confines of rubber. Boyhood crumbled, then shattered, rebuilding into young manhood as Terry jerked and hunched. It was over. Terry collapsed on the softness beneath him. His initiation into sex was over, and he could scarcely remember any part of it. He felt drained—which he was. He felt sick.

"Oh, God, I'm going to throw up!"

"No, you're not," Vera stroked his back, then pushed him off her. He lay panting on the bed.

He was still, watching her as she pulled the rubber from his slackness, got a towel from her dresser, and cleaned him. She looked out the window. Mother Kovak was nowhere in sight. Vera walked back to the bed, her breasts swinging with each step. Terry could not take his eyes from her pubic area. She had more hair than he would have imagined.

"Do you like looking at me, Terry?" She stood over him as he reached up to stroke her belly.

He nodded, not trusting himself to speak at this moment. He had read somewhere, or heard, that some men did not like to touch the woman after . . . after . . . what? What had they just done? Made love? Screwed? Fucked? Whatever it was called, Terry could not understand why men would not want to touch the woman.

Vera sat on the edge of the bed and put her hand on his hard stomach. "Don't say a word about this, Terry. Not ever. I know how boys like to talk. But you keep your mouth shut and there'll be other times. I'll show you things a woman can do for a man."

"I won't tell anyone. I promise."

She moved her hand to encircle his penis. "You're built up good, kid. You are what I said you are. A stud." Her hand left him and the moment was gone. Passion sated. Desire whipped into submission.

"Get up and get dressed and go wash yourself—get the smell of sex off you. Act natural at the supper table; don't give anything away."

Dressed, a bit shaky on his feet, Terry stood at the door for a moment. "Vera?"

"Yeah, kid?"

"Thank you." He said it shyly.

She laughed very softly, then grinned, shaking her head. "Terry, that's the first time a man ever said thank you."

"What does a man usually do?"

"They usually roll over and go to sleep. Now get out of here."

She clicked on the radio by the bed and Floyd Tillman sang the country hit: "Slippin' Around."

"Terry can't decide what to wear tonight," Mother Kovak said with a grin, as she spooned gravy over her meat and potatoes. "He's took two baths and changed clothes twice already." She smiled at her youngest son.

His father looked up from his plate to wink at Terry. "Got a hot one tonight, huh?"

"Poppa!" his wife protested, amused, but still feeling it necessary to object.

I had a real hot one about an hour ago, Poppa, Terry thought. "Yeah, Poppa, I got a date with Clarissa."

"That Baptist girl," Mother Kovak said, "from the ritzy part of town. Her father owns two big gas stations and I don't know what else. Property, I think. I'm surprised they let her go out with a Catholic boy." She chewed for a moment, then added: "If you marry her," and Terry choked on a piece of meat, "the children will have to be raised in the Church."

His father roared with laughter, banging his hard fist on the table. "Momma," he patted her hand, "the boy is just fifteen and a half; he's not thinking about marriage." He sobered and looked at his son. "Are you, Terry?"

"No, Poppa. What would I do with a wife?"

The family laughed, all except Mavis, and everyone helped themselves to more food. All except Mavis; she was on a diet—again. Just a small piece of meat, a little carrot for her. She ate in silence, seldom raising her eyes from the plate. She was on another of her religious kicks again. Hair pulled back tight in a bun, no make-up, gray, loose clothing to hide her figure: and she had a knock-out of a figure—better than Vera. Terry thought—and suspected that everyone else in the family did, too—that Mavis was a great big bore.

But Terry felt—sensed—something the others didn't about Mavis. When she looked at him, her eyes changed and she licked her lips. Now, he knew what that meant. He also suspected that

Mavis, unlike Vera, was not playing around, but, oh, would she like to.

She's a fraud, Terry thought. I bet she fingers herself and thinks about it.

Shirley excused herself from the table and went back into the playroom to look after the children. She loved children, and made her spending money baby-sitting around the neighborhood.

Mavis mumbled something about working at the church that evening and left the table. She gave Terry one quick, furtive glance, and did the same to Vera.

She suspects, Terry thought.

Poppa Kovak looked at her retreating back and shook his head in disgust. He had made the comment several times that his oldest son had really picked a ball of fire when he married Mavis. But this evening he said nothing, just shook his head and helped himself to more of everything on the table.

"You save room for apple pie," his wife gently scolded him. "You eat one more onion and you'll be up with gas all night."

The man grinned, patted her hand, rolled his eyes, and chewed, exaggerated groans rolling from his mouth. Under the table, Vera was rubbing her leg against Terry's. The boy knew if he stood up to be excused, a slight swelling just might be evident. He decided to linger over his huge chunk of apple pie, hoping his condition would go away.

"You be careful driving around tonight," his father cautioned him. "The weather man says more snow is on the way. The streets will be slick."

"We're just going to the movies, Poppa. Here in town." Vera had ceased her rubbing, and Terry was thankful for that.

"You still got to drive from here to her house and to the movies. Then you got to drive back to her house and get back here, so be careful." His father always got in the last word and then the subject was closed.

Vera and Mother Kovak laughed at the exchange and the Elder Kovak looked around. "Well, I'm right, ain't I?"

"Yes, Poppa," Terry smiled. His condition was gone and he stood up.

"Don't you be too late, now," his mother said, putting a large piece of pie on her husband's plate. He patted his flat stomach and grinned, smacking his lips.

"I promise I'll be in before dawn," Terry joked, waiting for the inevitable response from his father.

"When that hall clock strikes twelve," Poppa Kovak said, around a mouthful of pie, "you better be in bed, in this house, or you and me will have a talk about it at dawn, and you won't be sitting down all day. Now, then, we will all go to Mass in the morning. All of us. Awake and alert." He laughed at his own threat, but Terry knew it was very real. When Robert was eighteen years old, just before he joined the Marines during the Second World War, Poppa Kovak had thrashed him, and thrashed him good. When Robert had protested the whipping, trying to take the belt from his father, balling his fists and foolishly offering to fistfight his father, Poppa Kovak had shown his son how the Cow ate the Corn. He broke Robert's nose and knocked him out cold with a crashing right cross. The Elder Kovak was all muscle and gristle and bone—strong as a bear.

"Don't worry, Poppa," Terry moved around the table and put his hand on the man's shoulder. "I'll be in by two."

"Play games with your old man, huh? Twelve-thirty."

"One-thirty."

"Forget it. One o'clock at the most, and now the conversation about time is closed."

Vera winked at Terry, her eyes projecting a silent message as they sparkled with mischief: you'll be in something before one, Terry.

Terry returned the wink, kissed his mother's cheek, and went up the hall steps two at a time to get his coat. At her bedroom door, Mavis watched him, her breasts rising and falling as her breathing quickened.

Poppa Kovak met his son at the bottom of the steps. He held out two crumpled one dollar bills, then smoothed them with work-callused hands, tucking the money in Terry's jacket pocket.

"Thank you, Poppa." He had six dollars now. Enough to buy some whiskey.

"You're a man grown, Terry." His father was serious, no smile on his lips as he walked his son out the front door. They stood on the porch. "Grown at fifteen. I don't know how you did it, but you did. I've watched you these past months, and worried about you. You've come up faster than your brothers; there is a restlessness in you, a something I hope you can push back for a time. I mean nothing ugly when I say there is a . . . difference in you: a coldness in a hidden part of you that no one seems able to reach. I don't know how to say this. Your Momma don't believe it's there, but I do. You're moving too fast into manhood. I was like you, some, when I run off from home in the old country to join the AEF in France in '17. Stay a boy a little longer, Terry." He turned away, stepping back into the warmth of the house, leaving Terry to wonder what his father was talking about. A minute later, driving off down the snowy street, the young man was thinking about Clarissa, the conversation with his father forgotten.

Mr. and Mrs. Chambers had already left the house, to attend a party at the Country Club. Clarissa invited Terry in, asking if he'd like a Coke.

"Yeah," Terry said. Just looking at her brought the hotness to his blood. "That would be nice," He watched her swaying rump as she walked into the kitchen.

Coke in hand, she asked, "What's playing tonight, some old war movie?"

Terry took a drink from the bottle. "No, it's a Western. Duel in the Sun, something like that."

"I don't like Westerns, either," she made a face, pouting, her lips full and red.

"What do you want to do?"

"Well, I . . ." She looked down at the carpet, then moved to the window, glancing out. "It's snowing again. We can't go to the lake and park, listen to the radio. We might get stuck, then we would be in trouble.''

"Yeah, that's right." Terry shuffled his feet on the rich carpet, hooked his thumbs behind his belt buckle, and winced at the static electricity that jerked through him.

The boy and girl looked at each other, the unseen word moving between them, heavy as it touched them. "Whatever you want to do," she said.

"I bought a pint of Four Roses from this guy . . ." He let it drift off, leaving the final decision up to her.

"We could stay here, listen to the record player, maybe dance some."

"Got any popcorn?"

"Sure!"

Terry zipped up his jacket. "I'll go get that bottle."

The fireplace was blazing, logs popping and cracking, the Davis Sisters singing "I've Forgot More Than You'll Ever Know About Him," and Terry and Clarissa lay on the floor, under a thick blanket, the empty Four Roses bottle dead and pushed to one side. The young people were half looped.

Ten o'clock, and all was quite well, indeed, thank you. The dance at the Club was an hour old, and Clarissa's parents had called just after nine, concerned about her. She had told them she had decided not to go out, the weather was just too bad, and Terry had gone home. That's good. Going to bed, dear? Yes. Her parents were much relieved. They would be home about two. Have sweet dreams, dear.

Uh-huh.

The album changed on the Hi-Fi. Nat King Cole's "Too Young."

Terry French-kissed her, putting his hand under her sweater, snapping the bra hook free. He put his hand under the cups and touched her breasts.

She groaned. "I'm so hot, Terry," she said against his mouth and probing tongue.

"How hot?" he asked, a hopeful tone in his voice.

"Hot enough to do anything."

"Anything, Clarissa?"

"Do you love me, Terry?"

"Yes! I do."

"Do you really, really love me, Terry? With all your heart and soul?"

What is this? Terry thought: Hit Parade? "I love you, Clarissa. I really, really do." At that moment, he did. "More than anything else in the world, I do love you." It was not a lie . . . at the moment.

She kissed him, again and again, and Nat King Cole sang *Mona Lisa*. Suddenly, Clarissa was naked from the waist up, her young breasts exposed to Terry's mouth.

"You take your shirt off, too," she suggested, and he quickly obeyed. As an after-thought, and to save time when things got down right, he took his boots off. His big toe stuck through a hole in the right sock.

They kissed, deeper, searching; the young man felt sure his erection would rip his slacks. The room seemed to fill with the heady scent of musk, although Terry didn't really know what the odor was.

I hope it's not my feet, he thought.

She groaned. "Sex is not wrong when two people are in love, is it, Terry?"

"Oh, hell, no!" he gasped, almost sick at his stomach from desire.

"I don't want to have a baby, Terry. If we do . . . it, I'll have a baby."

"No, you won't! I brought some rub . . . I brought something." He began unzipping her plaid skirt and she sighed, grabbing his hand for a moment. She released his hand with a faint sigh of resignation and let him have his way. With her head on the pillow, eyes very wide and dark, she watched him. After much fumbling, he managed to slip off her skirt, then, with more fumbling, her half slip.

Jesus! Terry thought. *How many clothes do girls wear?*

She groped at his belt buckle, at his fly, and the boy was

stripped down to his boxer shorts, which did very little to hide his erection.

Putting her hands on his arms, she pulled him down to her, on the blanket. Young hands, soft and calloused, moved over strange flesh, exploring, feeling, touching heretofore forbidden places. Then, almost too suddenly for her, and almost too late for him, they were naked, underclothes in a heap on the floor.

She grabbed his penis as one might grab the handle of a hoe. "Ohh, it's so big!"

"Yeah, I guess," Terry said, embarrassed. He didn't know quite how to say it, but with her holding on to him like she was about to chop cotton, he couldn't reach his rubbers in his slacks. "Uh, Clarissa, would you . . . ah . . . mind . . . ah . . . you know, turning loose for a minute?"

"Ohh, I don't ever want to turn loose." She began pumping him.

"Oh, God! Don't do that, Clarissa!"

"Don't you like it?"

"Yes! But . . . ah . . . let me reach my pants—please?"

Terry, free for a moment, almost ripped his slacks hunting for the package of prophylactics. He broke the first one trying to put it on. He recalled that Vera had put the one on him hours before. Hell, he couldn't ask Clarissa to do *that!* He finally managed to get the sheath on and glanced over at the girl, to see if she had observed his clumsiness.

She had. Lying on her back, legs spread, eyes open, she giggled at him.

Damn!

He crawled between her legs and almost fell on her, catching himself with one hand.

He parted her and pushed, harder as something blocked his penetration. He was almost in a panic, thinking: *Now what?* He pushed; it was like trying to shove his pecker through a wet wall.

"What's wrong?" he asked, desperation in his voice.

"It's my maidenhead," she said from beneath him, beads of sweat clinging to her face. "You've got to break it! Oh,

Terry, don't you know: I'm a virgin. Do something, Terry, I can't stand this.''

She was almost in tears; he was almost in tears. "It's gonna hurt you," he said. He didn't think a cherry would be this tough.

She grabbed him with both hands, hunched her hips upward, and moaned as the tissue-thin maidenhead broke and he slid into her. She brought her mouth to his, kissed him, and let womanhood take the initiative. "Do it to me, Terry. Love me like I love you."

The act did not last long. He was moving, she was moaning and whimpering, and neither of them wanted it to end. She whined, shuddered, and he watched her eyelids flutter. She said something, but Terry couldn't understand the words. He slammed into her for the final time, his juices boiling over, exploding. The two teenagers lay panting in each other's arms, the flames from the fire highlighting the sheen of sweat on their bodies.

And Nat King Cole sang: *"Unforgettable."*

It was a cold morning; Terry lay snuggled under the covers in his room, the patch quilt pulled up to his eyes. *Did last night really happen?* he questioned silently. *Did yesterday really happen? Vera and Clarissa. I did it to both of them. Incredible.*

He knew the house was empty; he had heard everyone leave an hour before. He would have to make late Mass or really be in trouble with his father: trouble was, church bored him. But he had to go. Reluctantly, he got out of bed and stood shivering in the cold room at the very top of the old house, so far away from the coal-burning furnace in the basement that very little heat ever reached it. He looked out the window and was glad to see it had stopped snowing. It was unusual for it to snow this much before Christmas; everyone said so, especially all the old-timers.

In the bathroom, he showered, and stood for a moment before deciding he could get by without shaving. He needed a new blade for his safety razor, and he had never mastered the art of shaving with a straight razor, as did his father.

One thing Terry knew for certain: if he ever got away from home, he would not set foot in a church unless he felt he wanted to talk to God. What was the word for those people who went to church when they really didn't want to? Hypocrites. Well, he'd be damned if he'd play the part of one of them.

As he stood looking at his steamy reflection in the mirror, he laughed. "Yeah," he spoke to his likeness, "you'll probably be damned, all right." Somehow, he felt his words were true, and that knowledge frightened him.

In his room, dressing, he clicked on the radio. The song playing seemed to hold a prophecy, and a cold sensation swept over him, a chill he knew had nothing to do with the weather. It was a country song: *I'll Sail My Ship Alone.*

Two

February, 1954

It had been a hard, cold winter in North Georgia, and the old-timers said this snow would probably be the last big one of the year. Terry hoped so; he was tired of eating fried rabbit, baked rabbit, rabbit stew—with a squirrel thrown in every now and then. About one more month and Poppa would go back to work at the mill; things would ease up some.

Poppa had not worked in more than a month, and Momma said money was tight as Dick's Hat Band. Trudging through the snow, Terry wondered where that expression got started. He was just this day sixteen years old, and trying to keep three women happy.

Mavis had moved on him last month, telling him she knew all about Vera and him, and if Terry didn't do it to her, too, she'd tell. She'd tell Terry's father and mother, his brothers, and the priest.

Terry wondered how any one sixteen-year-old could get himself in so much trouble.

Not that Mavis wasn't something when she did it. She was a scratcher and a biter; wild in bed. But Terry wished his brothers would come home and take care of their own business. Everytime he turned around, somebody, it seemed, was expecting him to get it up and go to bed.

"Hell, I'm just a kid," he said.

He had passed Sergeant Tate earlier that morning: the new Sergeant at the National Guard Armory. Tate seemed like a nice guy; he'd have to get down there and talk with him some time.

"One more rabbit," Terry said to the white-covered earth and the cold wind that whistled around his face, "then I'll go home." He shifted his rifle from left hand to right, looked up from the ground, and found himself face to face with Ed Farago.

Crazy Ed Farago. That's what people called him. But still others said he wasn't so crazy—just mean as hell. Ed bootlegged and stole and gambled and did everything else that was dirty and mean, had been to prison twice. It was said Ed had killed two men but had never been convicted for it: the bodies were never found. Whispers said he'd raped more than once.

"Hello, boy," Ed grinned, exposing a mouthful of stubbed teeth, stained with tobacco. "I bet you got lots of big rabbits in that there bag. Right?"

I should be afraid, Terry thought. *But I'm not. Odd.* He backed up three steps, not out of fear, but to give himself some running room, or fighting room, if it came to that. *Or shooting room*—the thought jumped into his brain. The thought of having to shoot Ed did not really bother Terry, and *that* scared him. His thumb automatically slid to the safety on the .22 rifle and he thumbed it to the "Fire" position. Ed did not notice.

"Yeah, Ed. I got some pretty good-sized rabbits in here." *And I plan on keeping them in there,* he thought.

"I sure would like to have me some big fat rabbits for supper," Ed grinned. "They go good with fried potatoes. Why don't you jist gimmie them rabbits, boy?"

Terry was calm, cold in his thinking; he spoke his words carefully. "Hunt your own rabbits, Ed."

"Don't you sass me, boy!" Ed's eyes flattened, turning mean. "I'll slap you clear outta the county." His grin changed into a nasty smile. "You the one goin' with that Chambers gal, ain't you?'' He smacked his thick lips. ''That there is a prime little piece of ass. I'd like to have me a taste of that, myself. That there's eatin' pussy. You gittin' in her drawers, boy?''

''I don't think that's any of your business, Ed.'' Terry felt the coldness within him become tinted with fire and he did not understand what was happening in him. ''Now, why don't you just go on and leave me alone?''

''Naw, not yet. You got any money, boy? Some change, maybe. I'm busted and it's Saturday night soon—like to go out jukin' come dark, buy some 'shine, maybe. Gimmie them rabbits and empty yore pockets. Do it right now, boy!''

''No way, Ed,'' Terry stood his ground. He knew, with a horrifying clarity, what was coming, and just exactly what he was going to do. The image was clear in his young mind.

Ed looked around. There had been a hunter in these woods about an hour ago. That smart ass Paratrooper Sergeant from the Armory. The woods were silent. Ed turned back to Terry.

''You goddamn little snot-nosed punk! I'll whup yore ass like hit's never been whupped. Then I'll shove that pea-shooter up hit.''

''Come on, Ed,'' Terry said.

Ed took a step toward the young man, faking him out by suddenly shifting to the right, then lunged at him, backhanding him, knocking him to the snow.

Terry was faster than the bigger, older man, rolling to his feet and away before Ed could kick him, the boot just missing his head. Terry held onto his rifle, holding it at the ready.

Ed stumbled in the snow, off balance from his kick, and fell heavily to his knees. He rose slowly to his feet, reaching into his jacket pocket, producing a pistol. ''I'm gonna hammer on you, punk. Then I'm gonna kill you jist to watch you bleed and holler.''

Before the sound of Ed's words had left his tongue, Terry was moving, running through the snow, darting and zig-zagging, heading for cover.

Ed raised the pistol and cracked off a shot, the slug going wide by several yards, kicking up snow to Terry's left. The boy spun, dropped to one knee, and leveled the rifle just as Ed turned. The .22 slug hit the man in the upper arm, penetrating jacket and muscle, bringing a howl of pain and anger.

The boy and the man were less than seventy-five yards apart, Terry behind a stump, Ed behind a small tree.

"You shot me, you little son of a bitch!" Ed yelled across the snow. "Now you're in trouble for sure."

Terry was inwardly shaking from fear and excitement, but his voice was calm. "Come and get me, Ed."

Ed began blasting away at Terry, with the young man returning the fire, neither of them picking their shots, and no one was hurt during the exchange. Ed was firing a short-barreled .32; at seventy-five yards, he would have been lucky to hit anything.

There was a period of silence, almost audible after the gunfire.

"Your time has come, Punk!" Ed shouted across the distance, the words dull as they spanned the whiteness. "I'm gonna get you."

"So come and get me," Terry returned the shout.

They both had cartridges left, but Ed was confident he could handle the boy. "You'd better run, boy," Ed stood up, brazenly, his hands empty.

"That'll be the day," Terry stood up. Like Ed, his hands were empty.

Then, cold sunlight twinkled on polished steel: Ed held a long-bladed hunting knife in his right hand. The light twinkled again, and Terry's knife was in his hand. There was fear in the young man, but it was mixed with anger, and something else he could not define. The two moved toward each other, eyes locked, taking short, shuffling steps in the snow.

"One more for old Ed," the man said, walking toward the boy. Ed was smiling in anticipation of the kill, knife held sharp side up for a gut-cut. Ed liked to kill, liked the look of fear on men's faces as they went down.

They were two steps apart when Ed made his move. But he was too anxious; it was the wrong move. He lunged at Terry. Terry sidestepped him, then buried the blade of his knife in Ed's chest. He jerked it out and stabbed him again, in the belly.

Ed was still standing, his knife in the snow where he'd dropped it, when Terry pulled his knife out of the man's stomach. Ed slowly sank to his knees, blood staining his shirt and jacket. Pink froth formed in bubbles on his lips.

Ed screamed just once, spraying the snow with pink and red. "Goddamn you, Kovak! You little . . ." Then he collapsed on the snow, face down, to cough his way into his last adventure. Terry's first cut had nicked the heart of Ed Farago.

Terry walked up to the man, calmly wiping his knife clean as he went. He started to walk away, then remembered Sergeant Tate. Tate had seen him. More than that, almost every boy in this part of Georgia had a rifle, but almost no boy had a pistol. He stood for a moment, then reluctantly made up his mind. He rolled Ed over on his back. The man's eyes were open and he was still alive, but just barely.

Terry went through Ed's pockets, finding three more cartridges for the .32. He loaded the pistol, took careful aim, and shot Ed in the arm, in the exact spot his .22 bullet had hit. He then shot him in the spots where he had cut Ed. He put the pistol in his pocket and walked away. He knew where there was a deep, so far as he knew almost bottomless, hole in the ground on the way back to the road. He would put the pistol there. Terry had once dropped a large stone down that hole. He had never heard it strike the bottom.

He returned to the stump, retrieved his game bag, and began the long trek home. He did not feel sick—although that would come in a matter of minutes—and he did not feel numb or guilty. Ed had tried to rob him, tried to beat him, tried to stab him. Terry had defended himself. That was that.

Sixteen years old that day.

"Quite a birthday you bought yourself, Terry-boy," he said aloud, walking through the Georgia snow. The sole of one of his hunting boots had come loose, and his foot was wet and cold. The sole flapped as he walked. He dropped the pistol down the deep hole and kept on walking. Just before he came to the gravel road that would lead him to town, the young man knelt by a bush and vomited, trembling and shaking all over.

He did not want to go home and clean the rabbits. He wanted

to throw them away, but he knew his family needed the food, and he would have to pretend that nothing unusual had happened this day.

He had just killed a man. How did he feel? Terry wasn't sure. It wasn't like in the movies. When Johnny Mack Brown killed someone, it was a clean, quiet death. Nothing like what happened today. Or did Johnny ever kill anyone in his movies? Terry couldn't remember. Did Gene or Roy or Hopalong? He wasn't sure.

Neither was he sure just exactly how he felt about what had happened that day.

Sergeant Tate watched until he was sure Terry would not return to the site of the killing. He was impressed by what he had seen that afternoon and knew he must, after covering Terry's clumsy attempt at disguising his act of violence, contact his Colonel. Not the Colonel in charge of recruiting, but Tate's real boss: Colonel Perret, head of the Army's ultra-secret killing arm. The Dog Teams. Tate thought he had a fine candidate for those teams.

Kovak. That's what he'd heard the dead man call the kid. Kovak.

The sky began to spit snow, slowly at first, then abruptly disgorging huge, wet flakes. The snow would hide any tracks Tate made—if he moved quickly. He walked to Farago's body and pulled an Army issue .45 automatic from under his field jacket. He shot Ed three times in the chest with the pistol, then shot him in the arm, destroying what might have been left of Terry's .22 slug—he hoped. He shot Ed in the face with the .45, then twice in the chest with his own rifle.

Stab wounds, pistol wounds, rifle wounds. If the sheriff had any sense at all, he would figure three people had attacked Ed. Tate stepped back to review his work. It would have to do; he could not afford to linger in this area.

Yeah, he smiled, the Dog Teams. He believed Kovak would fit right in.

Tate walked, in a very roundabout way, back to his Jeep. He was smiling. The next couple of days should be very interesting in Flagler County, Georgia.

* * *

"You're not eating, Terry," his mother scolded him at the supper table. She softened her voice, adding, "What's the matter, son, you coming down with something?"

Terry wanted to scream out: *Goddamnit, I just killed a man! What's worse, I don't really feel anything. I don't think I'm normal.*

Instead, he smiled and shook his head. "No, Momma, just not hungry, that's all."

"Going out tonight, Terry?" his father asked around a mouthful of fried rabbit. His father never seemed to tire of the game Terry brought home.

Terry looked at his father, chewing, gulping, and smacking his lips, as if he were eating prime steak. "No, I'm staying in tonight. Clarissa's gone to Atlanta with her dad." Beside him, Vera rubbed his leg under the table with her stockinged foot.

Mavis shot hot looks at both of them.

Terry had told Vera about Mavis. She had laughed.

"Kid, you are something else. Screwing both your brother's wives, plus your teenaged girlfriend. God!"

"I really don't think it's all that funny, Vera. I don't feel right about this. What am I gonna do?"

She laughed. "Just keep right on humping us all, Terry-boy. Enjoy it while you can."

"Well, that's good," his mother said. "You need some rest, Terry. You're looking peaked. You and Vera can listen to the radio tonight while your poppa and me go visiting the Bensons. They invited us to play Monopoly. I know Mavis has got to go to work at the church. I don't know what Father Meranus would do without you, Mavis. You're such a help to him."

Vera kicked him under the table, but Terry refused to meet the gaze he knew was on him. Vera thought Mavis was in love with the priest. Terry thought that was stupid.

"He's a priest, Vera!"

"He wouldn't be the first one to stick it to a good-looking woman."

"Vera, you're going to go to Hell talking like that."

She laughed at him, fondling him.

"Be good to have some money in my hand," Karl Kovak said, looking up from his rabbit, "even if it is only play money." He touched Terry's hand. "You're a good son, Terry. A fine hunter. You've done us all proud this winter. We couldn't have made it without you."

Maybe I can join the Mafia, Terry mused. *Iceman Kovak. Gun for hire.*

Terry started to thank his father for the compliment. Before he could get the words out of his mouth, the outside air was ripped apart by the sounds of half a dozen sirens from fast-moving police cars. The highway was right behind the Kovak home. Terry's butt and the seat of his chair parted company by a good six inches. His father spilled his coffee, and the two babies, seated in high-chairs, began crying.

They found the pistol! Terry thought. Oh, shit!

"Good Lord in Heaven!" Mother Kovak said. "You don't suppose the war's started again, do you?"

"I hope so," Terry said, regaining some of his lost composure, "I'd like to go to Korea." *And if that isn't possible,* he thought, *I'll settle for the Moon.*

The family gathered outside, on the porch, while Shirley stayed with the babies, trying to calm them. Up and down the street, families were gathering on porches and sidewalks.

"Hey, there, Pearson!" Mr. Kovak yelled across the street to his neighbor. "What's all the fuss about?" It was six o'clock, full dark, spitting snow.

"It's Ed Farago," the neighbor called. "He's been murdered out in the Piney Woods area. Shot a dozen times and then stabbed. It's just terrible."

A dozen times! Terry silently mulled that over in his head. *What the hell . . . ?*

Pearson walked across the street to join the Kovak men. The women stayed on the porch. "It's bad," the man said. "A maniac is on the loose. Mrs. Webb's son, Don, he's a cop, you know, said Ed was shot in the face. Almost blew his head off. His left arm was almost shot off, and he had been shot with a high-powered rifle, too. All those stab wounds." The man shuddered. "The sheriff thinks a gang of big-city hoodlums is on a rampage in the County."

This was just about more than Terry could take. He got himself under control, knowing he had to be calm. But he didn't understand what had happened. He had shot Ed once, in the arm, stabbed him twice, then left him. Who would come along and shoot a dead man? And why? He left his father talking with Pearson and walked back to the porch to join his mother and Vera. Mavis had not come out of the house. Terry told them what had happened.

"Awful," Mother Kovak said, shaking her head. "Just terrible. But Ed ran with rough people. He was a hoodlum, a no-good. Everyone knew that."

"Yeah," Vera injected, "maybe he double-crossed some of his pals and they did him in." She looked at Terry. "Don't you usually hunt up in the Piney Woods?"

Terry forced himself to meet her gaze, his mind working hard and fast. Tate had seen him: he couldn't lie about being up there. "Yeah, I do—did. But I couldn't scare up any rabbits, so I went east, along the ridges."

So there it was. He would have to stick to that if he was questioned.

"Well," Mother Kovak said, "all this talk won't bring Ed back. If anyone wants him back." She crossed herself for saying and thinking such a thing. "I'm getting cold and we have dishes to do." She went back into the house.

Vera put her arm around Terry's waist, her touch brazen in the darkness of winter. "Shirley's taking the kids to her little friend's house next door and Mavis will be at the church tonight. We'll have the house to ourselves for two or three hours. Think we can find something to do, Terry-boy?"

"Yeah, Vera," Terry felt a cold/hot/strange rush of desire flood his groin. "Yeah, I think we can find something to do tonight."

She winked at him on the dark porch. "You being careful with Clarissa?"

He did not reply and she giggled softly. "Sixteen years old and gettin' it from at least three women. I'd really like to see

your track record when you're thirty, Terry. Come on,'' she
tugged at his arm. "It's your birthday and Momma Kovak
baked you a cake. I've got a little present for you, too—later.''

"Oh, baby!" Vera kissed his mouth, his neck, and his face.
"Stay with it.''

Terry tightened his arms around her. The memory of that
bloody afternoon was, for the moment, forgotten, lost in the
sweetness of woman and the heat of sex.

Vera shuddered under him. "That's number three for me,''
she panted.

A car drove down the street, tires crunching on the half-
frozen snow. Upstairs, in the second level of the old home,
with Danny's picture turned face down on the dresser, the
young man and his brother's wife would not have noticed had
a tank rumbled past.

Unfaithfulness, passion, and youth exploded on the old bed.
The springs ceased their tortured groaning as hot flesh began
to cool and hearts and lungs slowed.

On the street below the lovers, Sergeant Tate drove by once
more, slowly, gazing up at the run-down house. The Kovak
kid fascinated the military mind of the man. He had talked with
Colonel Perret and the Colonel had said to check him out. The
boy might have a good—if not long—future with the Dog
Teams.

"Damn!" the Sergeant swore softly. "The boy's a natural
killer. I've never seen any better, any calmer.''

Tate drove down the street, toward his rooming house. He
didn't want to do a thing out of the ordinary; the cops were
keyed up and tense over the killing.

With breasts pushing against his naked chest, Terry kissed
his brother's wife, gently, and she responded.

"What's going to happen when Danny comes back home?''
he asked.

"We act like nothing happened," Vera murmured, mouth
on his. "You're my kid brother-in-law, that's all.''

Terry chuckled as she moaned, his hands moving on her body.

"You're a real bastard, Terry Kovak." Vera laughed in his mouth. "You're going to make out okay, I think. But I worry about you, for some reason. You're . . . different somehow."

"What do you mean?"

"I don't know, Terry. It's not something I can put into words. You're not yet a man—but then, you are, too. There is a part of you that I can't touch. I don't know if anyone will ever be able to."

The young man lay beside the woman, knowing what she said was true, and wondering why that knowledge suddenly frightened him.

"You don't love me," Clarissa sobbed accusingly. "Not really, you don't. You just go with me for sex, that's all. Why don't you admit it, Terry? You don't love me at all."

"I don't know whether I love you or not," Terry tried to be honest with her. He may have been a sixteen-year-old rogue, but he was an honest scamp—most of the time. "You want to stop seeing me?"

It was the first week in April, 1954, and the teenagers were parked by the lake, several miles out of town. For the first time since that snowy winter's night in front of her parents' fireplace with Nat King Cole crooning in the background, Terry could not get Clarissa's panties off. He was almost desperate.

Robert and Danny had returned home, and Vera and Mavis had cut him off cold.

"My darling, darling Terry," Mavis had said. "I fear our little interlude must end. You're such a dear boy, and you've been so good for Mavis."

"Pussy factory's closed," Vera was much more blunt.

"Jesus!" was all Terry could say.

Ed Farago's case had been, for all practical purposes, closed. No one was charged in the murder. Really, no one had tried very hard to find his killer or killers. The opinion was: one hood bumped off another hood. Good riddance.

The lake rippled under the moonlight, soft in early spring, and a bird called out in the night. The pint of whiskey Terry had brought was gone, Clarissa was half drunk and on a crying jag, and Terry had a hard-on.

"You want to stop seeing me?" he repeated.

"No," she said, her reply so softly spoken Terry had to strain to catch the word. "Because I love you."

Terry slid out from under the steering wheel of Vera's car and over to Clarissa's side. He put his arm around her. "You want me to tell you I love you—whether I mean it or not?"

"Yes. Because you do love me. I know you do. You just don't realize it yet, that's all."

Terry pondered this peculiar logic for a moment. "All right, I love you, then."

The lie was foreign to his tongue, and he did not like the way it tasted.

"We'll be happy together, Terry." Her mood lifted and she was happy. She began unbuttoning her blouse. "We'll be happy, you'll see." She stopped at the third button. "Won't we, Terry? Be happy, I mean."

His patience was wearing thin. "If you say, so, Clarissa."

She kissed him while he shoved his hand inside her blouse to cup a breast. "Did you bring a blanket?" she asked.

"Two of them. In the trunk."

"Get them, and we'll make sweet love under the stars. Leave the radio on."

Later, tangled in each other's arms, Terry asked, "Clarissa, what did you mean when you said we'll be happy together?"

She snuggled closer. "When we get married, silly."

"That's what I thought you meant," he said, dryly.

"Mom and Dad like you, Terry. They really, really do. They say you're a good, hard-working young man. Daddy's going to offer you a job at one of his stations this summer."

Wonderful! The young man gazed at the Big Dipper.

"Did you hear me?"

"Yeah, I heard you." *That's just great,* he thought. *Working for the father, screwing the daughter.* He wondered if the mother put out, too?

And the radio played The Bunny Hop.

After school, an Army Sergeant met Terry just off the campus. Tate. Master Sergeant Tate. He shook hands with Terry. "I'm from the Armory. I was wondering if you'd like to come on down and look around the place. I heard you were interested in making the Army a career."

"Yes, sir," Terry said, excitement welling up. "That's what I'd like to do."

Tate jerked his thumb toward a Jeep. "Hop in, then," he smiled, adding, "Don't call a Sergeant 'sir.' We're non-commissioned officers."

"Yes, sir. I mean . . . Sergeant."

"There you go," Tate said with a grin.

A Colonel Perret was waiting for them in the Sergeant's office. He nodded to Tate, smiled at Terry. He seemed a nice-enough guy, in a rough-looking way. His face was tanned and his eyes were hard and flat, smoke-colored.

"Coffee, Terry?" he asked. "Maybe a Coke?"

"Coffee would be fine, sir."

The Colonel poured him a cup while Terry looked around the office. Tate had disappeared.

"First time I've ever been in here," Terry said. "The other Sergeant—I guess the one Sergeant Tate replaced—kept running me out whenever I'd look around."

"Ward was a shit-head," Perret acknowledged. "A Leg to boot."

"I beg your pardon?" Terry said. "What's a Leg?"

"SFC Ward was straight-leg infantry. A non-jumper." He smiled at Terry's look of puzzlement. "Ward was not a Paratrooper like Tate and me."

"Oh, I see," Terry sipped his coffee. "Well, I'll still be in school when I'm seventeen—old enough to join up—and I'm sure going to sign up."

"I'll tell you what, Terry," Colonel Perret smiled. He was anxious to get Terry into the Guard, while his mind was still young enough to be molded. Then, too, he had spent a good deal of his lifetime studying the Terry Kovak types, quietly pulling them into his Dog Teams. It took a special breed of man to work the Dog Teams, and Terry was the type. "If you tell me you're seventeen, I sure won't doubt your word. We'll enlist you—in the Guard, I mean. How 'bout it?"

"Okay," Terry smiled, not certain just exactly what was going on here; if this was some sort of game. "I'm seventeen."

"You see, Terry," Perret said as he sat on the edge of the desk, "we're way below strength in the Guard. All of us got hit pretty hard during the Korean Conflict. A lot of guys got wounded, got killed, got out. We need some good men, young enthusiasts, to build it back up." He leaned forward. "Does getting killed or wounded bother you, Terry? Scare you?"

"Naw," Terry shrugged it off with the arrogant bravado of youth.

"No sir," Perret gently reminded the young man.

"I mean no, sir," Terry reddened just a bit.

"Does the thought of having to kill someone scare you or bother you?"

This time, Terry's answer was quick and very honest, as Perret knew it would be. "No, sir. I don't believe it does." The memory of Ed Farago flashed through his brain. Terry dismissed the bloody picture with a blink and thought no more of it. He was too excited; he was really going to join the Army. Well—the Guard, at least. That was better than nothing, he supposed.

The Colonel pushed some papers across the desk. Terry looked at them, not stopping to think why his full name, birthdate, and all the other particulars of his life were already typed in. Or how the Colonel had managed to find out so much about him—or why he had done so. Perret's investigation had been quick, but very thorough.

OSS during the Second World War, Paratrooper, Ranger, British Commando; Perret now headed the most secret of all U.S. government groups: the Dog Teams. The President did not even know of their existence; only a handful of men did. The mission of the Dog Teams was simple: they were killers.

"Have one of your parents sign these, Terry. I'll be back in a week. If they're signed, we'll enlist you, and you'll be on your way." *If I don't get you, son,* he thought, *the law will.*

You'll be better off with me—for as long as you live, that is.
"See you, Terry."

Terry looked up from the papers: the Colonel was gone. Tate stood in the doorway, a strange expression on his face. "I'd do my best to get them signed, Terry."

"The Captain here knows I'm not seventeen." Terry spoke of the local Company Commander.

"The Captain will do what the Colonel tells him to do."

"I will *not* sign those papers!" his mother said, hands on her hips, unyielding determination on her face. "You're just barely sixteen, Terry. A boy. What a crazy idea."

"Oh, what the heck, Momma," Robert said. "Danny joined the Guard when he was sixteen, didn't he? Go ahead and sign them. The war's over, and it's not likely to kick up again. This will give the kid some extra money and he'll like it, to boot."

The woman looked at her husband and he smiled at her, remembering his own haste to join up in '17, and also remembering what it was like to be a boy, full of piss and vinegar. "Momma, you know the boy wants to be a soldier. That's all he's ever wanted to be—all his life. This might give him that little extra push up the ladder."

She held out the papers to her husband. "Then you sign them, Karl. Let whatever happens be on your head, not mine. I want no part of this."

Karl Kovak nodded, then slowly, laboriously, with his big, calloused hand, he signed the enlistment papers, looking up only once as his wife of many years walked out of the room and into the kitchen: her safe place, her sanctuary, her domain. When the father had signed the papers, he rose from his chair, to follow his wife, to make peace with her.

Danny put his arm around Terry's shoulders. "Well, kid, you're in the Army, now, on your way to being a man. All you need now is some pussy and you'll be walking tall." Robert joined in the laughter, but there was a cool look in the older brother's eyes.

Terry thought of Vera, Mavis, Clarissa, and the girl he'd

talked with at school just that day. "Well, don't give up on me, Danny," he said.

This time, Robert did not join the laughter. He sat looking at his younger brother, with a strange expression on his face, as if seeing him for the first time; as if this veteran of two bloody wars could see something in the young man that no one else had noticed. Terry met his gaze, saying nothing.

The boy's eyes hold no feeling, Robert thought. Except perhaps a little cruelty. *But maybe I'm wrong? Maybe he's just grown up while I've been gone? I hope that's it. But his eyes are as cold as a snake's. Where have I seen that look before?* Then he remembered: a few guys on a Marine Raider Team had that same look. And a few British Commandoes and American Rangers had that look in their eyes.

Robert finally cut his gaze, turned away, and left the room. Danny had failed to notice the silent exchange.

Three

June, 1954

It was hot and dusty at the National Guard Summer Camp, but Pvt. Terry Kovak didn't mind at all. He was probably the only member of the entire 319th Military Police Unit having fun that summer. Terry attended few classes; he was officially listed on the roster as part of the Special Weapons Team, spending his days on the rifle range, usually behind a Springfield 03 or an MIC sniper rifle. This day, he had been firing at 750 yards, knocking the center out of the target with boring regularity. The weapons he fired seemed to be a part of the young man's body: an extension of himself.

In a range tower, General Matt Wade put down his binoculars, smiled, and turned to Colonel Perret and M/Sergeant Tate. "Beautiful," the General said. "If everything else goes right, we'll have ourselves another shooter. What about Kovak's psychological profile?"

"We've only just begun that phase, sir," Perret was still watching Terry through glasses. The boy fascinated Perret. There was never any change of expression as he fired. "But, as Tate said, Kovak killed that Farago redneck with no more emotion than swatting a fly. He's a natural.''

"Keep him in high school; let him get his diploma. Bring him along slowly, carefully. When does your next class begin?''

"Next summer. Mine, personally, that is, General.''

"I want you to handle Kovak, Bill.''

"Yes, sir.''

"And I'm anxious to read his personality profile.''

"We'll get on that first thing in the morning.''

"Terry,'' the special Army psychiatrist said, "what would you do or think if you were ordered to kill for your country?''

"An enemy of America?''

"Yes.''

"I wouldn't think anything, sir. I'd just do it.''

"Disregarding the moral implication of right or wrong?''

"If the man was an enemy, how could there be wrong?''

The psychiatrist arched an eyebrow; that was not the answer he had expected. He knew this was another candidate for Colonel Perret's Dog Teams, and like most of the men and women Perret recruited, this one had a very high IQ. The psychiatrist wondered about that, pondered over it. What was it about these people that pushed them into dangerous and clandestine fields? (Although he knew Terry did not, as yet, know about the work he was being groomed for.) He knew some of the people had run afoul of the law, but most just volunteered for the work. Someday, perhaps, when he had retired from the military, and Dog Teams no longer existed—as such, for there would always be Dog Teams, in one name or the other—and what they had done had been declassified as much as possible: then, perhaps, he would, after carefully changing names, dates, and places, write a paper on his work with these men and women. If he could get away with it, that would certainly open the eyes of his colleagues. He suppressed a chuckle.

"Terry, haven't you wondered at all why Colonel Perret was so anxious to get you in the National Guard?''

"I've thought about it some, yes, sir.''

"And?"

The young man turned his cold eyes on the doctor. "I think . . . it's because I'm . . . different, sir."

He knows more than Perret thinks he knows. The psychiatrist smiled inwardly. "And how are you different, Terry?"

"Do I have to answer all your questions, sir?"

"Of course not, Terry. Do you like the military?"

"Oh, yes, sir. I'd like to make a career of it. Stay in for the full thirty, if I can."

"In what particular field, Terry?"

"Wherever I can best serve, sir."

"Doing whatever the Army tells you to do?"

"Yes, sir."

"Blind obedience, Terry? Come now, you're much too intelligent for that."

Terry cut his eyes, gazing at the psychiatrist for a moment, without speaking.

Strange eyes, the doctor thought. *Cold. The eyes of a killer? Not necessarily, he reprimanded himself, but what if that is true? What made him so? Why? A twist of the genes?*

Terry said, "It's not blind obedience, sir."

"What would you call it?"

"Serving my country."

"I see. Well, let's pursue that, Terry. Suppose, say, a person had some . . . ah . . . secrets in his or her possession and that person was going to sell them to the Russians. Now . . ."

"What kind of secrets?" Terry interrupted.

"Ah," the psychiatrist's face brightened. "You mean that might make a difference?"

"Sure. If they sold them the story of Jack and the Beanstalk, so what? But if the secret was something that could get an American citizen killed, or a lot of Americans killed, then that person would have to be stopped."

"Killed?"

"If that was the only way, yes."

"Suppose you were asked to kill them, Terry," the doctor said softly. "Would you do that for your country?"

"Yes," the young man said, unhesitatingly. "Yes, I would."

Damn you, Perret! the psychiatrist silently fumed. *How do you do it? How can you simply look at a man and know what's in his heart and mind? How do you do it?*

The Colonel had picked another one, unerringly.

"Thank you, Private Kovak. That will be all for today."

"You'd better tell him, Bill," the psychiatrist told Colonel Perret.

"Can he handle it? Hell, Doc, the kid's only sixteen."

"Yes, he can handle it."

"You don't approve of me or my work, do you, Doc?" Perret smiled.

"Morally? No. But I'm realist enough to know the work your . . . people do is necessary. But God help you if Congress ever finds out about your teams."

Perret laughed. "You mean, the good ole American way of justice for all would be tarnished?"

"What are you, Bill? You're married, you have a family, you love your wife, and I know for a fact you don't run around on her. Yet, if I may use a most unprofessional term, you're a goddamn killer."

Perret laughed louder. "Puzzles you shrinks, doesn't it? Killers are all supposed to be raving lunatics, with no emotions of any kind. Doc, I've never killed a child; I've never raped a woman; I've never mugged anybody . . ."

"But you can and have killed cold-bloodedly, and you train others to do the same."

"For my country, Doc. Not for personal gain. *For my country.* You can't understand that, but you know you can't look down your nose at me, or men like me, for you've been screening my people for eight years."

"Yes," the psychiatrist said.

"Going to write that paper someday, Doc?"

"How did you know . . . ?"

Again, the Colonel laughed. "Come on, Doc, you know this business as well as I. Everybody watches everybody else. We don't even have private thoughts."

"My phone; my office."

"Of course, they're tapped—wired for sound. So is my office. God, you're naive!"

"I should throw you out of here!"

Perret's eyes grew cold. "I'd kill you before you could ball your fists, Doc. Relax, man."

"If I should write my paper someday?"

"Don't."

November, 1954

"I never dated a soldier before," the girl said. "You look a lot older in that uniform, Terry."

With his newly acquired PFC stripes shining on the sleeves of his Ike Jacket, Terry smiled. He did look much older than his years. No one thought much about a sixteen-year-old joining the National Guard. In the 40's and 50's a great many young men did just that, for those were the days when the nation still possessed a degree of pride in the military: those were the days before overt liberalism; before serving one's country became nasty words—before Vietnam. In those days, it wasn't unheard of for parents to actually encourage young men to join the military.

No one knew, however, that this particular young man was on his way toward becoming a part of one of the most feared and highly secret units in the military; a unit that touched all branches of the military.

No one knew that Terry, during the final week of his stay at Summer Camp, had received some very intensive training on the Hand-to-Hand combat range, or that he had taken to it like a Pro, learning a great deal more than his instructors had believed possible in so short a time.

"The kid's a natural," a sergeant said.

"I'd hate to come up on him in a dark alley a few years from now," another remarked.

"Cold son of a bitch!" another said.

"Want some more bourbon with that Coke?" Terry asked, unscrewing the cap on the pint bottle.

She smiled, nodded, and held out her Coke bottle. Terry obligingly poured it half-full of bourbon and the two of them sat quietly in the car, listening to the rain pound on the roof. Robert had loaned Terry his '49 Ford for the evening.

Thanksgiving holidays blanketed the country, and the Guard meeting had been cut very short that evening. When roll was taken, only twenty men had showed up, and the meeting was canceled. Now, instead of having two hours to spend with Bess—as they had planned—Terry had almost four hours with her. His brain was working overtime, trying to figure out a way to get her panties off her.

"Terry?" Bess questioned. "Why did you call me for a date? You know I'm supposed to be going steady with J.A."

"If you're going steady with Cater, what are you doing out with me?"

Bess looked at him through the dim light of night and only shook her head. She didn't know, really, why she had accepted his invitation to go riding, have a drink. Something about Terry Kovak fascinated her; something else about him frightened her. He was not like the other boys; he was more like an adult in manner and bearing.

"You mean," Terry smiled, "I violated some kind of code by calling you?"

The thought amused him. J.A. Cater was the Classic Jock of Bishop High School. An all-around athlete from the tip of his toes to the point of his head, pushing through his always neatly trimmed flat-top. J.A. was the type of person who some-how irritated Terry, and he suspected that sports contributed only a small degree to that dislike. Cater was a born horse's ass.

"Well, I am wearing his ring," Bess sipped her doctored Coke. "And that's supposed to mean we're going steady."

"Why do you go steady with Cater?"

Bess giggled, the alcohol getting to her, spreading warmth in her belly and bringing a lightness to her head. She ducked his question. "Why did you break up with Clarissa?"

Terry shifted positions in the seat and took her hand in his. Her hand was very soft and warm. "We just decided we didn't like each other anymore. We wanted to date other people."

"She's pretty, but kind of false. You know what I mean?"

"Yeah," Terry grinned in the darkness, taking a drink of his Coke and bourbon. "And you don't like her very much. I feel the same way about Cater."

"Can I turn on the radio?"

"Sure, go ahead."

She leaned across him, her breast pushing against his arm. Terry didn't know if that was accidental, or not, but he figured it was intentional.

The disc jockey introduced a golden oldie: Tony Bennett's "Because of You."

Bess leaned back in the seat. "That's such a pretty song. I just love it."

"And the words are so true," Terry picked up the old line and spoon-fed it to her.

She drained her Coke and whiskey and snuggled close to Terry, the rain pulling them together, urging them, under its hammering blanket, to touch. She rubbed her cheek on the rough fabric of the Ike Jacket. "It must be exciting to be a soldier."

"Yeah," Terry whispered, kissing her mouth. Their tongues met, charging batteries that already did not need any more voltage in them.

"If J. A. ever finds out about this," she spoke against his mouth, "you two will have a fight." She nibbled at his lips.

Terry slid his hand under her sweater and caressed her bare stomach. She gasped, but made no attempt to remove his hand. "It won't be much of a fight," Terry said.

"It sure won't," Bess French-kissed him, as the song on the radio changed. Tommy Collins sang: *You Better Not Do That.*

"I want to talk to you, Kovak!" J. A. parked his bulk in front of the door to the gym, blocking it. He flexed his muscles a couple of times, and Terry laughed at him.

J. A. reddened and pointed a thick finger at Terry. "You better stay away from Bess, Kovak," he warned. "I'm not gonna tell you but once. Bess is my chick."

"And if I keep seeing her, you'll do what?" Terry grinned at him.

J. A. threw a punch at him, but Terry was ready for it, suspecting it was coming. Using the simplest of all Judo tactics, Terry used the heavier young man's weight against him and flipped him to the floor. J. A. got to his feet, cursing, and charged at Terry. Terry sidestepped, stuck out his foot, and tripped him, laughing as he did, thinking: *this is the easiest way to fight in the world.*

Roaring with rage, J. A. bounced to his feet and attempted to grab Terry in a bear-hug. Terry kneed him in the groin and the fight was over. J. A. lay on the floor, vomiting.

"STOP THIS!" Coach Murphy yelled from the door of the locker room. He ran to the side of his fallen right tackle, who was sprawled on the floor.

Terry stood to one side, arms folded across his chest. He was smiling.

The assistant coach ran in from the basketball court; he looked first at J. A., then at Murphy, finally at Kovak. His gaze took in Terry's smile, and that seemed to infuriate the man. There was disgust in his voice as he said, "If you wanted to fight, why didn't you call for the gloves? We'd have done it properly."

"Screw the gloves!" Terry blurted. "Fighting isn't a game to me." He pointed at J.A., huddled in a painful ball on the floor, hands cradling his cods. "He swung at me, coach, I didn't start the fight. At least I didn't swing the first fist." He laughed. "I didn't swing a fist at all."

Coach Murphy stood up from J. A.'s side. No one had asked if Terry was hurt. That amused the young man. "Scott, you take Kovak to the principal's office, tell him what happened. I've got to get J. A. to the hospital."

Coach Scott put his hand on Terry's arm and the young man shook it off. "Don't put your hands on me," he warned. "I'll go with you, but don't put your hands on me."

"You need a good ass-whipping!" the young coach told him.

Terry took a step backward, raising his hands, leaving his hands open. "Here I am," he said calmly.

"Both of you calm down!" Coach Murphy barked. "Kovak, get the hell over to Mr. Watkins's office. Move!"

The principal shook his head, clucked in distress a couple of times, and said, "Terry, Terry—this is shocking. I don't approve of violence, Terry, but there are times when it just has to be." He reached for the paddle on his desk.

"Is Cater going to be paddled, too?"

"I rather doubt it, Terry. Don't you think he's suffered enough?"

"I sure as hell don't! *He* started the fight, Mr. Watkins. Not me. If I get paddled, so does Cater. That's the way it's gonna be!"

"Are you refusing to take this whipping?" Watkins asked. He was angry, but he had heard several stories concerning this usually quiet and well-behaved, tough and very capable-looking young man standing in front of him. He remembered Robert and Danny Kovak: fine young men; good, if not great, athletes. But this young man was . . . different from his brothers. There was a coldness about him that was . . . he searched for the word . . . disquieting; somehow unsettling. He knew both Kovak parents, knew they were sometimes borderline poverty cases, and in a way he felt sorry for Terry Kovak. But discipline had to be maintained. If he just hadn't jumped on J. A. And Terry had to have been the one who had initiated the trouble; J. A. had never been in any serious trouble. Such a fine athlete.

"I asked you a question, Terry: are you refusing to take this spanking?"

"You damn well better believe it!"

Watkins nodded curtly. "Very well, then. You're on suspension until I can take this matter up with Superintendent White."

Terry spun around and walked out of the office without acknowledging the directive or looking back. He pushed past an astonished Coach Scott.

Terry walked to the Armory, located on the other side of Bishop, and told Master Sergeant Tate what had happened.

"And you didn't start this fight, Terry?"

"No, Sergeant, I did not. Cater swung at me; I just put him down, that's all."

"With Judo?" the Sergeant said dryly.

"Yes, Sergeant."

"You're too good, Terry. Maybe the best I've ever seen. You take to the killing arts like nobody I've ever seen. Go on home. Stay out of trouble. If your parents don't bring up the . . . incident, don't volunteer anything. Don't tell anyone you came to see me about this. I'll see it's worked out. No sweat."

The door had scarcely closed behind Terry before Tate was reaching for the phone.

Colonel Perret was at the Armory that evening; he had been training men not too far from Bishop, at an isolated training area around Dallonega, Georgia. Tate smiled at what the Colonel brought with him: in two paper bags, a rabbit and a rattlesnake, both live.

"A little object lesson, Colonel?" Tate asked.

"I thought I might be able to appeal to this White's sense of patriotism. But he doesn't have any, or so it seems."

"Military records?" Tate asked.

"None. Zip. Same with his kids. Two oafs he managed to keep in college so they wouldn't get drafted. Go get White. He'll be at the gym. There's a basketball game tonight."

When Superintendent White walked into the Armory, he had time to see the blurred image of Perret before the superintendent went flying through the air to land roughly, but unhurt, save for his ego, on thick close-combat pads on the floor. Yelling as he crawled to his knees, White felt himself jerked to his feet, then slammed down on the pads. This action was repeated several bone-jarring times. Badly shaken, hair disheveled, eyeglasses lost somewhere on the Armory floor, the superintendent was close to tears when Perret finally stopped flinging him about like he was a rag doll.

"My God, man!" White managed to say. "Are you insane? What is this?"

"Kovak," Perret said.

"Who? What?"

"Kovak, Terrance Samuel. Serial number NG 25434038. I don't want him expelled from high school. I want him to finish his education. Are you hungry, Mr. White?"

"What? What? Hungry. Hungry? God, no! I'm going to call the police!"

Perret reached for him again and the superintendent scrambled backward on the pads. "No, no! Maybe I won't. No, I *know* I won't call the police! Kovak? What, what . . . ?"

"Excuse me a moment, Mr. White," Perret said. "I'm hungry."

The Colonel reached into a bag, pulled out the kicking rabbit, and with one swift motion, brought the rabbit to his mouth. He tore open the animal's throat with his teeth, spat out a mouthful of hair and blood, then jerked the pelt from the still-twitching animal, tore off several strips of raw meat, and ate them, blood running down his chin.

Superintendent White threw up on the pads.

Perret tossed the bloody carcass beside White and opened the second bag. "Bring me a can of Sterno," he ordered. "We'll have dessert."

Carelessly—so it seemed to the fascinated and repulsed White—Perret reached into the second bag and jerked out a quivering rattlesnake. Actually, Perret's move was anything but careless but, to the untrained eye, it would seem rash. He cut off the snake's head, stripped the skin from it, and cut the white meat into strips, impaling the strips on bent coathangers, holding them over the blazing can of Sterno.

"You like rattlesnake?" he asked the superintendent.

Whatever else was left in White's stomach came up in a gush. Perret seemed not to notice, eating the seared meat with great relish.

"You ever eaten Long Pig?" he asked superintendent White.

"Long Pig?" the man gasped. "What in God's name is *that?*"

"Human flesh."

The superintendent started gagging.

"Yeah," Perret smiled. "Sometimes you come up on a burned-out tank—they go up like tinder boxes, you know—and you smell fried meat inside. Just take your knife and cut you off a whack. It's really pretty good."

The badly shaken man on the practice pads slowly nodded his head. "I believe I get your point, sir."

"I thought you would." Perret continued eating fried rattlesnake. "The incident with Kovak never happened, did it, White?"

"No," the man said softly. "No, it didn't."

"And you're going to forget anything that took place in this Armory tonight, aren't you? You're going to forget you ever saw me, aren't you?"

"God, I hope so!"

"Good. Now, get out!"

White found his glasses, put them in his pocket, and, walking as a man who had just bumped into death, left the Armory, waving away Tate's offer of a ride. "I'll walk, thank you. I need the air."

When the door had closed, Tate picked up a piece of rattlesnake and chewed it thoughtfully. "Forgotten how good it tastes," he said. "Colonel?"

"Uh-huh?"

"You went to an awful lot of trouble for Kovak, didn't you?"

"He's going to be awfully good, Tate. Maybe the best of us all."

"Yes, sir. But you were pretty damned rough on White."

Perret chuckled grimly. "I enjoy fucking these candy-ass civilians around from time to time. Shake up their smug little world. Especially these Holier-than-thou types who look down their noses at guys like you and me. To hell with them!''

Perret wiped his hands on a shop towel and walked toward the door.

''Colonel?''

Perret turned around.

''Did you ever eat Long Pig?''

Colonel Bill Perret laughed and walked into the night.

Terry was back in school the following morning. No mention was ever made of his refusal to take a paddling, or of the fight in the gym.

Superintendent White was out of his office for several days: not feeling well.

That same day, Karl Kovak was made a full foreman at the mill, and Robert and Danny both found good jobs in a local factory—one with a heavy government contract.

Terry wondered if the series of events in his own family were somehow related. He asked Sergeant Tate.

Tate looked at the young man for a long minute. He knew Perret had not told the boy why he was so interested in him, but Tate had broken the news to several old members of Dog Teams. He almost told Terry; then, at the last minute, held back, thinking: Let him get a few more months of age on him— maybe after Jump School this summer. If Perret doesn't tell him, I will.

''Terry,'' he said, ''it's called back-scratching.'' He smiled. ''Do you know what I'm talking about?''

''Yes, Sergeant. But what I don't understand is: why me?''

''In time, Terry,'' Tate poured them both cups of coffee from the ever-present pot in his office. ''I promise you, you'll understand in time.''

Terry sighed heavily. ''I think I've always understood, Sergeant. You saw me in the Piney Woods that afternoon.''

Tate's expression did not change. ''So what?''

''Come on, Sergeant, say it. You're the one who shot up Ed Farago after I . . . after I . . .'' his voice faded out.

"Killed him," Tate finished it. "Yes, Terry, I did."

"I'm being . . . schooled for something very special, aren't I?"

"Yes, you are."

"What?"

"In time, Terry." He then said something that would take Terry several years to fully grasp. "Guys like you and me, Terry, we belong in . . . special units. We need the protection our government can give us."

"I don't understand."

"You will, in time. Okay, Kovak, wear your Class-A's Monday night, we're having inspection. See you then . . . and stay out of trouble; stop all this fighting over pussy. There's plenty to go around."

Four

February, 1955

Once he was alone in his room, Terry looked in the envelope and shook his head in disbelief. Five, ten, and twenty dollar bills; three hundred dollars in all. He had never seen that much money in one place, especially in his hand.

"It's a birthday present for you," Tate had said, handing the envelope to him. "Don't open it 'til you're alone."

There was a short note from Colonel Perret:

> You're part of my Teams, Terry. And Tate tells me you know why you were picked. I take care of my men and expect them to do the same for me. I know you won't run out and start blowing this money all over Bishop; you've got a good head on your shoulders. That's just one of the reasons I chose you for my Teams. Happy birthday, soldier.
>
> P

On his way home from school, Terry ducked into some woods and burned the note from Perret. It seemed the right thing to do. He touched the money in his pocket. He would hide it in his room and spend it very carefully. A grin touched his young/old face as he thought of the upcoming weekend.

At the Kovak home, his mother met him at the back door, all smiles. "Seventeen years old this very day, Terry. I remember like it was yesterday, almost." She led him into the kitchen. "You was born right here in this house. And just look who come home for the event."

The family had not seen Virginia for more than a year and a half. In school in New York City, she worked there during the summers, on the weekends, and after school. Virginia rose from the table to greet her younger brother, to kiss him on the cheek. Terry was startled at her appearance, hoping the expression on his face could be controlled.

Virginia was dressed in tight black slacks and a black sweater. Her face was very pale. Her hair was long and hanging down her back: dirty hair, looking like it hadn't been washed or combed in a week.

"Damn, Terry," she said, ignoring her mother's shocked glance at her profanity. "I wouldn't have known you on the street—you've changed so much. Hell, you're a grown man, Terry."

"Did college teach you to curse?" Mother Kovak asked. "You going to swear in the courtroom when you start up your own law practice?"

"Oh, Momma," Virginia looked exasperated. "Loosen up, will you? It's the twentieth century. Women now have as many rights as men, although most of them don't realize it."

"What's that got to do with swearing? Your Poppa don't curse in this house . . . much—and neither will you, Virginia. That's my final word on it."

"Okay, Momma," Virginia winked at Terry, "no more hells and damns."

Mother Kovak mumbled something under her breath and turned away to resume peeling potatoes. Terry poured a cup of coffee and sat down at the table with his sister.

"I understand you're a big, brave soldier, now, Terry. You going to fight all the nation's capitalistic wars? Be a part of the subservient forces of the bourgeoisie, laying down your life for the power-people?''

"Ginny, I don't even know what that means," Terry looked at her. "What language is that, Communist?"

She laughed and patted his hand. Terry noticed her fingers and nails were filthy. "It's English, Terry—bourgeoisie actually coming from the French. But it's only natural, I suppose, for a military mind—young or old—to suspect a Communist plot in anything they don't understand."

"I don't suspect anything, Ginny." Or do I? Terry suddenly remembered the three hundred dollars in his pocket. "I just think it's all right to serve your country."

"Good for you, Terry," his mother spoke from the sink.

"Okay, all right," Ginny said. "We won't discuss politics. Tell me, what's happening in the bustling city of Bishop?"

"Well," Terry sipped his coffee, "I saw Joe the other day. He asked about you; when you were coming home."

"Good Lord!" his sister laughed. Terry noticed her teeth were stained with nicotine and could use a good brushing— several times. Ginny chain-smoked, lighting one from the butt of another. "Dear Joe. I haven't seen him in years—or thought about him. Tell me, is he still pumping gas and reading comic books?"

She was beginning to irritate Terry with her flip attitude, the way she constantly put everyone and everything down, as if she were so much better, so much smarter. Virginia and Joe Davis had gone together all during high school, with everyone assuming they would get married. Joe had told Terry recently that in the years since Ginny had gone to New York City, she had never once written him.

"I guess he pumps gas." Terry's reply was a bit testy. "He owns a little general store, sporting goods and all that, out on the lake road."

"And doing quite well," Mother Kovak said. "Going with a very nice lady." She seemed to put special emphasis on the word *lady*.

Ginny cut her eyes to her mother. "Momma, don't you think I'm a lady?"

"You were when you left here three years ago. Before you turned yourself into a. . . . into a . . ." She looked at her son. "What is the word, Terry? It's been in the papers and on the radio before."

"Beatnik," Terry said. "Greenwich Village beatnik."

"Yes, that's it." Mother Kovak nodded her head. "No-good-nik."

The young woman stood up, pouring another cup of coffee. She was very thin, and her hands trembled slightly. She stood with her back to the kitchen counter, looking first at her mother, then at Terry.

"Beatnik is just a word people use for something they cannot understand," she said. "Neither of you know anything about the true intellectual movement behind the word."

She was suddenly on the defensive and Terry could not understand why—if she believed so strongly in her way of life in the Village.

"Is it so wrong to read the great classics?" she asked. "Is it wrong to study the works of genius, past and present and future? To contemplate? To discuss?" She turned to Terry. "Don't you have something—anything at all—that puzzles you? That you would care to discuss with someone of intelligence?"

"Yeah," Terry said dryly, "this: how can a black cow eat green grass, then give white milk that can be turned into yellow butter?"

At first his sister was angry, a flush on her pale face. Then, slowly, a grin spread across her face. "Mother?" she asked.

Mother Kovak shook her head, shrugged her shoulders, realizing the hopelessness of arguing with her daughter. She scraped the carrots in silence, for she was still pondering her son's riddle.

Virginia looked at Terry. He shrugged. "It's your life, Ginny. You've got a right to live it the way you see fit, I guess. But," he met her eyes, "the rest of us have a right to live our lives, too, without being put down for it."

"You're pretty hip for a seventeen-year-old, brother, but I could punch holes in your logic."

"Putting the holes where you think they should go, Ginny?"

She sat down at the table. "Terry, go to college when you finish high school. You've got a good mind—a fine mind. Put it to some use."

"I'm going to. I'm going to be career military."

"Oh, my God! Talk about dumb-ass!"

Mother Kovak threw her paring knife into the sink with a clatter and left the kitchen, her back stiff with anger. Virginia followed her mother with her eyes: sad eyes, troubled eyes.

"I made a mistake coming back," she said. "I shouldn't have done it."

Terry thought he detected something awfully wrong with Ginny; something definitely out of kilter, but he said nothing about his suspicions. If she wanted him to know, she would tell him. "How long you going to stay, Ginny?"

"I was going to stay two or three weeks. Now, maybe three or four days. I don't really know." She touched the back of his hand. "Wolfe was right, Terry, you can't ever go back. Remember that before you leave. You can't go home again."

"I don't believe that. Robert and Danny came back after the war."

His sister's smile was gentle. "Bob and Danny never really left, Terry. Do you understand that?"

He shook his head. "No. I mean, I don't think I do, anyway."

"I have a feeling that someday you will—more than any of us."

The woman stopped him on the street and looked at him a moment before speaking. Terry could read the silent message in her eyes and the unspoken words made his knees feel just a little weak.

"How are you and Bess getting along?" she finally asked.

"Just fine, Mrs. Skelton." He didn't know what else to say.

She smiled at him, with mouth and eyes, and Terry felt a tightening in his groin. The woman was coming on to him. Good Lord! he thought.

"Bess seems to think the world of you," she said. "And

we're thankful, and grateful—Lee and I—for your breaking up Bess and J. A. I never really liked that boy. You and Bess have a date for tonight?''

''Yes, Ma'am.''

''Going to the movies?''

''Well, maybe . . .'' He was hesitant in answering the question. Actually, he and Bess were going to the lake to park and make out. Not something one wishes to discuss with the girl's mother.

''Well . . . I'll see you when you come to get Bess. Come a bit earlier tonight. I've baked you a cake. Yesterday was your birthday, wasn't it?''

''Yes, Ma'am.''

''For heaven's sake,'' she laughed, patting her hair. ''Stop calling me 'ma'am.' You're making me feel positively ancient.''

''Yes . . .'' He didn't know her first name.

''Carolyn. My name is Carolyn. Remember that, Terry.''

''Yes, Ma'am . . . I mean, Carolyn. Whatever you say.''

She smiled and patted him on the cheek with a gloved hand, then brushed by him, leaving just a hint of expensive perfume to drift into his head. He watched her walk away, and he knew she knew he was watching her. The woman's figure was sensational.

About thirty-five, Terry thought, *and, getting restless.* He had heard—and seen—that Mr. Skeleton was a boozer, and Carolyn probably wasn't getting enough at home.

He shook his head. *Here I go,* he thought.

Joe Davis's pickup truck was parked in the driveway with Ginny sitting in it, talking to Joe. Neither of them paid any attention to Terry as he took the porch steps two at a time.

''Joe sure didn't waste any time getting over here,'' he remarked to Shirley, who was sprawled on the floor reading a Hollywood scandal magazine.

''He's been here about two hours,'' his sister said, without looking up. ''Ginny's been crying, too.''

68   William W. Johnstone

"What about?"

"Beats me." She sipped her Coke, then said, "Sure is lonesome around here without Mavis and Vera."

Terry grinned at her, and the grin changed his face from a man to a boy. "They're only about six blocks from here."

"I know, but the house is kinda empty-like, now. You know what I mean?"

"Yeah. But it's a whole lot quieter."

Shirley would soon be twelve, filling out in female places. She was going to be a great-looking woman, and the thirteen-year-old boys in the neighborhood were looking at her the way boys do. And that worried Terry: he knew what boys had on their minds most of the time.

"Where's Mom and Dad?"

"Over at the Bensons'. They're going to have supper over there. Momma fixed some stuff for us before they left. She said Ginny probably doesn't know the difference between an egg and a potato."

Terry laughed and squatted down beside his sister. He grabbed her Coke and took a deep pull. "Momma doesn't understand Ginny, that's all."

"And you do?" Shirley frowned at the little bit of Coke he left in the bottle.

"I'm trying, little sister."

She turned the page of the movie magazine. "Rock Hudson is so good looking."

"What's Rock Hudson got to do with Ginny?"

Shirley giggled, rolling over on her back, holding the magazine to her. "Nothing, but he's still good looking."

"I give up," Terry said.

Conditions had greatly improved in the Kovak house since Mr. Kovak was made foreman at the mill, a year-round job. They now had a car, a 1950 Ford that Terry drove exclusively, since neither Mr. nor Mrs. Kovak could drive, and a TV set that was the pride of the household. They could get a station out of Atlanta, and sometimes get another out of Chattanooga. Mother Kovak liked the Perry Como show; Mr. Kovak liked to watch the boxing matches.

After a shower and a shave, Terry was buttoning his shirt as he came down the stairs to the living room. "What are you doing tonight?" He asked his sister.

"Staying home and watching TV." She did not look up from her movie magazine.

"Have fun," Terry slipped into his jacket. He expected no reply, and got none. Shirley was far away, in Hollywood, kissing Rock Hudson.

He waved to Joe and Ginny as he backed the Ford out of the drive, but they were too engrossed in each other to pay him any attention. Ginny looked like she was crying again. Joe put his arm around her shoulders.

"Better watch her, Joe," Terry muttered. "She didn't just pop back into your life for no reason." *But maybe he loves her.* Terry thought. *Hasn't seen her in three years and he just says Hello, I love you and let's pick it up again, like it was before.*

Terry grinned at the dusk that was settling over Bishop, Georgia. Love must be an interesting feeling, he mused.

"Like the cake, Terry?" Mrs. Skelton asked, standing close to him.

"Yes, Ma'am." Terry swallowed a mouthful of angel food cake. "I mean, yes. Carolyn."

Mr. Skelton sat at the table with them, lapping up beer as fast as he could drink one bottle and open another. He bobbed his head up and down and grinned, already half-drunk. "Don't forget that, now, Terry," he slurred his words. "I'm Lee, she's Carolyn. First names around here." He belched and his wife cringed. Bess was upstairs, still dressing and, as Carolyn had put it, "putting on her face." Terry wished she would hurry up and get him out of this mess. To make matters worse, he hated angel food cake.

Lee opened another bottle of beer and guzzled half of it. "Like you, Terry-boy," he said. "Didn't like that J. A. worth a damn. Had no manners—big stupid clod." He stood up, swaying slightly. " 'Cuse me, got to go be a little boy." Grinning, he left the room.

"Disgusting pig!" Carolyn said, as soon as her husband was out of the room. She poured Terry another glass of milk, and he declined another piece of cake. "Do you drink, Terry? Hard liquor, I mean?"

"Yes, Carolyn," Terry heard himself saying, "I do." Her name was coming easier to him.

She nodded, her brows knitting, as if she were deep in a process of decision-making. The young man and the older woman locked eyes, a silent message passing between them as she reached a conclusion.

"Lee will be gone to Atlanta all day Monday," she said, and said no more, leaving anything else up to Terry.

"Okay," Terry said.

She gathered up the dishes and took them into the kitchen, pausing at the barroom-type swinging doors to glance at Terry. Her eyes were a dark green, smoldering with fire. Terry's icy pale blue eyes under very blond eyebrows moved slowly over her body, from ankles to face and back again. He was bold, not at all nervous or shy. His gaze lingered at her full breasts, then moved upward to meet her hot eyes.

"You're pretty sure of yourself, aren't you?" she asked, a slight flush to her face.

"Yes," he said, "I suppose I am." He said it quietly, suddenly experiencing a strange sense of loss, as if realizing his boyhood days were almost gone. They would never return, and he sensed he was growing up too fast, doing things that should be waiting for him in the years ahead.

"Are you making love to my daughter, too?" she asked. Terry picked up on the "too" very quickly.

"Yes, I am."

"Be careful, hot-shot. The one thing I don't need is a bastard grandchild."

"Okay."

Lee stumbled into the dining room and the spell was broken. The quick look she gave her husband was one of contempt mingled with hate. Terry knew this marriage was broken beyond any repair; solely a marriage of convenience. He felt no sense of guilt for what he would do—or allow her to do to him—on Monday.

He wondered why people, who must have been in love when they married, would allow a marriage to crumble into this state of semi-warfare and disgust.

"Are you going to college when you finish high school?" Bess asked. She took a deep pull from her Coke—doctored with booze—and then a drag from her Lucky Strike.

"No. I guess I'm going into the Regular Army. You?"

She giggled. "Daddy thinks we're going to get married and go to college together."

"You and me?"

"Yes."

"Who the hell told him that?"

"Nobody; he just thinks it, that's all."

It was cold this night in North Georgia; the ground was spotted with white patches of snow, and the temperature was hovering in the low thirties.

"Terry?"

"Uh-huh?"

"Do you like school?"

"No. I hate it! Why?"

They were driving aimlessly. They had circled the town a dozen times, had a burger and fries at a local drive-in, and debated whether or not to see a movie. But the gas tank was full, the tires new, and now they were out in the country, on a blacktop road, driving deep into the hills of Flagler County.

"I hear kids talk around school," Bess said, lighting another Lucky and passing it to Terry. "Most of the boys don't like you for some reason, but they can't really say why. J. A. hates you. He swears he's going to get you if it takes him the rest of his life. I really think he means it."

Ed Farago flashed before Terry's eyes for the first time in months. He pushed the memory back into the dark regions of his mind, forcing the bloodiness into that darkness.

"I don't care for most of them, either," he said. "But I can't tell you why I don't." Suddenly, he chuckled.

"What's so funny?"

"I just thought of what a lot of people call J. A.—behind his back."

"What? I've never heard anything except J. A."

"Before his daddy sold out, they used to own a chicken farm. When J. A. was about twelve, his daddy was losing a lot of hens. Seems as though J. A. was slipping out to the henhouse and screwing the chickens at night. Soon as he did, they'd die. Someone hung the nickname on him: Needle Dick the Bug Fucker."

"That's awful!" Bess put her hand over her mouth to suppress her laughter. "Good Lord, Terry!" a giggle slipped through her fingers and soon they were both laughing.

She slid across the seat to sit close to him, her left hand resting on his thigh, warm where it touched. She put her head on his shoulder.

Terry slowed, pulled off the road, and drove down a gravel road for a mile. The road ended abruptly at a barbed-wire fence. The two of them were high in the hills of Flagler County. Far below them, the lights of Bishop gleamed in the cold night, diamond-like.

They got out of the warmth of the car and walked hand in hand to the fence. Terry stood behind her, his arms around her waist, the side of his face pressed against her hair. Her hair smelled fresh and clean, lightly scented from her perfume.

"It's pretty up here," Bess said, enjoying his arms around her.

"When I leave," Terry said, "I hope I never have to live in Bishop, Georgia, again. I don't even know if I want to see Bishop again."

"And—me?" she asked. She was crazy about Terry, but just a little bit afraid of him, too. That feeling confused her, because Terry had always been sweet to her. She thought maybe it was because of the fight. J. A. was bigger and stronger than Terry—a football hero—but Terry had handled him like he was a baby. J. A. had never landed a punch.

"I don't know how I feel about you, Bess. I really don't. I know I like you a lot."

"Boys aren't supposed to say that to girls. You're supposed to tell me you love me."

"I don't know whether I'm a boy—I don't know if I've ever been a boy, really. And I don't know if I love you or not."

Bess shivered in his arms; the wind was cold, coming off the mountains. She wasn't at all certain it was the wind making her shiver, though. She pushed closer into his arms.

"Terry, are you happy?"

"Kind of, I guess. I was happy—content is a better word— 'til about a year ago. Since then I've been kind of . . . confused about things."

Bess decided not to pursue that, thinking it might have something to do with that bitch, Clarissa. "I could fall very much in love with you, Terry."

"I'm not sure that would be very smart, Bess."

She turned in his arms and kissed him on the mouth, pushing her softness against him. "Then love me for just a little while, Terry. Love me until you have to go away. And I know that you will go away. You're not happy here."

"Okay," he said, and the image of her mother popped into his mind. He wondered what Carolyn would look like with no clothes on, and that thought brought him to semi-hardness.

She could feel his maleness pushing against her. She kissed his cold lips, tonguing his mouth. "Let's get in the car, Terry."

In the Ford, motor running, heater on, radio blaring, a new young rock-a-billy singer named Elvis something-or-another was vibrating the speaker with "Baby, Let's Play House."

"Are you going to church with us, Terry?" his mother called up the stairs.

"No," he shouted down to her. "Maybe I'll go later."

"Maybe we'll take the car away from you!" his father shouted up to him.

"Oh, 'way to go, people!" Ginny snapped at her parents.

They had not heard her enter the house. "That's cheap black-mail tactics. You think forcing him to go to church will bring him closer to your God?"

The parents looked at each other, not understanding the "your God" part of her statement. Before they could retort, Robert blew his horn in the driveway.

Karl Kovak took one more shot. "Terry comes dragging in at two in the morning and here it is a quarter to seven and you just now come home. What did me and Momma raise, a tomcat and a tart?"

Upstairs, Terry wanted to shout down that they would still all be dirt poor if it wasn't for their "tomcat." But he held his silence as he sat on the edge of the bed.

"A question like that doesn't even deserve an answer," Ginny calmly replied. "You're both assuming things that may or may not have occurred."

"Your Poppa and me will pray for the both of you," Mother Kovak said.

"Thank you," Ginny replied.

Karl Kovak snorted and stomped out the front door, leaving wife and daughter glaring at each other.

"I spent the night at Joe's," Ginny informed her mother, then braced herself for a good slap in the face.

The pop didn't come. Her mother said, "Your Poppa and me thought as much. You should go to confession, girl."

"Why? I have nothing to confess."

"God sees it different than you, Virginia. Did you come back here to mess up Joe's life?"

Ginny began crying, the tears melting the mascara and dripping down her face in dark streaks. She shook her head. "I don't know why I came back, mother. I just got on the bus one day and here I am."

"I think you know why you came back," the mother put her arms around the daughter and held her. It was breaking her heart to see her cry so. She patted Ginny on the shoulder. "You go get cleaned up and get some sleep. We'll talk when I get back. All right?"

Ginny pulled away, controlling her tears and sobbing. "For whatever good it will do, all right, we'll talk."

A smile creased the woman's lined face. "Good. I reached you; now, if I can only reach Terry."

Ginny shook her head. "No, Momma, no one will ever reach Terry—not for many years—maybe never. He lives in this house, but he's already gone away."

"Foolish words, girl. They make no sense."

"They will someday."

Five

Odd, Terry thought, driving away from school in the rain. Ginny suddenly deciding to stay. And she's the one who told me you can't ever go back. Or was it come back? Why would anyone want to leave New York City and come back here? Dumb hick town like Bishop.

He could find no ready answers to his questions, so he put them out of his mind and thought of the afternoon that stretched before him. And Carolyn Skelton. His young blood began to run faster and hotter as he drove toward her section of town. He parked in a wooded area behind the Skelton home, jogged the block to her back porch, and knocked on the door. The home was secluded, surrounded by woods that would hide him from prying eyes.

"Did anyone see you?" Carolyn asked, letting him into the kitchen.

"No." He removed his jacket and draped it on the back of a chair.

She picked up the damp jacket and hung it in the hall. "We shouldn't be disturbed," she said. "The Longs are at work and the Pattersons are out of town." She met his eyes, attempting to stare down his direct gaze. She gave up, cut her eyes, and flushed. "I may be a total fool for getting involved with a boy, but I'm not a tramp. You appeal to me. I can't explain it."

"I never said you were a tramp; never thought it, either. I saw your marriage the other night, not for the first time. You hate your husband, don't you?"

"You're pretty sharp for a boy."

"I haven't been a boy for over a year." Terry fiddled with a salt shaker on the table. It slipped out of his fingers and turned over, spilling salt on the tablecloth.

"That's supposed to be bad luck." Carolyn smiled, cleaning up the small mess. Her perfume drifted to Terry and he thought how pretty she was and how good she smelled.

"I don't doubt the bad luck part," he said glumly, suddenly depressed in spite of what lay before him that afternoon. "I think I've got more than my share coming to me."

"Well, I have a young prophet with me. What happened a year ago?"

Farago jumped into his memory. But, as it had been occurring of late, the memory was blurred, and did not seem as real. He pushed the picture back into the grave. "Nothing much, really. I just had a chance to grow up and I took it. Actually, I don't think I had much choice in the matter."

"You sound like you regret it."

"In a way; but I can't change it, so what choice do I have?"

"You don't talk like a boy, either." She touched his shoulder and her hand was hot through his shirt.

He shrugged.

"I'm thirty-five years old, Terry."

"I'm seventeen; so what?"

She laughed softly. "Let's go sit in the den. I have bourbon and ice in there."

Terry followed her through the house and into the den, his eyes never leaving the woman's full figure.

The den was large and warm and comfortable, a huge log blazing in the fireplace. Expensive carpet on the floor. Terry was suddenly ashamed of himself: his mother would really love something like this.

Someday, Momma, he silently promised, *I'll build you a home like this.*

"Drink bourbon with me," Carolyn broke into his thoughts, "and you'll drink it as it should be drunk, as an adult drinks it, with water."

He nodded, and she turned away, preparing the drinks at the wet bar. Terry sat on a low leather couch, watching her. Her belly and hips were firm, and her breasts swayed slightly under her dark sweater.

She took two coasters from a tray on the bar and placed them on the coffee table in front of the couch. Terry sipped his drink and decided he didn't like bourbon and water, but that he would drink it to please the woman.

"Bourbon with water is something a person must become accustomed to," she told him, smiling over the rim of her glass. "Drink it for a week and you'll like it."

"I'll take your word for that," Terry took another sip. He decided it wasn't all that bad. The whiskey was very smooth and easy to the taste. "What kind of whiskey is this?"

"It's a Canadian blend. Smooth, isn't it?"

"Yes, it is." He set his drink on the coaster and kissed the woman on the mouth.

Her lips, ripe and full and red, responded to his, her tongue sliding into his mouth, but her eyes remained open and cool. "Don't push me, Terry," she warned him. "I'm not a giggling schoolgirl in the back seat of a Chevy. This time, I'll be the teacher; you be the pupil. You may think you're a man, but there are many things you have yet to learn about a woman."

"And you're going to teach me?"

"I'll teach you. Now drink your drink and relax—we've got lots of afternoons ahead of us. This is just number one. Getting acquainted—saying hello."

Terry left the Skelton home a few minutes past four that afternoon. He was drained, almost exhausted, and had a brassy taste in his mouth. He had a headache, his legs felt weak, and he didn't know if he could ever get another hard-on. He didn't, at that moment, know if he wanted another erection—ever! He was very grateful for the fact that he had no date that evening, or the next. Bess was gone to a Home Ec. something-or-another. Terry hoped he wouldn't have to see another woman for at least a week . . . maybe longer.

The times with Vera had been nothing. The sex with Mavis forgettable. The moments with Clarissa and Bess nothing more than fumbling, quick releases, most of the time groping blindly in the back seat of a car. But Carolyn . . . she knew what she wanted, how she wanted it, and when she wanted it.

Terry never dreamed he could go so long without exploding. No wonder her husband drank!

He didn't want to go home just yet, so he drove up into the hills around Bishop. As he drove, he remembered . . .

Naked, in bed beside her, the young man took in all the wonders of mature woman. While his erection throbbed, she talked and stroked him, punctuating her conversation with soft kisses on various parts of his anatomy. Terry was quite certain he would keel over and die before the afternoon was over.

"You see, Terry," she had smiled at him, "you're ready to make love right now. It doesn't take any time for a man, but it takes patience when you deal with a woman."

Carolyn had knocked back several dark drinks before they went into the bedroom. She was far from drunk, but was feeling the booze.

She instructed him that afternoon, schooled him in sex. He busied his hands and fingers and she responded under his touch.

"It's automatic for you, Terry," she praised him.' 'You're going to be super. You've got the rogue born in you and the equipment to please a woman."

Just before Terry mounted her, sliding between her spread-apart legs, into the wetness of woman, Carolyn said, "I wonder why it is I worry about you?"

Terry parked the car and stood for several minutes looking down a long valley that gradually sloped downward and became the town of Bishop. The Chamber of Commerce said: "Big things going to happen in Bishop someday soon. Yes, sir. Big things."

"It'll happen without me," Terry said.

There, on that not-quite-a-mountain, but bigger-than-a-hill, the boy squatted down and allowed postcoital depression to hit him with all the force of a nine-pound sledgehammer, beginning between his ears and fanning downward to cover his entire body.

The rain came down in silver sheets, but Terry seemed oblivious to the downpouring. He thought: is this the end of youth? Is this all there is to it? When does youth stop and adulthood take over?

He lit a Lucky and blew the smoke to the elements while his mind worked. Did anything of any real importance happen today? he questioned. And if it did, what and why?

The wind sighed, the trees shivered their bare branches in reply, and a bird called out. Terry listened; the bird received no answer and sang again. No response. He watched the bird beat its wings against the sky and soar away, vanishing in the trees below, seeking some company in the dismal climate of late winter.

I should be happy, Terry mused, but I'm not. I should be proud—most guys my age spend their time jacking off, dreaming of someone like Carolyn. But I feel . . . sticky inside. Something is gone from me that I should not have lost so young. I know that, but I don't know what it is I've lost, or why I should feel so bad about it. What's wrong with me?

He hoped some Great Voice would boom from the sullen sky, answering his questions, erasing all his doubts, but nothing happened. The Heavens did not open; the rain remained the same: crystal gray and shining silver, falling to the earth, splattering on his head and jacket, dripping off his nose. He let sexual memories and bloody conflict in the rain wash away a youth he knew he had never had a chance to enjoy, and knew would never come again.

Terry sighed and stood up. "Hello, goodbye," he said. He walked slowly to the car.

* * *

"Ugh, Terry!" His little sister grabbed him as he walked into the house. She quickly released him. "You're all wet!"

"People get that way when they stand out in the rain." Terry grinned at her. A forced grin. He still felt very much like crying but knew, somehow, that he would never again shed a tear for anything or anybody. How he knew remained a mystery to him.

"I've got some really great news," Shirley beamed at him, wiggling with excitement, wanting to tell him, but wanting more to drag out the suspense.

"So, tell me. I know! Rock Hudson called. He asked you for a date?"

She giggled. "No, silly, it's Ginny and Joe. They're going to be married."

Terry sat down in a chair and stared at his sister. He could not bring himself to speak. Married! Just a couple of days ago Ginny had told him that a person could never go back home. Married?

He found his voice. "When did all this take place?"

"About noon. We've been looking for you all day. Momma didn't tell Poppa you played hooky from school. Where have you been, Terry?"

"I was on a field trip . . . sort of."

Joe was Baptist, Ginny Catholic, so they were married by a local JP, upsetting both families.

"It isn't proper!" Mrs. Davis told Mrs. Kovak over coffee. "People should wait a respectable time before marrying. We've had no time for invitations, receptions, teas, nothing. It just isn't proper."

"They should have been married in the Church," Mother Kovak responded. "The poor children. What will happen to them? This is terrible."

"If they have kids," Terry said, "maybe the kids can go their own way, find themselves, without being pushed and shoved without being asked if they want to go in that direction."

"You shut up your mouth!" Poppa Kovak said. "Mr. Know-It-All."

"Tell me, Ginny," Terry asked. "Why did you do it?"

His sister turned her gray-blue eyes on him. It was the weekend after the marriage; the short honeymoon was over. Ginny's hair was cut shorter, her face held some color, and she seemed more relaxed. She sat with her brother in the back of Joe's small country store, filling station, and bait house. Terry had driven out to see them.

"You told me a person can't go back," he persisted. "But here you are—back home."

"All right, Terry," Ginny poured them coffee, "I'll give it to you straight. I don't believe you're going to go to pieces and blab it to the family. God! They'll find out soon enough as it is. You're the age of a boy, but you're not, really. You're a man. Too soon, I think; but a man, nonetheless. So . . . I'm pregnant."

"Yeah, that's what I figured. And not by Joe."

Her laugh was bitter. "Not hardly, brother. I don't know who the kid's father is."

"Well, you must have had a pretty good time in the city." Terry sipped his coffee and waited for her reply. He had tried to keep his voice level, without accusation or innuendo.

"Implying that I gave it away wholesale? Or perhaps inferring is a gentler word. Either way, you're right. You see, Terry, in the Village, in my group, sex is not considered dirty. It's fun, healthy. A dozen or more men and women together is not unknown. Oh, I've narrowed it down to four or five men, for whatever good it will do." She sighed. "Maybe our philosophy is all wrong—was all wrong in the Village. Look at me: when I got in trouble, who did I turn to? Hell, I came running straight back to Bishop."

"How far along are you?"

"Three months, I think."

"Did you consider . . . ah . . . doing away with it?"

"Abortion? Sure, most definitely. But those crumby back

rooms and that coat-hanger routine scared the hell out of me.''
She shuddered, shook her head, started to speak, then abruptly
changed her mind.

"I'm glad you didn't go through with it. Does Joe know?"

"Yes, I've leveled with him." Her eyes widened. "Would
you believe the man still loves me? After all I've done, all I've
been, he still loves me. Joe is quite a man, Terry.''

Her brother wondered what it was like to be in love. Wondered if he would ever experience the sensation. "Do you love
him?"

"I like him," she stated honestly. "And I believe that's a
better basis for a marriage. I've been in love; and it's not all
that wonderful. I prefer not to go through that again. Besides,
there is an old Arab proverb that reads: It is better for a woman
to marry a man she likes and a man to marry a woman he
loves.''

Terry thought about that for a moment. "Ginny, you've
been in college for four years—off and on. How about your
education? You shouldn't waste all you've done.''

"You're very wise for one so young, brother. I don't understand how you reached that plateau this quickly. But you're
right. Joe and I have discussed it. After the baby is born, I'll
go back to school—I guess here in Georgia. I can take my bar
in about eighteen months. She touched her brother's hand, hard
and calloused for one so young. She knew he had done odd
jobs and worked at hard physical labor for years. The work
ethic was deeply instilled in the Kovak boys.

"I've put my troubles on your young shoulders, Terry. Is
there anything you'd like to tell me?"

The killing came to him, moving about in his mind, but not
as vividly as before, gradually having become, over the months,
a cloudy thing, hazy and surrealistic. Terry had accepted the
killing and knew he could live with it. It was rapidly becoming
no big deal to him. If he was to be a professional soldier, in a
top unit, he was certain there would be more killings on various
battlefields. He could live with those, too.

"No, sis; I just feel a little lost, a little confused, at times,
that's all.''

Ginny didn't believe him; didn't believe there was nothing wrong; but she didn't push it. "Okay, Terry, and thank you for listening to me. A sister couldn't ask for a better brother."

Carolyn touched her mouth to Terry's bare stomach, her tongue tracing wet designs on his flesh. Outside the bedroom window, the signs of late spring were evident, with green leaves and bright blooms and puffs of warm air blowing gently through the North Georgia hills and valleys.

"Tell me how you like this, Terry," she said, then opened her mouth and took him.

Disjointed words and half phrases floated through his mind, but his reply was to groan aloud and tangle his fingers in her hair.

Both the young man and the woman sensed that this day was the beginning of the end for them. Terry had been making up excuses not to see her. He felt very real pangs of guilt, making love to Bess after making love to Bess's mother the day before. The last time the woman and the young man had made love, Carolyn had cried and told him she was in love with him, quickly adding that she knew nothing could come of it. She was growing increasingly jealous of her daughter's relationship with Terry. This day, Terry was going to tell her it was over between them.

She brought him to near climax, pulled away, then mounted him. When completion drained them to a sweaty truce, they lay side by side in the bed, smoking.

She seemed to be reading his thoughts. "Go ahead and tell me what's on your mind, Terry."

"I don't think we'd better see each other after this, Carolyn," Terry said, putting into words the unspoken thing that had been building between them for weeks. He felt much better after saying it.

She abruptly snubbed out her cigarette and knocked back a half-full tumbler of warm whiskey and water. She set the glass on the night stand with a bang. "Well, if that's the way you want it, lover-boy, you can damn well stay the hell away from my daughter.''

The dark humor of it all hit Terry. Unintentionally, the laughter bubbled out of his mouth, uncontrolled. ''Excuse me,'' he said.

''What's so goddamn funny?!'' she demanded, up on one elbow, her breasts swinging just above Terry's nose.

''You! Jealous of your own daughter. Come on, now, it is funny. You have to admit that.''

She lay back on the bed and pulled the sheet up to her chin. Her eyes were dark with fury. She adjusted the sheet to cover her body fully. A moment of sudden propriety had swept over her. ''I know you've been making love to Bess. I want it to stop.''

''What do I tell her?''

''Tell her any goddamn thing you like! Just stay away from her and this house.''

''Sure, I will, Carolyn, but not because of any threats from you. What would you do? Tell Lee I've been screwing his wife *and* his daughter? I've got a mental picture of you doing that.''

''You sorry punk!'' she hissed at him. Then she began to cry.

''Carolyn,'' Terry sat on the edge of the bed, swinging his feet to the thick carpet. He pulled on his pants. ''This . . . affair has been going on for months. Look, I'm seventeen and you're thirty-five.'' He was feeling as if he were her age and, sensing that, for a few moments, she had regressed to his. ''You knew all that when we started. How did you think it would end? Just One Big Happy Family?''

She turned her face from him, her tears staining the pillow. ''Put your clothes on and get out. Don't look at me, don't touch me. Just get your ass out of here and don't ever come back.''

''Whatever you say, Mrs. Skelton, ma'am. Just please let me find my socks.''

''Smart ass!'' she mumbled into the pillow.

''That's not true,'' he challenged. ''I just don't understand why you feel this way. It had to end—we both knew that. Why do you hate me?''

"Get out!" she yelled.

"Yes, ma'am, Mrs. Skelton. I gonna steady be shuckin' and jivin' out of your fine house."

She threw her empty highball glass at him as he was moving out the bedroom door, hitting him in the back. "Goddamn you!" she squalled. "I love you. Don't you realize that? I need you! Get out!"

He could hear her screaming and throwing things about as he hit the back porch then the yard, moving swiftly. Shuckin' and jivin.'

BOOK TWO

BOOK TWO

Six

"Terrance Samuel Kovak." The Principal called out his name, and Terry walked across the stage to receive his high school diploma while his family sat in the audience, grinning and punching each other in the ribs.

Superintendent White breathed a slow sigh of relief, very glad, most happy, in fact, to see this senior go. He still had memories of the night in the Armory, watching that disgusting man eat raw rabbit and rattlesnake.

Later that night, stretched out on a blanket by the lake, Terry stroked the skin of Bishop High's Home Ec teacher, a twenty-three-year-old, red-haired, green-eyed Kentucky girl in her first year of teaching. They were both drunk, and the sweat from their lovemaking had not yet dried on their bodies.

Stretching in front of them, the lake shimmered under the moonlight, alive in the night: a fish jumping, smacking the water; a bird calling out; insects in the woods humming. From across the lake drifted the faint sounds of laughter from a graduation party in full swing. The young High Society of Bishop in their parent's expensive lakefront houses were whooping it up.

"Having fun," Terry muttered. "Well, if they're having

more fun than I'm having, I don't see how they're standing it.''

Ruby softly laughed her agreement.

But the thought rushed through his mind: *Am I having fun? How long since I've had a good old-fashioned belly laugh? Really, how long since I've laughed and meant it, enjoying the humor?*

''What am I going to do next year, Terry?'' Ruby asked. ''You won't be in school.''

He lit a Lucky and they shared it, along with the last few swallows of whiskey from the pint bottle, chasing the booze with Coke. Terry had no answer to her question, and really didn't much care what she did the next year—or the rest of her life, as far as he was concerned. He knew she was leaving town.

Their affair was based on sexual need, nothing more. Neither of them really liked the other.

The wind off the lake grew chilly in the May night, and Ruby snuggled deeper into the warmth of the blanket and Terry. With her head on his naked shoulder, she dozed, while Terry listened to the sounds of young people having fun across the lake.

''Dare ya to go skinny-dippin'!''

Then the shril laughter of a girl caught up in the challenge.

Terry forced the sounds out of his head and thought of things past and present.

Bess had put the word out on him at school after her mother poisoned her mind against him. Terry couldn't get a date with anyone at Bishop High. The girls refused to speak to him. All that summer and into fall he had been ostracized by his peers. Terry accepted it stoically, withdrawing into himself. J. A. flexed his muscles and strutted about, puffing hot air about what he was going to do to Terry . . . if he ever caught him out. But nothing came of the threats: J. A. had tasted Terry's cold method of fighting once—that was quite enough.

Then Terry met Ruby.

* * *

It was a Friday, and Terry sat on the steps of the high school, wondering what he would do with his weekend. He did not look around as the door behind him hissed open and closed.

"Ah," a female voice said. "Mr. Terry Kovak. The baaad boy of Bishop High School. Are you doing penitence for all your whispered sins?" She sat beside him on the steps.

"I don't know. What does that mean?"

"It means," she smiled at him, green eyes sparkling with mischief, "are you sorry for what you've done—or are rumored to have done?"

Terry shrugged. "I haven't done anything, that I know of." He lit a cigarette, offering it to her. She took it, inhaling deeply, then handed the cigarette to Terry.

"Rumor is," her smile broadened, "you not only jazz all the girls, you also jazz their mothers. My, my. Any truth in that, young man?"

"No comment."

She took the cigarette from his lips and smoked it, leaving a trace of lipstick on the end. She put it back between his lips. The paper tasted slightly of peppermint.

"My car's in the garage," she said. "For a valve job. Whatever the hell that is. Will you give me a lift home?"

Terry grinned. "Aren't you taking a chance? I might assault you . . . or something."

She huffed out smoke and said, "The assault I could handle. 'Or something' intrigues me."

"What's your name?"

"Miss Mathews."

"Bullshit!"

She laughed at him. "Okay, how about Ruby?"

"That's better. Come on, Ruby, let's go."

She had expected him to make a pass at her. Terry had not. She had invited him in for a Coke, and he had accepted. He

drank the soft drink, chatted with her, then left without touching
her or making any kind of proposition. He left Ruby wondering
if her lipstick was smeared, her breath bad, or if she had B.O.?

On Saturdays Terry worked at a local service station from
seven in the morning until five in the afternoon. At noon, Ruby
strolled in to buy a package of cigarettes. Kools. Terry was
handling the front by himself while the owner went to lunch.
Ruby had a Coke and chatted with him, while the small radio
played softly.

"You don't live up to your reputation, Terry," she said,
plopping her soft rump on the Coke case. "I felt insulted when
you left the other day."

"What'd you expect me to do? Rape you?"

There was a spot of grease on his cheek and she wiped it
off with a Kleenex from her purse, "If you're the stud you're
rumored to be, I'd expect you to ask if you could come back
sometime."

"Okay."

"Okay? Okay, what?" His answer irritated her and she
almost walked out on him. She thought: *what am I doing fooling
around with this boy?* But she did not leave. "Don't be flip
with me, Terry."

He smiled, but his eyes remained noncommittal, cool, knowing. "Can I come back and see you?"

"May I come back?" she corrected automatically, and they
both laughed.

"Yes, teacher," he said.

"I'll be home tonight. Anytime after seven. Park in the back
so no one will see you."

"Yeah," his smile faded, "I'm getting used to back doors."

She set her Coke bottle on the cooler a bit harder than she
intended. "I don't think I like you very much, Terry."

"Your privilege," he said, then walked into the back to fix
a flat tire.

"Bring a bottle," she called after him. "Scotch."

"I hate Scotch," he said, not turning around.

"Then bring whatever the hell you like!"

He acknowledged her remark with a careless wave of his hand.

"Got a date tonight, Terry?" his father asked at the supper table.

"Maybe," Terry grinned at him. "Thought I'd drive over to Westfield. There's a girl over there who kind of likes me." He was amazed at how quickly the lies came, once a person began living one.

"A nice girl?" his mother looked up.

"Sure, Momma."

Terry did not see the look that passed between his parents. "Be careful, Terry," his father said.

"Where are you from?" he asked Ruby. "You don't have a Georgia accent."

Her apartment was small and very neat. Private, with a back entrance that was convenient for any kind of midnight tête-à-tête. The door to her bedroom was closed, and Terry hid a smile at that.

"Kentucky," she said, and a faint wistful look passed quickly over her face. "The Western part of the state."

"You're a long way from home. Why Bishop, Georgia?"

"They needed a teacher and I needed a job. It's a nice little town." She handed him a drink and sat beside him on the couch, close, but not touching.

"This town stinks and you know it," Terry said, after taking a sip of his drink.

"It's quiet, and no one bothers me here," Ruby said, with a finality that signaled the end of conversation as to why she had settled in Bishop, Georgia.

He placed his drink on a coaster on the coffee table and kissed her. Her mouth moved on his. She abruptly pushed him away and brushed back a strand of hair from her forehead.

She stared hard at him. "I guess the rumors are true, after all."

"I just kissed you," he picked up his drink. "There's no harm in a kiss, is there?"

"Maybe. When one takes into consideration some hard facts: I'm twenty-three and you're not quite eighteen. I'm a teacher and you're a senior in high school."

"Come on, Ruby! You didn't invite me over here to help me with homework."

"Maybe I made a mistake?"

"Maybe you did, at that." Terry stood up to leave and she grabbed at his arm.

"Stay, Terry." Her eyes were soft as she looked up at him. "I'd like to get to know you: understand you. And I need someone to understand me. I . . . ah . . . have special needs from time to time."

"What needs?"

"In time, Terry."

"I'm getting used to hearing that, too. You feel sorry for me?"

"Yes, in a way, I do."

"Interesting," he said.

"We've got to keep this quiet," she warned him. It was late, and they were in bed in her apartment. "I'd lose my job if the school board were to discover I'm dating a student—especially you, Terry. You have got to be the most disliked young man I've ever heard of."

"Thanks a lot," Terry said, snubbing out his cigarette, chuckling.

She stiffened beside him, leaned over him, and clicked on the bed lamp. "I fail to see the humor in being disliked."

"Lately, I fail to see the humor in anything," he retorted.

She lay back on the pillows and rubbed his flat, hard stomach with her hand. "Terry, you don't behave as a high school senior should. You act more like a grown man. What is it with you?"

"Nothing," he said, his tone holding no feeling.

She felt his mood shift. The boy/man beside her fascinated the woman, yet somehow frightened her as well. He was both repelling and appealing to her, as a swaying, silent cobra is to its fabled hypnotized victim, held enthralled until the final darting strike.

There were whispers around Bishop High. Talk that Miss Mathews was seeing Terry Kovak on the Q.T. The school board quietly looked into the matter and decided it was just talk, though Miss Mathews dated no one openly. Superintendent White played the story down; he wanted it over and done with and forgotten as quickly as possible. He could not get the memory of that evening at the Armory out of his mind.

"Let the kids talk," he told the school board. "It's just talk, nothing more."

The subject was closed.

The laughter from across the lake had faded and died into silence. Ruby dozed beside him while Terry inspected the stars far above him. The woman stirred, and he felt her hand moving on his body.

"Terry?" Ruby spoke against his skin, her breath warm, her hand busy at his groin.

"Uh-huh?"

"I'm leaving town in a few weeks. I won't be back."

"Yeah, I heard. I'm glad for you if that's what you want."

"What will become of you, Terry? Despite the way I know you feel—and I know you don't like me—I do worry about you."

"I'll make out, and who said I didn't like you?"

"Don't lie, Terry. A woman can sense some things that a man cannot."

He did not reply and she moved on him, her hands making him hard. "Let's make tonight the last time for us, Terry. We'll say goodbye this way."

As she brought him to full hardness and mounted him, Terry wondered what had happened to his boyhood. As she swung into an easy rhythm, straddling him, moving up and down on him, her face contorted with pleasure, Terry's body occupied itself with sex and his mind finally moved free, away from philosophical meanderings he did not understand.

He laughed in the night as the old song came to him: No more studies, no more books. No more teachers' dirty looks.

"It's good, baby!" Ruby moaned on him, her breasts bouncing. "It's the best ever."

"Yeah, Ruby," he agreed, and let his mind race away from the present.

In a week he would be leaving for Fort Benning, Georgia, and Jump School, then off to some other post for five months more of training. Phases One and Two of Perret's Dog Team training. He viewed the upcoming training with mixed emotions.

Ruby picked up her rhythm, groaning in the early summer's night, sweating in the lake breeze, fucking on graduation night.

Terry put his hands on her naked hips, enjoying the smooth feel of her—for the last time. They had used each other up.

"Hurt me, Terry!" she cried out, and he dug his fingers into the softness until she whimpered. "More!" she called, and his hands bruised her flesh.

Crazy woman, he thought—pain and sex, all mingled together. He recalled the time in her apartment, weeks back, when she had handed him a thick leather belt.

"I've been a very bad girl," she told him, unbuttoning her housecoat. She stood naked in front of him. "I want you to punish me."

Terry looked at the belt in his hands, then at her. "What the hell are you? Some kind of nut?"

"No," she told him, green eyes alive with a strange kind of light. "At least not much of one and not very often. I told you, Terry, I have special needs, that's all. I need to be disciplined every now and then."

Damn weirdo. Terry thought.

She knelt in front of him, buttocks elevated. "Whip me!" she ordered.

"I'll be damned if I will. You don't need me, Ruby, you need a doctor—a head doctor."

"Terry, you don't understand. I've got to be punished. If

you don't do it, I'll go out and find some . . . thug. Please punish me.''

He hit her lightly on the rump with the belt, feeling very much the fool. She laughed at him, her laughter muffled against the carpet.

"I don't need love-taps, Terry," she said. "Put some muscle behind it."

"Ruby . . . I can't do it. This is not normal. You're sick. You need some kind of help."

She rose from her submissive position on the floor, faced him, then slapped him on the face. Instinctively, he returned the pop, backhanding her to the floor; a tiny trickle of blood leaked from a corner of her mouth. She smiled up at him, her hands squeezing her breasts, pinching the nipples.

She rolled to her knees, assuming the position. "Punish me, Terry. Now. Please!"

He looked at the belt in his hand, then dropped it on the floor. "No way," the young man said.

Ignoring her pleas, he walked out the back door, got in his car, and drove off. He did not see Ruby for a week; she called in to the school, telling them she was very ill. When Terry next saw her, her body still carried the marks of the beating.

"I told you I'd find someone to do it," she reminded him.

"Your choice," he told her. "Just don't ask me to do it."

The stars began to fade and the moon was covered with clouds. The night had turned moist. Terry dressed, then stood looking down at Ruby, asleep on the blankets. He felt nothing for her. He sensed she had added more confusion to his life at a time when he least needed it. Reaching down, he shook her awake.

"Come on, Ruby. I'll take you home."

Seven

"My son will be gone for six months at some faraway Army Fort!" Mrs. Kovak was upset. "Karl, he's just a young boy."

"He's eighteen, Momma," Karl tried to comfort his wife. "And he's in the Army—sort of. He'll be learning his skills. He's a man, and he's not ours, alone, anymore."

"I don't like it, Poppa. I just don't like it. Nothing good is ever going to come of this. I feel it in my bones."

"Yes, Momma," he patted his wife's arm. "I know."

Second only to the first time he made it with a woman, this was the high point in Terry's life; this sprawling base in the South, filled with Infantrymen and Paratroopers and Rangers and super-secret special groups of highly trained men and women. Terry would soon be a part of them, but first he would undergo Jump Training. He looked up to the sky, watching as planes spat out men, tiny under the blossoming silk as they floated to their Drop Zones.

His stomach did a little kick.

* * *

Sixty boots hit the ground in unison as the group of men ran to the airstrip, chanting verses of the seemingly endless Airborne training songs.

"Hey, hey, haven't you heard?

"We're gonna jump from the big-assed bird."

"I wanna live a life of danger,

"I wanna be an Airborne Ranger."

At the strip, they were allowed to rest and smoke (if you have 'um) before chuting up with main back packs and belly reserve chutes. They were, to a man, all frightened, but not a one would admit it—aloud.

Picking up their static lines, they received a short lecture, then climbed into the planes. In a few minutes they were circling the Drop Zone, and two men had already puked in the plane, vomiting up their fright.

Terry leaned close to the man next to him and said, in a whispering shout, above the roar of wind and engines, "I'm scared shitless!"

The man rolled his eyes and nodded his agreement. Lights flashed on, bells rang, and the sticks of soon-to-be-paratroopers waited for the word.

It came all too quickly. "Stand up and hook up! Check equipment, and sound off!"

"Stand in the door!" came the call from the Jumpmaster. The light changed, and the time was now.

The first man in the left stick was in the door, in position, his mind racing, trying to remember all he'd been taught: *Keep your feet together; don't crack your spine; roll . . . Oh, Jesus, what else? What have I forgotten?*

The light came on, a slap on the butt. "Go!" And the men were moving through the door, stepping into nothing. Some of the men went pissing in their shorts, some shitting, some puking. All went out the door.

On the ground, in the DZ, the men gathered up their silk, laughing, cursing, pounding each other on the back. There were only a few minor injuries: bruises, scratches; no broken bones.

The landing was perfect all the way around. A few more jumps and they would earn their Blood Wings.

Terry wasn't sure where he was. The men had loaded at dusk, landing after a ten hour flight. They had flown west; Terry knew that from the stars, but exactly how far west, he had no idea. The country was rugged—desert, with mountains in the not-too-far distance.

Colonel Perret, dressed in camouflage field clothes, greeted the new arrivals. "Welcome to Utah, men." He split them up into small groups, gave them each a number to replace his name, and turned them over to some of the meanest-looking men Terry had ever seen. He faced Terry, alone at the strip.

"Well, Terry," he returned the young man's salute. "We're going to see if we can break you during the next several months. Think you can take it?"

"Whatever you dish out, sir."

"Is that right?" Perret grinned. He liked this young man.

"Correct, sir."

"Good," Perret's grin faded and his face turned hard. "From this moment on, your name is number five. Remember it. Now hit the ground and give me twenty push-ups."

"I beg your pardon, sir?"

"HIT THE FUCKIN' GROUND AND GIVE ME *THIRTY* PUSH-UPS AND ONE FOR AIRBORNE!" he roared.

Terry dropped to the ground and began pumping out push-ups, adding one for Airborne. He jumped to his feet to stand at attention.

"YOU FORGOT TO COUNT THEM! DO IT OVER!"

Again.

"Good," Perret said. "Very good. Now then, you listen to me. From this moment forward, you obey orders instantly. You will not think about them—just obey them as if they came from God. If an instructor of this group gives you an order to climb the nearest pole . . . you climb it! If you're ordered to run until you drop, do it! If I tell you to kill a man—do it! Do you understand all that?"

"Yes, sir!" Terry shouted.

"Move out!"

"Where, sir?"

"MOVE OUT! Run! I don't give a goddamn where to—just move it!"

Terry moved it, at a flat lope. Unfortunately, he didn't look where he was going and ran into a barracks, knocking himself unconscious.

Terry had never been so completely physically and mentally exhausted in his life. As if the physical conditioning wasn't bad enough (it was terrible), the mental conditioning was brutal. Terry knew he had run over a hundred miles the first week; an average of sixteen miles a day—eight in the morning, eight before evening chow. In between: push-ups, sit-ups, duck-walks, hand-to-hand combat training, rappelling down steep mountains until he was dizzy. One man died. Close combat training with K-bars: fighting knives with brass knuckles welded to the handles. One man had been seriously hurt during the second day's knife training.

The men spent three hours a day, seven days a week, in mental conditioning classes, hardening them to pain, blood, suffering, and killing. They ate raw meat from freshly killed animals (they did the killing, sometimes with their bare hands), until the men began to feel like cannibals. They were being systematically reduced to the level of savages, with only one thought uppermost in their minds: SURVIVE. Several men would crack under the extreme pressures.

Of the sixty men who had begun this training cycle, thirty had dropped out, cracked up, been wounded so severely they had to be hospitalized, or died. More would quit. More would die. Terry lay in his bunk, feeling his legs tremble from the strain of training. He silently swore he would never quit; he'd die first. He would take whatever Perret's people threw at him, and he would make it. He rolled over on his side and dropped off to sleep, exhausted.

*   *   *

At the end of sixteen weeks, there were eleven men left in the group, and they were a rough, hard-bitten lot, honed down to muscle, bone, and raw nerve. The next week they would graduate from phase one of their training. The eleven survivors sat in bleachers, listening to Colonel Bill Perret speak.

"You've made it, men," he grinned at them. "I think you'll be able to make it through the rest of it. We've weeded out the ones who couldn't take it . . . for whatever reason. But, don't ever look down on those men, not for one second. Those men will go on to become your 'solid citizen types.' They're the ones who'll pay the taxes and make this country work. As for us," his grin became a hard slit, "we'll fight their wars for them; usually in some stinking little back country no one ever heard of. Or in alleys, gutters, swamps, or jungles. And we won't receive fifteen cents worth of praise for our efforts. The public won't give a shit when you die . . . because they won't know about it. Most of our fighting will be done in the shadows. Don't expect to be made heroes, because you won't be. Even should the public hear of us, they'll be appalled at the work we do—the majority of them. They don't give a good goddamn about men like us, but there are many reasons for that. Paramount, I believe, is simply that they cannot comprehend what we've gone through, and what we will go through for them." He waved his hand, indicating the outside world.

"Those people out there, they read spy novels, they see movies about hit men, professional assassins, and so forth, but most of them don't believe anything like that could exist in America, especially government-paid assassins." he smiled. "Little do they know.

"All right, men. I'm proud of you. You've put yourselves through Hell for something you believe in: America. Well, I believe in her, too. Unfortunately," he smiled, ruefully, "the courts won't take that love into consideration if you get caught after dropping the hammer on someone.

"Now, then, you all know that graduating from this school does not entitle you to any special badges, flashes, or patches.

It will not show up on any 201 file. You all know what that means: you've all taken the Secrecy Oath and the Oath of Silence. Officially, Dog Teams do not exist. We're the bad boys of the military. The top brass, most of them, those chair-borne warriors, get nervous twitches just thinking about us. And they should. We're the best in the world at what we do. Since 1948, I've pushed twelve groups of men and women through this training, incorporating them all into various branches of military and civilian life, ready to do a job for their government, whenever there is a job to be done. Questions?''

A hand shot up.

"Yes, number ten?"

"You mean, sir, that when I leave here next week, I'm to go back to my duty assignment as Signal Officer?"

"That is correct, number ten. All of you men will have cover stories as to where you have been. Most especially, where you have not been: here.''

Terry raised his hand and the Colonel nodded. "I understand, sir, that if we—any of us—run into each other outside of here, we don't know each other.''

"That is correct, number five, you've never met. How could you? This place does not exist.''

"But we've all mailed letters home," a man said.

"You've mailed letters, yes, but your mail was opened, censored, rewritten, and post-marked from another base. Those of you who called out of here or received phone calls should know all calls were rerouted.

"We'll spend the next week going over your cover stories: why you were selected to come here, what you'll be doing when you leave. As soon as you've been briefed, you'll leave this camp, without communicating with each other. You will not, I hope, see each other again—unless you are assigned to work a job together. Remember this, men: you all have a great deal of training still ahead of you. But you'll make it.'' He wheeled about smartly and walked away.

A Master Sergeant took over. "The rest of the day is yours to spend as you please. Since you can't leave the camp area, weve put beer in he barracks. If you wish to get drunk, feel free to do so . . ." There was a cheer at this news. "You'll fall out at 0700 hours tomorrow to start your briefing. That's all. Take off."

Colonel Perret came right to the point. "You see, Terry, Sergeant Tate was about a hundred and fifty meters from you on the day you killed that Cracker, Farago. He reported to me; I liked your style."

"Yes, sir, I know. Tate told me, some months ago. In so many words, sir: you've got me by the balls."

Perret laughed. "You're a natural, Terry. In all my years, I've never seen a more natural killer than you. And I mean that as a compliment, not implying at all that you are a homicidal maniac. None of my people can be called that. But you can kill without remorse, to protect yourself, or your country."

"I know I'm not like other people," Terry admitted. "If that's what you mean."

The Colonel's face turned serious. "Make the military your life, Terry, just as I've done. In special units; crack units. You won't always be in my teams, but understand this while you are: less than one tenth of one half percent—and that may be exaggerated—of the military is made up of men like us. But we're protected in here, Terry; needed to do a specific and very important job . . . for the time being. When you're ready to get out, ready to return to civilian life, we can down-train you and make you acceptable to civilian life. I can almost guarantee that. But out there, Terry," he waved his hand, indicating the world and life beyond the military, his version of the military, "they'll shit on you and you'll end up in the gas chamber or a cell for the rest of your life. Let me channel your natural tendencies to work for your country. I guarantee you Buck Sergeant in a month, plus . . . ah . . . more money, under the table, so to speak."

"I intend to make the military my career, sir."

"Good. Then we'll speak no more of it."

* * *

It was over in the pump of two heartbeats: number seven lay dead on the floor of the barracks, his neck broken, spleen ruptured, and one side of his skull indented from a kick with a heavy boot. Terry stood over him, startled, but not shocked, at what had just transpired. He felt no pity for the man— number seven had started it.

No one in the room seemed unduly upset about the incident; their training had been too thorough. One man looked up from his bunk and girlie magazine, grunted, took a sip of beer, then returned his attentions to the pictures of half-naked women.

"I'll go get the Colonel," the man said.

There were a few moments of silence while several men milled about the body of number seven.

"You're good, kid," a dark-complexioned soldier said. "You're real good."

"He started it," Terry looked down at the dead man. Blood leaked from the nose and mouth of number seven.

"Don't worry about it," number nine said. "We all saw him come at you when your back was turned. I've heard him say, more than once, that he was gonna kill you if he ever got the chance. Seven's had a hard-on toward you for weeks. Every since you bested him on the close-combat range."

"Yeah," the man with the girlie magazine laughed, "every time the two of you met you put him down. Seven was a horse's ass."

"How'd you know the swing was coming?" Colonel Perret spoke from the door of the barracks.

Terry met his eyes. "I sensed it."

"He reminds me of a pet wolf I had," number three said. "Up in Wisconsin. Big mother: a buffalo wolf. You wanted to trust him, wanted to pet him, but something in his eyes made you pull your hand back at the last moment." He looked at Terry. "If push ever comes to shove, number five, I sure as hell want you on my side."

"That'll do," Perret said. He looked at Terry. "Come with me, number five."

Terry matched the Colonel's stride as they walked away from the barracks into the night. An ambulance would arrive and number seven's body would be taken away. Listed officially as killed in a training exercise. The two men walked in silence for more than a mile, finally turning onto the now-deserted training area.

Perret spun, angry, facing Terry. "It cost the government many thousands of dollars to train number seven. All for nothing. Wasted!"

Terry opened his mouth to speak.

"Shut up!" Perret snapped at him. "You've got to learn to control what we taught you here, and what we'll teach you in the future. We can't have you out in civilian life running around killing people with your hands. Goddamnit, you'd scare those candy-ass civilians to death. Those aren't warriors out there," he jerked his thumb toward the outside world. "Those people out there are pussys and duck hunters. They're not like us. They cannot comprehend people like us. And I've got to make you see that. I know only one way to do it."

Terry never saw the blow that knocked him sprawling on the gravel and sand. He tasted the salty favor of blood in his mouth. When his vision cleared and the ringing in his head abated, the Colonel was standing over him.

"You think you're dangerous, now?" Perret said. "You think you're bad? I'm going to show you what dangerous really is. Get up!"

Clouds hid the moon as rain splattered on Terry's face, urging him to consciousness. He ached all over. The memory of the short but very savage fight with Perret came to him in a rush of colored emotions. He crawled to his knees, then to his feet. How long had he been there? How long had he been out? An hour, surely—maybe longer. He began his walk back to the barracks, slowly, for his ribs hurt, each step bringing pain to him, fanning over his entire body.

Despite his pain, Terry grinned in the light rain. He had gotten several pretty good licks in on the Colonel, bringing grunts of pain and anger from the man. Then Perret really lowered the boom on him.

Terry knew this had been an object lesson, the colonel choosing physical rather than verbal means. At this juncture, Terry fervently wished the Colonel had merely lectured him. But words fade within hours; this lesson would stay with him for a long, long time.

"Okay, Colonel," Terry spoke to the night and the mist, "you got your point across, sir."

He limped on, with no one challenging him. The small camp was void of life. The barracks were empty, except for Perret. Everyone else was gone—shipped out. Perret said nothing to him, just pointed to his locker. Terry's duffle bag was sitting forlornly on the mattressless bunk. His class-A's were hanging on the locker door. He showered, dressed, then walked out to meet Perret.

The Colonel pointed to the airstrip, where a plane sat, its engines ticking.

The two men walked into the night, boarded the plane, and flew off to the east.

Eight

"Where are we, sir?" Terry asked, looking around the wooded area.

"Maryland. It's very quiet here, very secluded. A training area for my people. This is where we get down to the serious business of teaching you to kill."

"When I leave here, sir . . ."

"*If* you leave here."

". . . what will my job be?"

"The unit in Bishop is up to full strength. Tate needs an assistant—you. Your records will show you as graduated from NCO school at Benning. As of 0800 this morning, you're a Buck Sergeant. Okay?"

"Yes, sir—fine."

He couldn't breathe! The wire around his neck was cutting into flesh and his vision was dimming. It was useless trying to get his fingers under the wire, and he had only a few seconds left. Terry relaxed and drove his elbows back into his assailant's stomach, at the same time bringing the heel of his boot down hard on the top of the man's foot. A howl of pain, and the wire loosened. Terry slipped from the noose of the wire, rolled to the ground, and came to his feet, hands open and held in a defensive position, just before killing.

He moved forward, blocking a chop from his assailant and driving stiffened fingers into the man's lower belly, at the same time bringing his right hand up, heel of hand raised like a snake, to smash the man's nose and drive the cartilage into his brain. He pulled his blow at the last split-second.

"Very good, Kovak," an instructor told him, walking between the two men, allowing them time to cool their blood before training became reality—as it sometimes does in harsh close-combat schools. "You broke free and killed him. Outstanding! Work out with the Kindo stick for fifteen minutes and then take a break."

Terry nodded, walking away.

"That kid's almost too good," Terry heard another instructor say. "I've never seen anything like him."

"I have," the chief instructor said. "I helped train some of Wild Bill Donovan's boys in England during the war. I've seen some just as good, but none any better."

Terry walked away.

"This place is something, isn't it?" the young woman said.

There was a bruise on her right cheek, and her left hand was swollen. Terry had seen her around the training area a dozen times, but never closely enough to speak to her.

"Yeah," he said, taking in her figure, which was shapely, and her face, which was cute. "How'd you hurt yourself?"

She shrugged. "I got careless on the Close-Combat Range." Big brown eyes looked at him, inspecting him, accepting him after a few seconds. "My name's Sally."

"Terry." First names were preferred at this Camp. "You're the only woman in my cycle, aren't you?" It was not a question. "How old are you, Sally?" Terry blurted out the last. More than half the trainees were young, scarcely out of their teens. Easier to train, to mold, Perret said.

"Twenty." Lovely brown eyes never left his face. "You can't be much older." They shook hands warily, for one never knew who to trust in training; when friendliness might be a trick and the unsuspecting would suddenly find himself flat on his back with a knife at his throat. ''There are two other women in the camp that I know of,'' she said. ''But they're in the final phase. I understand that's pretty rough. Two guys were killed over there last week.''

''Yeah, I heard it was tough. I got to go through Army Ranger school before I take on that phase, though.''

''You'll make it. The word around camp is you're tough.''

''So I'm told.''

It was late Saturday afternoon, the training over until Monday morning. The men and women could relax for a time; some even went home if they lived nearby. Back to a normal life for thirty-six hours. Perret had gone fishing . . . the instructors back to their homes just off the small government-owned base . . . and the training areas were silent. No grunting of humans locked in deadly training; no shots from the more than thirty weapons each Dog Team trainee was required to learn; no booming of explosives from grenades and homemade bombs.

A softness lay on the land, belying the truth about the camp, as if the place had never seen sudden death, violent training: preaching it, teaching it.

''My last name's Malone,'' Sally said, then looked around to see if anyone else might be listening.

''Kovak,'' Terry followed suit.

''We wouldn't be breaking any rules by just talking or walking around together, would we?'' she asked.

''Not that I know of.'' Terry took her hand and gently pulled her to her feet. ''Come on, let's walk down by the creek. It's quiet down there.''

With approaching twilight, the shadows had grown heavier, deeper, bolder, silently slipping through the afternoon to grasp the countryside in a darker embrace, to close around the young man and young woman who sat chatting by the tiny, rushing creek. Enjoying a few moments of peaceful intimacy.

''How'd you get into this outfit?'' Terry asked. ''Don't worry,'' he quickly assured her, ''I'm not from ASA or the Agency.''

"Or from DOD or CIC or NSA?" she smiled.

He laughed. "Yeah, there's a lot of them."

Sally sighed, as if the remembrance was a weight on her thoughts. "It's not a very pretty story."

"Neither is mine. Hell, I don't suppose anyone has a pretty story, really."

"I was with some guys in New York City," Sally said. "We got drunk and decided it would be fun to steal a car and joyride. It was a big, long Cadillac, black. If we'd had any sense we'd have looked at the license plates." She snorted a bitter chuckle. "If we'd had any sense we wouldn't have taken the car, to begin with. Anyway, the car belonged to a diplomat: English, I think. Some big-wig. We wrecked it and the guy driving got killed, but not before we ran down two kids who were playing in the street—at one o'clock in the morning. We banged them up pretty bad. Almost killed one of them. Suddenly, it was all hush-hush, like being in a super-spy movie or something. I only talked to one cop, really, plainclothes, and he had a funny accent. The guys with me were booked, but I wasn't. They never knew my last name—I wasn't using Malone at the time. They went to prison; I went to Perret. It was only recently that I began to realize just how big Perret's group really is—I mean, how much scope it encompasses."

"You mean, about how he has people in a lot of big-city police departments—stuff like that?"

"Yes," she seemed surprised, and a bit cautious. "How do you know that?"

"I guessed it."

"Anyway, the next thing I know, I'm up at Camp Drum in New York State, and Perret is talking to me, telling me everything is going to be all right. You know, I thought I even saw the President up here last month. Perret really has a big operation."

"I think we're needed," Terry said, tossing a pebble into the creek. "I really believe that. Don't you?"

"Yes. I guess so. Oh, I suppose deep down I know so." She lay back on the grass and moss, looking up at Terry in the dim light. "I'll tell you one thing, though: it's a hell of a lot better than going to prison. Tell you the truth, I don't mind it all that much. I'm a Lieutenant, I'm paid good—if you know what I mean—and I'm beginning to enjoy my work. I've been on two assignments. You?''

''No, I haven't done anything but train—so far.''

''I mean, how'd you get into the Dog Teams?''

He told her, leaving nothing out. Afterward, he felt more relaxed, getting it out of his mind, sharing it with someone.

''That took guts, standing up to that man with just a knife. I guess the talk is true about you.''

''What talk?''

''That you're the Colonel's fair-haired boy; that he's got you picked to be one of his personal Guns. You're going to be one of Perret's Smoky Boys. Maybe I shouldn't have told you that.''

''It's okay, I guessed that a long time ago. After I did some thinking about how easy it was for me to get in the Guard.''

Just before Terry kissed her; just before they made love on the grass and moss by the whispering creek in the Maryland hills; just before they began an affair that would last—off and on—for many years, Terry said, ''I think I was born to it.''

Sally

"I won't tell you to stop seeing the Malone girl," Colonel Perret said, "but I wish you would."

Sergeant Kovak stood impassively in front of Perret's desk. He did not speak.

Perret rubbed his hand across his face. "Sergeant Kovak." He spoke slowly, chosing his words carefully. "You've been here for twelve weeks. You know what you're being trained to do. You're going to be a member of a very special group of people—made up of all branches of the military. Call it what you will: counter-espionage, counter-insurgency; spy, spook, secret agent; you know, and I surely know, what we really are. We're guns for the government of the United States. Paid killers. That's it. And I'm sure you know, by now, that we've been training you, off and on, mentally and physically, for quite some time. After you take a short Ranger course, you'll be ready.

"Now, I know you've been involved with the Malone woman. Hell, you've been humping her every chance you get for over a month. Suppose I sent you both on assignment—together—and it came down to the nut-cutting: you had to sacrifice her or blow the mission. What would you do?"

Terry grinned his little-boy grin, but it was wasted on the Colonel. "That's simple, Colonel: don't send us out together."

"I ought to get up from behind this desk and stomp your insubordinate ass!"

"Meaning no disrespect, sir, and begging your pardon, but are you sure you can whip my ass?"

"Yeah, Kovak," Perret grinned. "I'm sure. I've still got the edge on you. I'm polished by years, you're still a diamond in the rough." He glared at Terry and shook his head. "I'm going to regret the day I brought you into this outfit—I can feel it in my guts. You're just too cool; too good to be real." He waved the thought away with a jerk of his hand. "Okay, Kovak, go on seeing your cunt, 'cause in a couple of weeks I'm going to ship her pretty dimpled ass so far away from here you'll never see her again."

"What do you want me to do or say about that: break down in tears?"

Perret chuckled and Terry added, "By the way, Colonel, how do you know her ass is dimpled?"

"Maybe I got some, too?"

"You sorry ass—you dirty old man."

Perret laughed until tears rolled down his tanned cheeks. He slapped his hard hand on the desk top. "By God, Kovak, maybe there's some hope for you, still. God, you're a rogue bastard. I thought you were falling for her. I should have known better."

"No, sir, not at all. She's just handy, that's all. Fun to be with."

"Got no feeling for her, Terry? No deep feeling at all?"

"I don't guess so, sir. I mean, I don't want to marry her."

"Ever been in love?"

"No, sir."

Perret knew then—sensed it—the personality profiles on Kovak only scratched the surface. Terry was as many-sided as the Pentagon.

Perret smiled. He had never fooled around on his wife. Not in almost twenty years of marriage. "I hope I'm around when you finally fall for a woman. Oh, Lord: great the fall thereof.''

"What the hell does that mean, Colonel?''

His answer was a chuckle. "Go on back to your training, Terry.''

"Terry?'' Sally spoke to the night, its shadows, and to the young man beside her.

"Ummm?''

"I wonder what Colonel Perret would say if we both told him we wanted out?''

"Why would I want to ask him that?'' Terry sat up. "I don't want out. I'm perfectly happy doing what I'm doing.''

She looked away from him. "What would you say if I told you I love you?''

"I'd say you were a fool!'' Terry gazed at the dark waters of the small creek, then glanced at the dim shape of the creek bank. She started to touch him, then drew back her hand.

"But I do love you. I gave myself to you, didn't I?''

"I wasn't the first. Don't try to tell me I was.'' His words were cold.

"On second thought, I don't love you, I hate you!''

"Good. That will probably be best for both of us.''

"I feel sorry for you, Terry.'' She sat up, adjusting her clothing, patting her hair. "You're going to be such a miserable, totally rotten bastard!''

"What is it with you women? I don't know why you all have to complicate things. Why did you say that? I haven't done anything to you.''

"You don't have any feelings, Terry. You think a woman values her sex that lightly?''

"Oh, hell, I don't know.'' Terry rose and walked away from her, following the creek bank back to the path, ignoring her calls for him to come back to her, 'cause she was sorry for what she'd said.

Her life should have—could have—been so different. Sally had had it all going for her, growing up in Binghamton, N.Y.

Successful parents whose income placed them in the super upper-upper middle class, just short of wealthy, almost, but not quite, rich, with a swimming pool and a tennis court. At age sixteen, Sally had traveled in Europe, spoke several languages—if not fluently, at least enough to get by—owned a sports car, a horse, was in the top five of her class, had had her debutante's ball, and the future looked good stretching before her.

Then she met a hot-shot, horse's-butt college boy named David.

"Come on, baby!" he panted in her ear, his breath hot. "If you won't give me some, at least jerk me off. You got me so hot I can't stand it."

His father's Cadillac was parked along and above the Susquehanna River. It was early December and the windows were steamed up, and so were the two occupants. The sixteen-year-old girl and the twenty-year-old college boy grappled and groped in the front seat. They sweated and pawed and pushed at each other. Sally touched his erect penis, which was sticking out of his pants, and imagined a snake felt pretty much the same. She couldn't envision how that thing would feel inside her; but the way some girls talked, it must feel pretty damn good.

She let David remove her panties and paw around between her legs, with her skirt bunched up around her waist, her blouse open, and her bra unhooked.

David kissed her with lips and tongue and wetness. She held onto his penis, made up her mind, and then released the stiffness, removing the rest of her clothing.

"The back seat, David," she whispered.

He got stuck between seat and roof and managed to fall ingloriously on top of her.

He *is* in her, groaning, hunching, and mouthing inanities, none of which Sally believed. Meaningless words of endearment in a moment of young passion.

The sliding in and out *is* rather pleasant, and she clutched him; now it is she who whispered love words. Then it was over too quickly, and she was filled with a gush of liquid and a slight sense of loss. David collapsed on her, recovered, and took her home—quickly.

A few months later she discovered she was pregnant. She never saw David again.

New York City frightened her. The name of the doctor was written on a piece of paper in her purse. The money for the abortion, in hundred dollar bills, was tucked safely in her bra. It chafed her breasts.

Her parents have told her not to worry: what she is doing is the right thing.

Back at her hotel, the operation over and the whole ugly bloody mess flushed down NYC's sewer system, Sally stretched out on the bed and cried.

"Son of a bitch!" she cursed David, but it did feel good while he was doing it to her, she remembered.

Later that night she woke in a pool of blood and pain . . . hemorrhaging. Unable to stop the alarming flow of blood, scared witless, she stumbled into the hall and collapsed at the feet of a totally astonished couple from Iowa, on their first—and probably last—trip to the Big Apple. At the hospital, the doctors told Sally she would be all right, but she'd never be able to have children.

"No daughter of mine is going to sleep around like some whore!" her father yelled at her. "I wish to God I could send you to a military school."

"Hey, that'd be super," Sally said. "Must be about five miles of cock at the average military school. When do I leave?" She didn't mean it, and she wasn't a whore; not really promiscuous. She just got caught with a boy with his hand up her dress.

Her face stinging and reddening from the open-handed slap from her father, Sally looked up at him from her newly and quite suddenly attained position on the living-room floor.

"I hate you!" she glared at her father. "God, you don't know how I hate you."

She is eighteen.

Just for an instant, her father's eyes softened, then his features hardened as he made his decision. "You've got a younger sister and brother here in this house. I can't have you corrupting them. You're just no good, Sally. You're a little tramp. I'll pay the rent on an apartment and give you an allowance until you can find a job in the city. Pack your clothes, take your car, and get out of here. Sell your butt on the streets of New York City with the rest of the street-walkers."

Sally picked herself up from the floor. There was a slight trickle of blood from one corner of her mouth. "You won't object if I tell mother goodbye?"

"Your mother does not wish to see you," he lied. "Not ever again."

Sally glanced in the rearview mirror. She had just passed the city limits sign. "Hello, Binghamton," she said, tears forming in her eyes, welling up, running down her cheeks. "Goodbye, Binghamton."

She clicked on the radio as the disc jockey intro'ed a Goldie Oldie. *Daddy's Little Girl.*

This time, New York wasn't so frightening. Sally found an apartment in the Village, sharing it with two other girls. One was from Ohio, the other from Tennessee. *Ohio* worked as a full-time waitress and part-time writer. *Tennessee* was an artist, peddling her painting and occasionally her ass.

Sally sold her car, or rather, what was left of it after she parked it on the street her first day in the Big Apple—Fun City. The car thieves took the tires, wheels, seats, and radio. Sally sold what was left.

For a year, Sally worked, part-time, at a dozen different shops and cafes and stores. She wasn't qualified to do very much. Her only contact with her parents was a check each month. No notes, messages, or social amenities from father and mother to daughter.

Then the money stopped coming.

She began drinking more, and was sometimes into drugs:

snorting coke and smack, smoking mary jane, Sally took her night ride in a stolen car.

Sergeant Kovak propped his Jump Boots up on his desk and twiddled his thumbs. Tate grinned at him from behind his desk, where he was occupying his time concentrating on a crossword puzzle.

"Sometimes we get busy, Terry, and, when we do, we work our butts off. But most of the time we just piddle around at makework projects."

"Hell, it's boring!"

Tate put away his crossword puzzle book. "Yeah, but you just came off months of hard and fast training. Don't worry, the Colonel—the Head Dog—will call on you soon enough."

Terry looked at him.

Tate matched his glance. "I've been with Dog Teams—of one name or the other—since 1944. Now that you know, you can forget I said it."

Terry wouldn't leave it alone. "How did you get in with Colonel Perret?"

The Master Sergeant sighed. "I'll make it short, then we won't bring it up again." He smiled, a sad moving of the lips. "Back during the war—the Second one—I was on leave in England in 1943 when I got word my wife was fucking around on me in the States. I went a little nuts. Banged up some MP's and then assaulted an Officer of the Crown. Wound up pulling hard stockade time. Perret came to see me. You can put the rest of it together yourself."

"Wonder how many people are in this thing?" Terry mused.

"In what thing?"

"Dog Teams."

Tate smiled. "Never heard of them. By the way, how was Ranger School?"

"Rough."

"Of the four hundred chosen in pre-Ranger testing, only eighty made it through the most grueling training—at this time—ever devised by the U. S. Army."

"Yeah," Terry said, almost in a whisper. "It was rough."

"I know," Tate said. "I was with Darby in '43."

"March or die."

"You better believe it."

Nine

The crisp and often lovely days of fall moved into the cold and sometimes lonely days of winter. Rain was mixed with bits of snow and ice; steamy breath shone against a backdrop of white-covered ground—people hurried along from one warm spot to another.

When Terry entered the Armory that morning, Colonel Perret was sitting at his desk, a cup of coffee and a folder before him.

"Good morning, Sergeant Kovak." The Colonel was all business and Terry quickly sensed it.

"Morning, sir. Haven't seen you for a few months." He sat down in front of his desk and waited for the Colonel to lay it on him.

Perret opened the folder and tapped a blunt finger on an 8×10 photograph. "Gene Hubbell," he said. "Employee of the government. Top secret clearance; just last month granted Eyes and Ears Only rating. Then, last week, it was discovered he's been working for the Russians, passing high-level information to them. That passed information just cost two men their lives in East Berlin. The men worked for the Agency."

Terry knew his months of training and studying were at an

end. Gene Hubbell was to be taken out, and he was to do the taking.

"May I have the bottom line, Colonel?" Terry asked.

"The agent, Hubbell, is to be dealt with in an extremely prejudicial manner."

Kill him. "Yes, sir."

"Very well. Now then, Hubbell has taken two weeks leave time from his post in Washington. He'll be visiting his sister in Kansas. Western Kansas." He told Terry the name of the small city. "On February the first, Hubbell is to link up with a Red agent at the zoo. He'll be exchanging papers for money. We've managed to juggle the date around so Hubbell thinks the meet will take place on the last day of January. The man he'll meet is you. There is a very slight chance the Red agent might be around, waiting. If so, *don't* kill the Moscow man." He met Terry's steady gaze. "He's a double agent. Those orders come from The Golfer. You understand?"

The President. "Yes, sir."

Perret handed Terry a slip of paper. "When you get to the city in Kansas, check into the motel named on that paper. The next morning, you won't get ten miles out of town before your engine will lock up: the oil plug will have worked loose. There will be a tow truck happening along. You'll have four or five days in the city while your engine is being replaced. Plenty of time to deal with Hubbell. Rent a car to run around in. Your car will be repaired by late afternoon of the last day in January; that's a Thursday. That night, meet Hubbell, then get the hell out of there. Your false ID, driver's license, money, all the other paraphernalia you'll need, including your orders, are in this envelope." He pushed a manila envelope toward Terry. "Memorize your orders, then burn them. Understood?"

"Yes, sir."

"Any qualms about this job?"

"The man's a traitor, isn't he?"

"Most definitely."

"Does he need the money he's getting selling secrets?"

Another side to Kovak, Colonel Perret thought. "What do you mean, Sergeant?"

"Just what I said, sir. Does he need the money to support his family? His parents? Sickness that's got him in a bind—that sort of thing."

"Would it make any difference?"

"It would to me."

Perret thought: *I'll have to be very careful where I send Kovak.* "No, Sergeant, Hubbell makes a very good living at his position. No sickness in the family. Parents are dead. What he's doing is attempting to support both a wife and a mistress."

"Then I have no qualms, sir."

If Terry thought winters in North Georgia were rough, it was only because he'd never been in Kansas in January. The wind, coming straight out of Canada, cut him with a thousand icy knives.

For lack of anything else to do, Terry went to the small zoo—almost deserted in winter—and prowled about. The seals were playing in their watery cages, enjoying the cold weather, and they fascinated Terry. One would actually come up out of the water and take a small fish—purchased from a converted Coke machine in the zoo—right out of Terry's hand. He made friends with the seal, naming him Pete. Terry spent as much time as possible in the zoo, playing with Pete, feeding him fish, until it was time to do the job he'd been sent to do.

He found a spot out in the country to bury Hubbell—officially, Hubbell would be listed as having defected to the Russians—and in the trunk of his rent car Terry found bags and bottles of lime and lye and acid. He spent one cold afternoon digging a hole in the ground, far out in the country, in a clump of trees, and the hole was ready and camouflaged.

Terry did not know all the particulars about his assignment, but he knew his meeting with Hubbell had been set up from Washington with the help of a foreign embassy; a double agent planted in the embassy. Terry didn't understand it all; he knew very little of the tricky maneuverings of governments. But he knew that security at the zoo would not bother him that night. He wondered how Perret had managed to pull that off?

That night, he carefully investigated his own thoughts and feelings as he drove toward his rendezvous point at the zoo. The radio in his newly repaired car was turned down low, playing country music.

Did he have doubts about this mission: this cold-blooded killing he was about to perform in the night, in a zoo in Kansas? No. Hubbell was a traitor—a spy, selling out his country, a turncoat, working against the government of America. Terry had no misgivings about killing the man.

It was eleven o'clock when he reached the zoo and parked his car near a small building. He killed his engine and picked up a special preset walkie-talkie from the seat beside him.

"Everything Go?" he asked.

"Green light on," came his reply. The two men who waited just outside the zoo compound were not Dog Team personnel. They worked for a civilian agency, there to take care of the small details of Hubbell's disappearance. These men were not the Smoky-Boy type, Perret had told him. They did not soil their hands with gunsmoke, and, the Colonel added, they looked with contempt upon Dog Team personnel.

"Fuck them," Terry had said.

"My sentiments exactly," Perret agreed.

Terry fitted the silencer onto the Colt Woodsman .22-caliber automatic and jacked a round of hollow-point ammunition into the chamber. He got out of the car and walked up to the meeting point, the pistol held close to his right leg.

A shadowy, bulky figure stepped out from behind a tree. "Hubbell?" Terry spoke, sensing that the man had a pistol in his hand.

"Yes, I'm Hubbell. Has Freeland lost his mind? You're not the man I was supposed to meet. Who the hell are you?" Hubbell raised his gun.

"Dog Team," Terry said, and brought his silenced automatic up, shooting the spy four times in the chest. The little pistol made flat hissing sounds in the night.

Terry heard the man gasp in pain as the small slugs flattened when they struck him; the gasping ceased abruptly as one slug tore into his heart, stilling it forever.

Hubbell fell forward, settled on one knee for a few seconds, then toppled over on his face. He twitched several times, then was still. Vital functions ceased their life-supporting work. His bladder relaxed and the smell of urine was sharp in the cold air.

Terry walked to the man, nudged him with his shoe, and was satisfied Hubbell was dead. He removed all identification from him, and took all papers. Back at his car, Terry spoke into the walkie-talkie.

"You can have his car in five minutes."

"Okay," the same voice as before replied. "Is it done?"

"That's why I'm here, hero," Terry said sarcastically.

Terry removed a heavy tarp from the trunk of his car, rolled the body in it, and carried the grisly bundle to his car, stuffing the dead man into the trunk. The other men would clean up any bloodstains on the ground. Technicians.

Terry hesitated, then walked over to the seal pool. There, he purchased several fish from the machine, and softly called out for Pete. The seal refused to come to him.

"Come on, Pete," Terry urged. "It's me. Come on."

He called and called until he knew the seal would not come. Pete ignored him, remaining in the far end of the pool, aloof, oblivious to Terry's pleas. Terry dropped the fish over the fence, very much aware he had just lost another friend.

"Who says animals are dumb?" he said, walking back to his car.

At the burial site, Terry stripped the body naked, working swiftly in the cold darkness. He stuffed the clothing into a plastic bag, dropped it into the hole, then poured acid over the bag. He dumped Hubbell into the hole, and covered his body with layers of lye and lime, acid over that. The stench was awful. A half hour later, he was satisfied his job was done. The ground was patted down and covered with rock and earth. The body—what was left of it—would not be found. Terry's first lethal assignment for Dog Team, unit 12, was done.

* * *

On the seat of his car in Benning, Terry found an envelope containing a message and a thousand dollars in twenty dollar bills. The note was typewritten, congratulating Terry on a job well done. It was signed with the letter P.

Terry drove back to Bishop and the next day resumed his duties at the Armory.

On the last day of February, Terry was sent to an Air Force base in Arkansas.

He was met by several unsmiling and grim-looking Air Police at the back gate, escorted to a sedan, and driven to a huge hangar. The young Airman in the hangar was frightened, his face pale. He made no attempt to run, not even when the door closed and he was alone with Terry.

"Don't you even want to know why I did it?" he asked Terry.

"I know why you did it," Terry said.

"Hey, man! The government's got no right to draft me. I just barely got under the wire in time to join this chicken-shit outfit. But it's better than the Army. I was doing okay in college; just busted a couple of courses, that's all."

"So that gives you the right to sabotage a fighter-bomber and kill three men who had done nothing to you?"

"Ain't no point in tryin' to talk to you. You gonna beat me up, huh? Teach me a lesson? Well, you go right ahead. But, mister, I'm going to the press after you do. So you better have your fun while you can."

"No," Terry said, "I'm not going to beat you up."

"Yeah? Whatcha gonna do, then?"

Terry pulled out the .22 automatic. The young man's eyes widened. He panicked. "You gotta be kidding? Don't I get a trial? Man, this is America! All I did was mess up a fighter-bomber."

"And kill three men."

"Big deal."

Terry shot him between the eyes, picked up the empty brass

from the weapon, and walked to the side door of the hangar. The Air Police were waiting for him.

"Done," Terry said, and got in the back seat of the sedan.

During the ten-minute ride to the back gate, the Air Police said only one thing to Terry. "You're a cold motherfucker," a Sergeant said.

"So I've been told," Terry replied.

"You want to do WHAT?" Colonel Perret was astonished. He sat open-mouthed behind Terry's desk at the Armory. He held Terry's unsigned reenlistment papers in his hand.

"Get out for awhile," Terry repeated. "See how normal people live. Hell, I might like it."

"Kovak, the government's got a lot of money invested in you," Perret reminded the young man. "Not to mention," his smile was grim, "I know where the body is buried."

"Hubbell?" Terry returned the dour smile. "No, you don't. I didn't follow your orders to the letter." Perret's smile faded. "I picked a different spot to plant him, miles from the original plan."

"I should have guessed it," Perret sighed, allowing a rueful smile to crease his tanned face. "Kovak, you are a natural-born horse's ass."

Terry shrugged off the insult. "I'm not going to sign those re-up papers voluntarily, Colonel."

"What do you want, Terry? I'll confess, I don't understand you. I thought you wanted to make the Army your career?"

"I do, Colonel, believe me. But . . . I want a chance to be a kid . . . again. If I ever really was. To have some fun. Then I'll be back. I promise you that." The Armory was empty, Terry's voice hollow in the huge building.

"I believe you when you say you'll be back, Terry. But isn't it a bit late to be thinking of boyhood?" Perret's voice was soft. "You're no longer a boy. Listen, Terry, I *know* what you're going through, son; believe me, I do. Our lives almost parallel. I, too, killed a man when I was just a kid. I killed a cop who was beating me up. Shot him right between the eyes with his own gun. Now you know something on me. Oh, he had it coming—but that's beside the point. I took off, changed my name; it was easy back then. Lied about my age, joined the Army. That was in '38. The year you were born, son. I'm a Mustang, worked my way up the ranks.'' Perret stood up, putting his hand on Terry's shoulder. ''Son, listen to me: we're alike, much more than you realize. After one hitch, I left the Army. I was back in less than four months. I killed a man in a bar in Kansas City. Like you, Terry, I was searching for the youth I never had. But it's gone, son. And when it goes, it's gone forever.''

''You're probably right, sir, but I sure would like the opportunity to find out for myself.'' He looked into Perret's eyes. ''Colonel, if you order me to sign those papers, I'll do it.''

Perret was thoughtful for a moment, then slowly tore the re-up papers in half, dropping them in the wastebasket. ''No,'' he sighed, ''I won't do that. You've got to find out for yourself just who you are; just how different you are from other men— just as I had to find out. We enjoy the high of combat, Terry. The seeking out of danger. And, whether we'll admit it or not, we enjoy killing those who would destroy a way of life we believe in.'' He smiled. ''Notice I did not use the term *democratic* way of life. What will you do, Terry?''

''Get out of Bishop, for one thing, and more than likely never come back—at least not to stay.''

''Yes.'' Perret's smile was sad. ''I did that, too. I want you to stay in touch with me, Terry. You have the number where I can be reached, day or night. When you get in trouble with the civilian law—and you will—call me.'' He hesitated, then said, ''You have a talent, Terry. Whether it's good or bad is a moot point—it's there. I'd hate to see you wind up in the bucket.''

''I have no intention of going to prison, Colonel.''

Perret held out his hand. ''Goodbye, Terry.'' The two men shook hands.

Perret sat for a long time, far beyond the point where the sound of Terry's car had faded into traffic. ''You'll be back. Just as I came back. Just as men like us always do. Maybe,

Terry, maybe when you're forty years old, and the wildness in you is tamed, maybe then you can live a semi-normal life—alone. But you'll be back.''

"I got some money stashed away," Poppa Kovak said. "Some money your Momma don't know about. It's yours if you want it."

Terry shook his head, embarrassed by the offer. "I have money, Poppa. I'm 'way ahead on my car payments and I don't owe anyone in Bishop, so I'm in pretty good shape." He had said his goodbyes to his mother and sister, and he could hear them crying in the kitchen.

"Where will you go, son?"

"Well, I don't want to go to Atlanta, so I think I'll try Memphis. I'll be in touch."

Poppa Kovak shook hands with his son, then embraced him. "Good luck, boy."

"Yes, sir."

Just outside of Bishop, Terry parked his car and stood for a long time looking at the city limits sign. He knew then that he was cutting all ties, for he felt nothing, leaving the town where he had been born and reared.

"Goodbye, Bishop," Terry said. "I wish I could say it had been fun."

Paula

She was drawn to the young man the moment he walked into her office at the shoe factory in Memphis. His eyes fascinated her: cold as ice even when he smiled. Something about him brought a touch of fear to her, but she was still drawn to him. He looked twenty-five and Paula was startled when she read on his application form that he was only nineteen. She did some quick arithmetic. She was five years older than Terrance Kovak, but she suspected that he was much older than she in many, many ways. Miss Paula Askins, Assistant to the Personnel Director of the shoe factory, hired the young man.

"Can you start on Monday?" she asked. "It won't be much, and you'll be working in the stock room to start." She told him the starting salary.

I made four times that much in one minute, Terry thought. *Putting a hole in a man's head.* "Okay, Monday will be fine."

"Where are you staying?" That was none of her business, but the question popped out of her mouth. Paula felt her face flush hot under his gaze. She got the impression he might be mentally undressing her.

Which he was.

"I don't know, yet. I just got in town a few hours ago. Haven't had a chance to look around."

"There's a small garage apartment behind the apartment complex where I live." His eyes held hers. "Why don't you try there?" She put her hand on the phone. "I know the lady who owns it. Would you like me to call her for you?"

"Sure, if you want to. Yes, that would be nice."

It took four trips to the car before Terry got all his gear unloaded. His mother had packed him to the top with towels and sheets and pots and pans and knives and forks and spoons and curtains and dishes. He stood in the center of the apartment living room, looking around, waiting for some kind of excitement to hit him. Nothing. His only sensation was a dead feeling in his stomach.

This is not what I want, Terry thought. *Not at all. But . . . what do I want? Where do I belong? And who in the hell wants to work in a goddamned shoe factory?*

He thought of his brutal training, and the excitement of it all. The months of hand-to-hand combat; learning to kill with every conceivable type of weapon.

No, he thought: *I've got to give this a try.*

His thoughts were interrupted by a knock on the door.

Terry sighed. "Come in, Paula. It's open."

The Assistant Personnel Director of the shoe factory opened the screen door and viewed him with cautious and somewhat surprised eyes. "How did you know it was me?"

She carried a flat box in her hands. "I thought you might like a pizza. . . . I mean, to share one with me."

And away we go, Terry thought. "Yeah, that would be nice. I am kinda hungry."

Terry wondered if perhaps this would be the woman with whom he could experience love. And how would he know when and if that elusive sensation struck him?

But the flame was not to explode. They ate the pizza, licked their fingers, smiled at each other, and later drove to a small bar in South Memphis and drank dark beer out of heavy frosted mugs. Paula told Terry the story of her life—not that he was particularly interested in hearing it. But he listened patiently, nodding in all the right places.

Later in the evening, as he had known would happen, he made love to her in his newly acquired apartment. She moaned and cried and shuddered as she experienced climax after ripping climax, marking his back with long fingernails.

"Damn!" he said. "Any more of this and I'll be eligible for combat pay. Why don't you cut those fingernails?"

She laughed as she met his stroking with upward moves of her hips. "If you want to stop what you're doing, I'll cut them."

Afterward, they shared a cigarette and a cold bottle of beer as they lay in bed, amid the sweaty, tangled sheets, her flesh warm against him.

But Terry felt nothing for her.

"You're the first man in months for me, Terry."

"Why me?" he asked drowsily. "You just met me about eight hours ago."

"I . . . feel something for you. Something I haven't felt for a long time."

"What?"

"I think . . . pity, perhaps."

"Pity?" he rose up on one elbow. "Why would you feel pity for me?"

"I don't know, really. Or really if that is that right word. But I sense . . . something about you."

"What?"

But she would not answer. She rolled over and went to sleep.

That night, Terry's sleep was punctuated by dreams of his mother and father, alone in the big house in Bishop, worrying about their youngest son.

Saturday, the shoe factory closed for the weekend, and Paula showed him Memphis: the ducks in front of the Main Street hotel; the Zoo (Terry remembered the seal in Kansas and wondered if Pete had found another friend to feed him fish); Sun Studios, where Elvis had cut his first record for his mother (so the story went), launching him in his star-bound career.

Terry was not overly impressed with any of it. *But then,* he remembered, *I haven't been overly impressed with anything in my life, and I don't understand why I'm young; I should be full of piss and vinegar, happy to be alive in my youth. Why am I not?*

He turned off the sights and sounds of Memphis, and the searching of his mind, to concentrate on Paula.

A tall young woman, five-seven, with a truly magnificent figure. Dark brown hair, green eyes, a tiny sprinkling of freckles across her nose that seemed just right for her. High, full breasts that Terry remembered quite well from the night before. A Mississippi girl who grew up on a farm in the Delta. A degree in Business. Several thoroughly rotten love affairs (she hadn't dated in months) left her with the impression that most men were beasts.

They walked along the main drag, window-shopping, and she asked Terry if he owned a suit.

"No, just a couple of coats, that's all. Got my Army suit, but I left that in Bishop."

An hour later he had bought a suit from Goldsmiths, a white shirt—button-down collar—and a tie. Terry wondered if perhaps this wasn't all a dream? Maybe he was back in Bishop and he would soon awaken.

Paula took him to dinner that evening, shocking him by giving him thirty dollars to pay for the meal.

"Goddamnit, I've got money! I've never taken money from a woman before and I don't want to start now." He tried to return the three tens.

She waved away his protests. "So, when you go on to a better job you can pay me back. Let me do this, Terry; you're the first man I've really wanted to be with in a long time. Let's have fun for as long as this lasts." Her eyes were very dark and serious as they rode up the elevator, alone, to the rooftop restaurant.

"You act like I'm leaving tomorrow," Terry was puzzled. "Hell, I just got in town."

"You won't be here for long," she informed him, as if she were a mystic, peering into a glowing ball. "You're looking for something you'll never find in Memphis. And for someone. That someone isn't me, Terry.''

''How do you know that?'' he questioned, but he sensed she was right.

She laughed softly as the elevator bumped to a stop. Smiling at his puzzled expression, she said, ''I took a lot of psychology in college.''

''Wonderful,'' he said.

The work at the factory was not difficult, and it certainly wasn't mentally stimulating. Terry tired of it in a month, wondering if he was sorry he'd left Perret and the Dog Teams. A part of him said yes. The men he worked with—most of them his age or just a bit older—were total bores. Their conversations were limited to pussy and sports—in that order. None of them professed any desire to willingly serve their country. They were also afraid of being drafted.

Terry had a recurring dream, a curious dream: a mixture of graves, yawning open at him, of blood, and of Hell. After awakening from these nightmares, he would feel drained and sweaty, somewhat apprehensive of the twists and turns life might hold for him. He found he missed the camaraderie of the military. And, he finally admitted, he missed the action of the Dog Teams.

He awakened one morning, several minutes ahead of the alarm clock, with Paula asleep and warm beside him. He looked at his hands and for the first time realized he could kill as easily with those hands as most men could pick up a pen and write a check.

What if he got into a fight while he was a civilian and killed someone? Who would protect him? Nobody!—the chilling realization fell on him. His mind locked in on that thought.

They've got me boxed in tight, he thought. *Colonel Perret knew it; that's why he let me go without a fight. He knows exactly what I am. He recognized the quirk in my make-up that allows me to kill without much—if any—remorse. I've got to fight it . . . keep it under control.*

Yeah, Perret, I'll probably be back, but I've got to try it my way for a time. Stay out of trouble for as long as I can.

He stroked the warm flesh of Paula and she stirred in her sleep, responding to his hands; turning, moving against him.

A few months later, on a Friday, two things happened that would change Terry's life forever.

"Well, I guess we get married," Terry told her. "That's the right thing to do."

"No!" Paula shook her head. "No, Terry, we *don't* get married. That's not really what you want and you know it."

"It's my child you're carrying. He . . . she . . . whatever, has got to have a name." *A child might settle me down. Yes, I believe that might do it.* He thought of returning to Bishop with a wife; his mother and father would be so pleased. *But would he be pleased?*

Paula slashed his fantasy to bits. "It would be a marriage without love," she said. "A name without love. It would not be fair to us or to the baby."

"Are you going to have an abortion?" That thought sickened Terry.

"No. Absolutely not! I have money saved, so I'm going to work until the time it's . . . obvious, then quit and have our child. After that," she shrugged, "I don't know. But I don't want you worrying about it."

Terry opened his mouth to speak and Paula shushed him quiet. "I've taken the liberty of packing your things while you were at work this afternoon—after I came home from seeing the doctor. It's probably best if you leave this evening. Terry," she touched his cheek with a cool hand, "you've been wanting to go for some time. I sensed that. There is something restless in you, pushing you on. You're a young man . . . but, then, you're not young. You were a mystery when I met you; you're a mystery as you leave. I think it's best for us to say goodbye. Just as we said hello." There were tears in her eyes.

"You're sure this is the way you want it?"

She kissed him. "I'm going to visit my folks in Mississippi

this weekend, Terry. Please be gone when I get back. Don't make it harder on either of us. It's for the best, believe me.'' She turned and walked away. Terry made no move to stop her.

As he watched her walk away from him, a sense of loss hit him in the pit of his stomach. He could not understand the sensation. Why should he feel anything? He did not love her. He knew that, she knew that, so what was the big deal? *She's giving you a way out, so take it.*

He stood in the doorway of the apartment and watched her walk down the steps to her car. She backed out into the street. Paula raised her hand in farewell and Terry returned the gesture. Then she was gone from his sight and his life.

I'm going to be a father, Terry thought, *and I'll probably never know when it happens. I wonder what she'll look like.*
She?

His car was packed with his belongings, parked outside the bar. Inside, Terry picked up his third beer. Frosty mugs of beer to occupy his hands and attempt to dull his mind. Absentmindedly, he watched a woman walk across the barroom floor to the restroom area. Tight jeans encased her swaying rump, full breasts jiggled under her blouse, and his were not the only eyes on the woman. He watched her until she entered the restroom, then returned his attentions to his mug of beer.

''Don't get any cute ideas about her,'' he heard a man say. Terry paid no attention to the voice, the warning, assuming it was not directed at him.

''I'm talkin' to you, sonny-boy!'' the voice came from behind him and to his left. Terry stiffened slightly, then swiveled on the stool as he realized the warning was meant for him. He looked at the man.

A drunk redneck: a construction worker, in dirty jeans and a dirtier shirt, faced him, fists balled in anger, eyes alive and shining with meanness. Trouble whispered and moved about in the smoky, country-music-filled air of the barroom.

Terry's smile could have chilled a rattle-snake.

''That's right, blondie,'' the man said, pointing a dirty finger at Terry. "Keep those nasty thoughts about my wife out of your mind. I know what you're thinkin,' but she ain't that kind of woman."

Rage swelled up in Terry, running hot and wild. He had done nothing; the man had no right to call him down like this. Terry's words were blunt and very much to the point. "Fuck off, buddy! I haven't done anything."

The redneck moved closer to Terry, fists swinging at his side. "I seen you in here before," he said, "eyeballin' my old lady, grinnin' at her. I 'bout had all I'm gonna take offa you."

Terry wasn't about to back down. He sensed what was coming and was ready for it: wanted the man to come on and take his best shot.

Terry despised these types of people. His father had repeatedly told his sons: "We're poor, yes, but we're not trash. Your Momma and me, we bring you boys up right. But there are people of low degree out in the world. My boys will not be one of them. White trash is something no Kovak will ever become."

"I've never been in here before in my life," Terry said. "Even if I had, what goddamned business is it of yours? Why don't you go take a bath? Decent people don't want to smell your stink."

The man trembled with rage. He was big, rough, did hard work, and no one had ever talked to him in such a manner.

"Decent people do not enter a public place without clothing on their bodies," Poppa Kovak had said to his sons. "No one wants to see a man's hairy belly hanging over his belt buckle, or his shirt open, or, worse, no shirt at all. Wash yourselves, be neat. Trashy people do not care about other people's feelings. I better not ever catch one of my boys acting like trash."

"You smell like a goat," Terry told the man. "And look like an ape."

No one made any move to stop the two men. Besides, everybody present knew ole Luther was bad. Be a real short fight: everybody would have a good laugh when the kid got his face busted.

"Git up, you smart-mouthed punk! I'm gonna kick your teeth in."

The jukebox changed tunes: *Yonder Comes A Sucker.*

Terry slipped off the stool and faced the man, getting set. The redneck swung at him, a looping right. Grabbing the man's arm, one strong hand around his wrist, the other hand clamped just above his elbow, Terry tossed him over his shoulder, over the bar, and into the glasses and mugs, shattering the mirror, sending glass flying about the room.

He looked at the bartender. "If you want any damages"— he jerked his thumb at ole Luther, struggling to get up from behind the bar, thrashing and cussing in the broken glass— "get it from that bastard! He started it."

Terry picked up his change from the bar, then walked out the door and into the warm Tennessee night.

He was almost to his car when he heard the construction worker pounding the gravel behind him, lumbering and huffing up to him in the night.

"MOTHERFUCKER!" the man screamed, and Terry spun to face him.

All Terry's training, still fresh in his mind, activated in his brain, roaring at him in a silent tongue: SURVIVAL KILL.

The world about Terry froze in time and space. There were only two people left in the world: himself and the redneck. Terry saw, heard, remembered nothing but his training. His eyes locked upon his assailant and held him close to death's door, with a gaze as cold as the grave.

Terry jammed stiffened fingers into the man's throat, cutting off the scream as the larynx ruptured. He ripped the man's face into bloody shreds with claw-fingers and -nails, jerking out one eye with his downward rip. He lashed out with a powerful Judo chop to the man's neck, paralyzing the muscles. He brought the knife edge of his hand down, breaking a collar bone. Pivoting, he broke the redneck's nose with the side of his hand, then brought the lower palm of his right hand up in the classic Cobra Strike, driving the nose cartilage deep into the man's brain.

Terry stepped back as the world began revolving and time ticked into reality. The construction worker flopped on the gravel parking lot, his damaged brain not yet transmitting the message that he was dead. He trembled, his legs jerking. He grunted, snorted, then died.

Terry stood for a few seconds, looking down at the man. The door to the bar remained closed. The parking lot was dark. A truck rumbled by. Terry felt no emotion as he looked at his work, lying on its back, one eye staring into nothing, blood leaking from its mouth, nose, and ears.

The man had attacked him, Terry had defended himself, and that was that.

Terry walked to his car and drove off without looking back. He did not stop—except for gas—until he reached Chicago. There, he bought a Memphis paper and learned that a John Doe warrant was out for the arrest of the man who had wrecked a Memphis bar and killed a construction worker. The man was obviously a maniac, the paper implied.

Fifteen minutes after reading the paper, Terry was on the phone to Colonel Perret.

BOOK THREE

Ten

The officer in charge of the team called a halt: a rest period for which all were grateful. It gave the men time to remove the leaches that had worked their way up their boots, under their field pants, and onto their flesh, puffing up to three and four times their normal size, sucking the blood of the men. A South American officer moved down the line of sprawled men to stop in front of Terry. He squatted down, sipping water from his canteen.

"It won't be long now, Sergeant. Three miles. Are you ready?"

"I know who to kill, if that's what you mean," Staff Sergeant Kovak took a sip of water from his own canteen. "Are you certain our man is there?"

Major Pizarro shrugged. "If my informant is correct. That's the problem with torture: people will tell you anything you want to hear just to make the pain stop. But, yes, I believe the general will be at this camp." His eyes shifted to the still-sealed gun case, part of it resting on Terry's leg. "The weapon, you are certain of its reliability? It will do the job?"

"You get me to the man," Terry said calmly, "and I'll do the rest."

"The bullet—it really explodes on contact?" The Latin was not fully convinced.

"Yes, it's tipped with an explosive. Don't worry, Major. Just get me to the target."

The Major regarded the Sergeant. "You're very young to be so highly rated by your government. I had expected a much older man."

Terry was not disturbed; his age had come into question many times before. "I have good eyes, calm nerves, and a steady trigger finger, Major. I'll do my job."

The Latin nodded. "Yes . . . well, rest now—sleep if you can. I'll wake you in about an hour."

Terry closed his eyes. To the amazement of the Major, he was asleep in less than three minutes, sleeping as peacefully as if he were on his way to a ballet instead of an assassination.

"General Flores," Perret had briefed Terry, showing him the man's picture from a thick dossier. "Hard line Communist, stirring up trouble among the masses. The Man says send a gun—you're the gun."

Terry nodded, studying the face of the general he was to kill. "This is an Agency shoot. Why don't they send some of their own people?"

"Because they asked for you, hot-shot. Now, listen: the way this thing sounds to me, you'll have time for two shots, maybe three. The friendlies can get you to within maybe five hundred meters." Perret showed Terry pictures of the camp and aerial photographs of the terrain surrounding the camp, marking an X where Terry would shoot. "Can you do it?"

"No sweat, Colonel."

"There'll be plenty of sweat, all yours, with much pain— if you miss and get caught."

"Colonel, if you have doubts about me, send someone else." Military or not, Terry spoke his mind, and pulled very few punches.

Perret smiled. "Kovak, this country is very important to us.

We need all the friends we can get in South America. I can't make it any clearer than that. Do you read me?''

"Loud and clear, sir. When do I leave?"

"Sunday. 0800."

Everything was going wrong with the operation. General Flores had twice as many men in the rebel camp than they had anticipated, and Major Pizarro's troops were having a difficult time holding against the heavy odds. Terry could get no closer than six hundred meters from the main building that housed Flores, and if the General didn't show soon, the mission would have to be scrubbed and it would be bug-out time . . . with every man for himself.

Terry adjusted his scope for the extra yardage and sighted in, steadying the cross-hairs. Six hundred meters. He'd hit targets at much further distances, but never under these conditions. He waited.

General Flores made a break for it, heading for the protection of the jungle, moving swiftly, for a man of his bulk. Terry led his target, gently taking up trigger-slack, then let the rifle fire itself. The weapon pounded his shoulder. When he again got Flores in the cross-hairs, the General was lying on the ground, blood spurting from a massive hip wound; the mercury-tipped bullet had torn a huge hole in the man's leg and hip. One of Flores's aides attempted to help the General to his feet, and that was all the target Terry needed: he blew a cup-sized hole in the General's chest, and it was all over except the mop-up. The Rebels scattered. Major Pizarro's men cut them down, giving no mercy, no quarter.

Terry unloaded the rifle, stored the cartridges in the case, and locked the weatherproof carton. He dug in his pocket for a candy bar, chewing slowly while the mop-up went on around him.

Later, the fight over, Terry sat with the Major, waiting for a helicopter to take him out. He was aware of the Major looking at him from time to time, studying him. Finally, Pizarro spoke.

"You're a cool one," he said, and Terry assumed that was

a compliment, of sorts. "With Flores out of the way, his men scattered, we can dry up his source of Red money and move closer to a democracy—our form of your government, that is. You are a truly magnificent shot and a brave man, Sergeant, but I don't think I would want you for a friend." He chuckled. "However, I don't think I would want you for an enemy, either."

Terry chewed a piece of gum from his accessory pack and remained silent.

"It's a job to you, isn't it?" Pizarro asked. "This killing, I mean? Just a line of work."

"I'm a soldier," Terry said. "Just like you. I had my orders and I carried them out—just as you did." He shrugged. "You tortured a man, then probably killed him, to find out where Flores would be—so I could kill him. I don't enjoy killing, not really; I don't feel anything about it, one way or the other. Did you enjoy torturing the man?"

"No," the Major said softly. He sighed. "No, I didn't. It's a disgusting business. But one must believe that one is doing . . . all this," he waved his hand, "for one's country, no?"

"The end justifies the means."

"Si."

Both men were silent for a time. "You have a family?" Pizarro asked.

"I have no one."

For a moment, in the steaming jungles of South America, amid the cawing of various brightly colored birds, Terry allowed his inner joylessness to show on his face.

"You are not a happy man," the Major observed. "And you are far too young to be so unhappy and yet so worldly. I think perhaps the latter is the reason for the former, amigo. Don't you agree?"

"I don't know," Terry smiled. "But you just called me 'friend.' I thought you said you wouldn't want me for a friend."

Pizarro laughed. "Ah, now I can add mental quickness to your other talents. Well, we Latins are unpredictable—changing like the wind. At least that is our reputation." A chopper coming in cut off the conversation. Both men rose, Pizarro holding out his hand. "I will not be returning with you, Sergeant, so I will say the words at this time: Adios, amigo."

They shook hands, and Terry climbed aboard, strapping himself in, adjusting his headset as they lifted off. He waved to the Major and Pizarro saluted him, then was swallowed up in the jungle. Any Communist rebel still alive was being shot.

Terry had not been back to Bishop in more than two years. The town had changed: there were several more factories, two shopping centers, and a huge housing development that gave the old town a more modern look. Many streets had been changed into one-ways, and Terry almost got lost before he found his bearings.

The Presidential campaign was over, and JFK looked pretty good to SFC Terry Kovak. Twenty-two years old and Sergeant First Class. He had come up fast.

He drove slowly past the high school; his thoughts, for the first time in months, swung to Ruby. He wondered where she was and how she was doing? Ruby, with the sometimes-kinky sex habits. Terry hoped she had found someone to love and understand her. He smiled as the school faded in his rearview mirror. He had no desire to stop and visit.

He drove to the Armory and went in, wanting to say hello to Tate, but his friend was gone, replaced by a Master Sergeant Terry did not know. A straight-leg, too, unlike Tate, who had been a Jumper. This one wore a sour expression on his face.

"Sergeant Tate around?" Terry asked.

A full half minute passed before Terry received any reply. The Master Sergeant—his name tag read: RICHMOND—gave Terry a long once-over with little mean eyes, taking in the Silver Wings on his chest, resting above his decorations; the Airborne/Ranger tabs on his shoulder, and his highly polished Jump Boots.

"I thought some of you rough-tough glamor boys had taken to wearin' them berets?" Richmond asked, no friendliness in his voice.

Terry smiled. The hostility was nothing new to him; he had

met it many times before from both officers and EM's of the old-line Army. Many of them resented change of any kind—possibly they were afraid of it, certainly they were envious of it.

"Special Forces wears them. Is Tate around?" Terry got back to his original question.

"Naw, he retired, shipped out—something. Hell, I don't know where he went and really don't care. He left me a mess here."

"Thanks for your cooperation," Terry said sarcastically. Richmond only glared at him as he left. Just outside the door, he said, loud enough for Richmond to hear: "Asshole!"

"Screw you, pretty-boy!" The words drifted out to Terry as he walked to his car.

Terry laughed and shouted. "I wanna live a life of danger—I wanna be an Airborne/Ranger."

Richmond appeared at the door, his face red with anger. "Get outta here, you son of a bitch! Took me fifteen years to make SFC. You wouldn't have made it in the old Army!"

Terry laughed and drove away.

He didn't believe Tate had retired. Tate had told him too many times he was in for three times ten, and 1960 would be his twenty-first year in the Army, over fifteen of those with Perret and the Dog Teams. No, Tate had either gotten killed, cracked up, or been moved by Perret to another post—probably the latter. Terry made a mental note to find out. He and Tate had gotten along; they understood each other.

He drove past the mill, from a distance seeing his father walking across the mill yard. He would be home and surprise his father when he came in from work. Terry smiled; it would be a good homecoming.

The old house looked pretty good: a fresh coat of paint shining on the wood, red trim around the windows, a new porch. A very lovely young lady sat in the porch swing, reading a book. She looked up as Terry pulled into the driveway.

My God! Terry thought. *That's Shirley. She's a grown woman.*

Then she was in his arms, kissing his face, crying. His mother ran out of the house, wiping her hands on her apron, crying, throwing her arms around the neck of her son.

Terry was home.

"You sure aren't much for letter-writing, Terry," Poppa Kovak gently and jokingly chided his youngest son. He smiled at his wife. "What, Momma—eight letters in two years?"

"Yes, but I saved them all. Such nice long letters." She winked at Terry. "I tied them up with a ribbon around them. At least a page and a half each. And your handwriting, son, it's terrible." And the family laughed.

With all the family present, the big house seemed to overflow. Robert slapped Terry on the back and grinned at him. "You look good in that uniform, kid. Real good. Kind of makes me sad I didn't stay in this last time."

Terry returned the smile as he looked around the room at the family. One was missing. He cut his eyes at Robert.

"If you're looking for Mavis," his brother said, "she's not here and won't be. She ran off."

"Aw, hell, Bob." Danny jumped into the conversation, blunt as always. "Tell him." He looked at Terry. "It's just one of the things we're not supposed to talk about." He ignored his mother's efforts to shush him. "She ran off with the priest. They're living up in Detroit."

Vera had been right all along. "The priest?" Terry asked.

"Yeah . . . Danny's voice trailed off.

No one said anything more for a moment. Shuffling of feet on the carpet, much inspecting of the ceiling, avoiding of eyes, clearing of throats, lighting of cigarettes.

"Shameful," Mother Kovak said. "Not to mention her leaving the children. Sad excuse for a mother."

"Well," Robert said, "it's over and done with. I've met a nice lady. She'll be over here tomorrow night and you can meet her."

The subject was closed.

"Exactly what do you do in the Army?" Joe asked. He sat

with his arm around Ginny. She had just passed her Bar and would soon go into practice in Bishop.

"Too bold!" many of the local men said. Damned if they'd go to a female lawyer. But Ginny had the support of almost all the women in the County, and she didn't seem to be too terribly worried about her future.

"I'm in weapons," Terry said, not a lie on his part.

"Stationed where?" Shirley asked.

"Fort Bragg—for awhile, at least. I get shipped around quite a lot, instructing all over the world." *And blowing dudes away,* he thought.

His answers seemed to satisfy the family, but every now and then Terry would feel Robert's eyes on him, gazing at him rather curiously, a puzzled look on his face, perhaps wondering how a twenty-two-year-old could make Sergeant First Class so quickly and could afford to drive a new Thunderbird on that salary. Hoping to put an end to further discussion of his military career, Terry changed into civies.

After the family had returned to their homes, promising to get together the next night for a real family reunion, Terry drove around Bishop. He realized he could not spend much time here: the place depressed him. He did not fit in Bishop society—if, indeed, he ever had. He drove by the Skelton home and saw Carolyn working in the yard, fussing over her blooming flowers. She looked about the same as he remembered her: still a good-looking woman. She was bending over, her jeans tight on her rump. But Terry had no desire to stop and chat. He wondered if she was still married, or if she had finally gotten enough of Lee's drunkenness and tossed him out? And Bess? Where was she?

He swung into the service station where he had once worked, and bought gas from a kid he didn't know. He felt even more depressed: old for his years. Terry knew he would have to leave this town very soon.

"You're Terry Kovak, ain't ya?" the young man asked, wiping his runny nose with the sleeve of his shirt.

"Yeah, that's me."

"Man, it must be great . . . what you do, I mean. Jumpin' out of them airplanes."

"It's a job, partner."

"Huh?"

"You can get used to anything." Terry wished the kid would just shut up, blow his nose, and fill the tank with high-test. Maybe check his oil, if he could find the dip-stick.

"I been thinkin' 'bout joinin' up, myself. Gettin' me a pair of them big shiny boots." The gas ran over, spilling on the pea gravel of the drive. "I been readin' 'bout them Green Berets guys. Them Special Forces Troopers. Maybe that's for me. What'd you think, Terry?"

Terry looked at the young man and wanted to laugh and cry simultaneously. Terry spoke German fluently and could get by in Russian, Vietnamese, and, Pali—having just returned from four months' duty in Burma. This kid was having trouble with English and he wanted to join SF.

At this juncture, Special Forces was perhaps the finest guerrilla fighting force in the world, its men required to speak several languages and be familiar with dozens of weapons—including garrote, knife, and cross-bow—and they were considered to be the best jungle fighters, the best mountain men, the best dog-sledders, the best desert fighters, and the most murderous ambushers in the world. But, as usual, the military potentates of the United States Army would eventually attempt to turn the fighting men into sanitation engineers, bridge builders, and diplomats, and royally fuck up the finest fighting force anywhere in the world.

But, for several years, the men of the Green Berets—Special Forces—would be considered the best guerrilla fighters in the world.

"You can give it a try," Terry told him. He paid for his gas and drove away, thinking: *Damn stupid Cracker. Jesus, I've got to get out of here.*

Terry went to the local drive-in for a Coke, and was startled to find it gone, a Serve-Yur-Self store in its place.

He drove around until he found the new location of the now very modern drive-in. He walked in and ordered a milkshake.

The place was full of chattering, giggling high school girls, the boys seated around and among them, flexing their muscles, running their mouths, and all the time wondering if their acne medicines were working, and hoping they could cop a quick feel from one of the girls without being seen or getting their faces slapped. Terry smiled and concentrated on his shake.

The door opened and closed behind him. A vaguely familiar voice said, "Hello, Kovak."

Terry turned and looked at the bulk of J. A. Cater. He nodded to him and turned around, his back to Cater.

"Bastard turned his back on me," Cater mouthed to his buddy, standing beside him, grinning like an idiot.

One of the boys with the girls said, "Man, that's J. A. Cater, All-American tackle. He's a hero. There's gonna be trouble, I betya."

Another boy, with more sense than the rest of his peer group, took a closer look at Terry, taking in his carefully trimmed, close-cut hair, his low-quarter shoes, his burned-in tan, and his thick wrists. The young man smiled, put his back to a wall, and pulled a chair close to him.

No trouble here, Terry cautioned himself. *I can't bring attention to myself.*

"Where's your pretty little soldier suit, Happy Warrior?" Cater laughed maliciously.

Terry ignored him, hoping the two neanderthals would go away and sit in a tree somewhere, eating leaves and picking fleas from each other.

J. A.'s friend, about the same size and, Terry was sure, of about the same mentality, wandered off to the jukebox, carefully studying the selections, his lips moving silently. J. A. sat down beside Terry. Terry pushed his milkshake away and laid both hands, palms down, on the countertop.

"I've been going to college for the past five years, Kovak, improving my mind." J. A. boomed the words at him. "What have you been doing, besides strutting around in your soldier suit?"

Terry's smile was sad for a few seconds. *Homecoming,* he

thought. He looked at Cater, then slipped the insult to him. "Seen Bess lately, Needle-Dick?"

Cater's face paled, then reddened with anger. "Wanna step outside, Kovak?" He had lowered his voice.

"No." Terry said, "Not now. Tonight, J. A., out by the lake, north side. Just you and me, Cater. Leave your ape-man friend at home, I've got nothing against him. Tonight, Cater, eight o'clock, if you've got the balls."

"Just you and me, Kovak?"

"Just you and me, hero." Terry slurred the word "hero."

"I'll be there."

Terry waited by the lake. He was dressed in old fatigues, jump boots on his feet. He sat patiently on a stump. Terry did not want to really hurt Cater, just humiliate him, although *why* he wanted to humiliate Cater was not clear in his mind.

This is high school crap, he thought. Wouldn't I be a much bigger person if I just went home and forgot it?

But Terry had no more time for mental ruminations. Headlights flashed on the dirt road and cut off; a door slammed shut.

"Kovak?"

"Right here, hero." Terry stood up.

Cater walked to him, bulky in the night. "You're a damned fool, Kovak! Don't you ever read the papers? I'm an All-American, man."

And Terry knew then why he wanted to humiliate Cater. "God, I hope American means more than that." Then he hit him.

No man who plays on the Front Four can be a coward—that just isn't possible. But football is controlled violence. America probably has the world's finest athletes—our sports writers tell us that often enough—but there is a great difference between being a fine athlete and being a warrior.

Cater was in superb physical condition; Terry knew how to cripple with his hands. Cater could stop anything—short of a freight train—from coming through the line; Terry, had he been a civilian, would have had to register his hands as lethal weapons. Cater had spent years learning a sport; Terry had spent years learning how to kill.

As any gunfighter knows: make the first shot count, for you might not get another one. Terry made his first shot count.

He hit him in the throat with stiffened fingers. Not hard enough to kill or do permanent damage; just hard enough to take some of the steam out of Cater.

The fight was downhill from that point.

Cater was no fool; he knew after thirty seconds that he was outclassed. But man has so much macho bullshit fed to him that pride makes him go forward when common sense tells him to quit.

Terry chopped at Cater with short, brutal, painful Judo blows; he kicked him with hard-learned *savate* techniques; he punished Cater's nervous system with jabbing fingers. When Cater would swing a fist, Terry would flip him over a shoulder, slamming him to the ground, bouncing him off the earth, bringing grunts of pain. When Terry wanted to play, he would use variations of the Jamaica come-along: applying pressure against bone and nerve, causing excruciating but temporary pain.

Finally, Cater had no more fight left in him. He squatted on the ground, unable to believe a smaller man had handled him so easily. He listened to Terry speak.

"You see, J. A., the one great difference between us is this: there is no one writing glowing newspaper accounts about what I do for a living, so I have no press releases to live up to. Nobody gives a lousy damn what I do; I'm just a soldier.

"But you listen to me, Cater, 'cause what I'm about to tell you just might save your life, if you ever decide to fuck with me again. I've killed men with knives, guns, piano wire, and with my bare hands and fingers. I did it all for very little money and absolutely no gratitude from the public I serve. I and a lot of other men do it, so assholes like you can run up and down football and baseball and basketball fields—and be heroes in the eyes of the public. And, more importantly, Cater: be free to do so. We do it so you can work at a job of your choice, vote freely and openly, move around without papers and border guards to hassle you and, in most cases, speak your mind without fear of punishment.

"Now then, you thick-headed jockstrap, you have anything you want to add to that?"

"You didn't fight fair," Cater mumbled.

"You're an idiot!" Terry said. He walked to his car and drove away.

Eleven

"I'm still going to be a doctor someday, Terry," Shirley told him. "The counselor at school says I'd be a good one."

They sat on the front porch, just the two of them, enjoying the night air of summer in North Georgia. Terry drained his beer, and opened another bottle. He said, "I remember when you were in the fifth grade, Shirley; that's what you wanted to be then. I told you I'd help you, and I will. Now then, what can I do to help?"

"Write me a letter every now and then. Tell me how you are and what you're doing."

He nodded, the darkness hiding his sad smile. *Tell you I've just killed a man for my country, or that I'm plotting to kill one.* "I'll do that, little sister, and also send you some money from time to time. Okay?"

"Oh, pooh! I don't want your money, Terry. I . . ."

He waved her quiet with a quick slash of his hand. "Everyone needs a little money, Shirley. Buy yourself something pretty. Wear it just for me."

She kissed her brother's tanned face and hugged him. "Just for you, Terry."

They were silent for a time, enjoying the closeness of kin.

Terry's thoughts drifted away from Bishop and settled on Sally Malone. They had seen each other a half dozen times in two years: in Munich and Bad Tolz; in Hong Kong and the Philippines; and several months back, in Denver. Both had been on assignment for the Dog Teams.

Terry suspected he might be a little bit in love with Sally, and she with him, but when they were together, that word never came up. They took whatever few moments were allowed them to make love and talk of small things and of people they knew: who had been killed serving their country, and whose body was never found and would never be spoken of. And then they parted. Sally was not yet ready to settle down, and Terry knew damn well he wasn't ready.

His sister had dozed off, her head on Terry's shoulder, his arm around her. He suddenly thought of Paula and the baby. His baby. He had found out, quite discreetly, and with the help of Perret, that his child was a girl. Correction, he smiled in the night. Their child. Patsy.

He lit a cigarette and sipped at his beer. Patsy would be . . . two years old. Paula had married a farmer in the Mississippi Delta and was quite happy, so the dossier had read. Terry would have liked to have seen his child, though. He would like that very much.

The invitation was there, shining in her eyes, his for the taking if he would but ask. Instead, he said, "You're certainly looking well, Clarissa; marriage must agree with you."

Womanhood did look good on her, having matured and deepened her beauty. She studied his face and said, "I think about you from time to time, Terry. You were the first person I was ever in love with. Really, you were."

It was awkward for him, not knowing what to say, wishing he were back in Germany or Burma or some damned place, anyplace other than on the main street of Bishop, Georgia, standing in front of Cindy Lou's cafe, with the jukebox blaring. "I Can't Stop Loving You."

The situation grew worse when Bess walked by, glanced at

them, paled, her hand going to her throat. She managed to say, "Hi, Clarissa. Terry? Is it really Terry Kovak?"

"Yeah," he found the word, wishing he had stayed in bed that morning. "It's really me, Bess. How have you been?"

"Fine, Terry. Just fine. I didn't recognize you at first—you've changed so. You're bigger and more muscular and . . . where did you get that terrific tan?"

"Well, I work outside a lot," he said, thinking: *Shooting people.* He noticed the golden ring on her finger. *Jesus! Is every female in this town married?*

The trio looked at each other and suddenly the moment was shattered for them. Terry was both saddened and grateful when it died. Both women studied the other's wedding ring, realizing their time for anything other than inward, silent remembrance of old lovers was gone. They parted to go the way fate had chosen for them, saying they must all get together some evening while Terry was in town, 'cause he would like Carl and Ken, and they would talk of things past and those old bittersweet days of their youth. But they each knew they would not do that, could not do that, must not.

Old memories are so much more precious when they are kept in the mind, fuzzy and deliberately vague, carefully treasured against the half-light of dimming years. Precious memories tend to tarnish and diminish in value when cast under the full brilliance of reality, like a valuable gem, with a flaw marring its beauty.

They had said hello; now they must say goodbye.

Terry watched them walk away, these two young married ladies, strolling out of his life for the second time. They chatted of this and that: the Jaycees and the Jaynes, Little League Baseball, what detergent gets diapers the cleanest, and wasn't it just awful about Mrs. What's-her-name getting caught in the back seat of a Buick with Mr. What's-his-name—and now there's going to be another divorce in Bishop.

Terry stood alone on the sidewalk of Bishop, in front of Cindy Lou's cafe, and knew the words of the man were right: You can't ever go back home. Not really. It's so much better if a person stays away, just remembering the good times, or what you thought were good times.

I'm marked, he thought, just as surely as if I wore a caste mark on my forehead. I can never live here. I just don't fit—not any more.

Suddenly, Terry looked into the eyes of Clarissa, standing in front of him.

"I've just got to see you one more time, Terry," she said, urgency in her voice. "I've got to. Please?"

All Terry's great philosophical meanderings turned to dust. "When? Where?"

"It has to be tonight. My husband's out of town. There's a new motel outside of town—you passed it coming in. Out by the interchange. The Tuck-em-Inn. Rent a room there and I'll call you and come to you."

"All right, Clarissa. I'll be waiting."

"I have such a shitty sex life," she told him, as she removed her blouse and reached behind her to unhook her bra. Her breasts, larger than Terry remembered them, swung free.

Terry lay on the bed, in his shorts, waiting for her.

"Three and a half years of marriage and two kids," Clarissa complained, "and now my husband thinks it's wonderful if we have sex once a week—at best." Impatiently, she pulled his shorts from him, grasping his half-erect penis. "God, I wish I'd married you, Terry." She moaned as she took him without foreplay; mounted on him, straddling him, she took him to her depths, groaning her pleasure. She rode his erection, running her mouth constantly.

"Aren't you afraid you'll get pregnant?" Terry asked, finally able to get a word in.

"I don't give a damn if I do. I hope I do! I hope it's a son, I hope he's like you, you goddamned stud!" She almost screamed her pleasure. "Oh, God, that's good, Terry!"

* * *

He said his goodbyes to the family, shook his father's hand and kissed his mother while she unsuccessfully fought back tears. With all of that behind him, Terry tossed his luggage in the trunk of his Thunderbird and drove away from Bishop, Georgia, leaving behind him his sad-eyed family, memories of a not-too-pleasant youth, and discontented, sex-starved (to hear them tell it) housewives.

He was depressed until he drove past the city limits sign. A mile farther and he began whistling a tune from the mid-fifties, his spirits lifting.

"Okay," he spoke aloud, "so you have no real home. Big deal. You don't know where the Army will send you—but what damn difference does it make? You can't go back, can't stand still, so that leaves only one direction: straight ahead."

So, Terry thought, let's do it!

Four o'clock in the morning, and it was snowing in the Kentucky hills of Fort Knox. Terry shook his head at the decision of a higher-up to send him to Fort Knox. Jesus, it was cold.

Men who had gone into the Army in 1940 and '41 were getting out after twenty or so, and there was a shortage of Drill Sergeants. Basic training camps were being shuffled around, and Terry—after a mini-course at DI school—was pushing troops.

Colonel Perret thought it amusing when a dozen of his personnel in Dog Teams were chosen to train troops at various bases around the country.

"It's only temporary," he reminded them. "One or two cycles at the most. Besides, all you guys are getting soft"— that was a lie and Perret knew it; there wasn't an ounce of fat on any of them—"it's time for you men to remember you're soldiers. Get back with the troops." He laughed at their long faces. "Get the hell out of here, I'll see you all in a few months. Providing you can keep up with those kids you'll be pushing." He was still laughing as they filed out of his office at Fort Bragg, a dozen men, bitching and cussing.

Sergeant Kovak stood by the window of his room in the barracks and thought about the men—boys, really, most of them—in his platoon.

Ninety-eight percent of them would make it. One or two he might have to recommend for recycling. One, a draftee, too fat to keep up with the others, was dragging them down. Terry felt a little sorry for him. There should be a special program for men like that, he thought. A three- or four-week course to get them gradually into shape; all we're doing now is humiliating them in front of guys in better shape. That's not right. The other guy was just plain dumb. Stupid. He had no business being in the Army. And the kid named Jones had him worried. He had something on his mind that was nagging at him, tearing his concentration apart. Terry could empathize with him; a seventeen-year-old with problems. He had a hunch it was a woman: a girl back home in Pennsylvania who just might be screwing Jones around. For a moment, Terry toyed with the idea of sending Jones to talk with the Chaplain. He forced Jones out of his mind; Terry had fifty-nine other recruits to worry about.

Hours later, Terry wearily pulled off his boots and sat down in a chair in his room. He had driven the men hard that day—both before and after their time on the rifle range—and driven himself just as hard. Terry would not demand of another man something he could not do himself.

He showered, put on clean clothes, and ate in the mess hall behind the barracks; he returned to his room to work on the day's reports, and then, he hoped, to relax a bit before putting the troops to bed.

There was a knock on the closed door, timid tapping. "I can't hear you!" Terry called. Heavier knocking. "I still can't hear you!" The door rattled under the pounding of knuckles. "Come in," Terry called.

Private E-1 Jones stood in the doorway. Terry could tell he'd been crying. There was a letter in his hand that had been crumpled, then smoothed out, several times. The young man looked completely miserable. Jones was small, and his fatigues never seemed to fit him properly. He looked like the original Sad Sack.

"What's on your mind?" Terry asked, after the young soldier had closed the door. Terry pointed to a chair and Jones sat.

"I . . . I'm all messed up, Sergeant. It's my girl back home. She's . . . pregnant!" he blurted out the words.

Terry grunted. He had been right. "Want me to try to arrange some emergency leave for you? I don't know if I can, but I can try."

Jones shook his head. "It wouldn't do any good, Sergeant." He held up the letter. "She got married a few days ago. I swear to God in Heaven I didn't know she was pregnant when I joined up. We had a fight, that's all."

"I believe you." Terry leaned forward and patted the young man on the shoulder. "Look, Jones, talk to me. Get it all out of your system. If you want, we'll go out back of the barracks and you can yell at me. Cuss me out if you think that will help. Jump up and down. Kick things. Call me every name in the book—I don't care." He reached into a dresser and got a bottle of whiskey. "You want a drink?"

"No, Sergeant. I don't drink?"

"What can I say, Jones? I don't know what to say. You want to see the Chaplain?" He reached for the phone on his desk. "Say the word. He'll see you tonight. It's got to help."

The boy/soldier shook his head and began to cry. Terry felt useless in this situation.

"I love her, Sarge. I really do love her." He sobbed into his hands.

Having never been in love, Terry had no comprehension of the word; did not know how the emotion could tear at a person's guts. However, he did not like to see a man cry and he almost told Jones to knock it off. He held his tongue at the last second.

The young man stood up. "I'll go back to the room, Sarge—maybe try to get some sleep."

"You can stay and talk to me the rest of the night if you want to."

"Thank you, Sergeant. I don't think so. But I really do appreciate the offer."

A few minutes after lights out, Terry walked down the hall of the barracks to a room full of recruits. He heard one of them say: "What's the matter, little boy? Gonna cry yourself to sleep? Little boy got his girl knocked up and she married someone else. What's the matter, Jones: didn't you have a big enough cock to keep her happy?"

Laughter.

Wild with fury, Terry savagely kicked open the door and flipped on the lights. Wide eyes, frightened faces, and open mouths mutely expressed the shared sentiment that Drill Instructor Kovak was mightily pissed off.

"YOU SHIT-HEADS!" he roared at them. "If I hear one more goddamned word from this room, I'll drag your asses out in the street and we'll do close-order drill the rest of the night. You understand me?"

The next morning, Jones's letter was missing, stolen. At noon, the weather turned so rotten that the day's training was canceled. At three o'clock the letter was thumbtacked to the bulletin board and the entire Company read it. Terry's Platoon Guide ripped the letter from public inspection and brought it to Terry.

"Some of the guys are really giving Jones a bad time of it, Sergeant. Especially Jordan. He's saying that tonight Jones can sleep with him. He's saying that . . . ah . . . he'll . . . ah . . . fuck Jones in the ass—that'll take his mind off his girl. Jordan's getting pretty raunchy, Sarge."

Jordan from Ohio. A college-boy jock who flunked out of school and got drafted. An asshole with a capital A. Jordan reminded Terry a great deal of Cater. He was constantly complaining about his knee; an old injury suffered—supposedly—on the gridiron. He bitched about being in the Army.

"All right, Clark," Terry said, "thanks. I'll take care of it."

Terry called the Chaplain's office. The man was out for the rest of the evening. He told the Chaplain's assistant about Jones and his troubles.

Terry walked over to the CO's office, really not expecting the Captain to be there, and he wasn't. Gone home. The XO was a natural born nitwit who couldn't lace up his own boots properly: Second Lieutenant Slate. A Reserve Artillery officer fulfilling his military obligation. Slate had about as much business being the XO in a training company as Daffy Duck would have had. Slate knew it, and admitted it.

Terry found First Sergeant Deale sitting behind his desk reading a novel. Deale was a fifty-year-old semi-alcoholic with thirty years in and no place to go if he got out. Deale stayed in because he was scared to death of civilians. First Sergeant Deale had spent thirty years in the Army, through two wars, and had never heard a shot fired in anger. He admitted that violence frightened him.

"Well, now, Sergeant Kovak," Deale said, after Terry had explained the situation and Deale had reluctantly listened. "It's a sad story, truly depressing, I admit that. But I have great faith in your ability to handle it." He sucked on a cigarette. "However, we must both understand that Jones is now a man— a man among men. The barracks humor—however salty—will die down in a few days, Jones will recover from his sniffles, and all will end happily. Perhaps, Sergeant Kovak, I might arrange for Jones to slip into Louisville and find himself a prostitute. That way he could wet his dipstick and he might feel better about the entire dismal matter? During the interim, let's you and I stroll over to the club and have a few beers and some more enlightening conversation."

Terry looked at the First Sergeant, not believing what he'd just heard. "You know, Deale," he said slowly, "you're a real prick!"

The First Sergeant did not take offense. At least not visibly. Drill Sergeants—especially DI's such as Kovak—scared him just a little. "Of course I am," he smiled. "I gather by your most defensive reply that you do not wish to imbibe with me?"

Terry put his hands on the First Sergeant's desk and glared at him through cold eyes, frustrated in his efforts to help Jones. "Shove it up your ass, Deale!" He walked out of the Orderly Room.

Terry knew he could not show any favoritism toward Jones; that would be disastrous for both of them. He walked back to the barracks through the heavy snow.

Jordan was needling Jones as Terry walked past the squad room. He stopped and entered the room. "Get off his butt, Jordan. He doesn't need your smart mouth."

Jordan grinned. "Yes, Sergeant Kovak." But it was a very greasy reply.

Terry gave them no time to needle the young man, keeping them busy mopping and waxing the floors, running through inspections, and field-stripping and cleaning weapons. It was eleven o'clock before Terry allowed them to hit their bunks, too tired to hassle Jones.

At one o'clock, Terry woke, went to the latrine, and on his way back looked in on Jones. The young man was wide awake. "Go to sleep, Jones," Terry ordered him in a whisper.

Sometime during the night Terry thought he heard Jones cry out, but he wasn't certain whether it was a dream or real. He lay in his bed, listening, but heard no more cries.

He rolled them out at four-forty-five, a little surprised to find Jones up and dressed. His face was pale and he was walking stiffly. Terry started to say something to Jones, but the boy only looked at him with pain-filled eyes and walked away. Terry could not find his Platoon Guide to ask him what had happened.

It was snowing when Terry lined his men up in front of the barracks, preparing to move them out to breakfast. Jones approached him. "I'm not hungry, Sergeant," he said dully. He looked tired . . . and something else Terry could not pinpoint. "Can I be weapons' guard this morning?"

"Okay, Jones. Is there anything you'd like to talk about?"

"No, Sergeant."

Terry nodded, and the young soldier assumed his lonely position over the packs and weapons of his platoon. Terry looked at him just once more before moving his men to breakfast. Jordan wore a nasty grin.

Sergeant Kovak was midway through his breakfast when a recruit came running into the mess hall, face white, eyes wide. Flecks of vomit spotted the front of his field jacket.

"Somebody come quick!" he yelled. "He's dead! Oh, my

God, half his head is gone!'' The young soldier sat down on the floor of the mess hall and threw up the rest of his breakfast.

Regimental Sergeant Major Terrian stood up and shouted the mess hall quiet. ''You will *not* leave this building without permission,'' he told the several hundred recruits. He talked for a moment with the young man on the floor, wiping his mouth with a handkerchief. He rose, and turned to Sergeant Deale.

''Get your lard-ass in gear, Deale. And close your mouth. You're supposed to be a leader of men. You look like Chicken Little. Call Captain Young and then call the MP's. Sergeant Kovak, come with me.''

It was Jones. Terry knew that the instant the recruit came rushing into the mess hall, yelling and puking. Lying face up on crimson snow, fists clenched, the entire back of his head gone, eyes open in that final shock of death. Blood and brains were scattered over many of the packs.

''Stuck the barrel of the M1 in his mouth and pulled the trigger,'' Sergeant Major Terrian observed. ''Where in the hell did he get the ammunition?''

''From the range, I would imagine,'' Terry said. ''We fired out there day before yesterday.'' Then he told Terrian about Jones.

The Sergeant Major questioned Terry hard. ''You did try to see the Chaplain? It's on record?''

''Yes, Sergeant Major.''

''You did try to see Captain Young?''

''Yes, Sergeant Major.''

''You did try to counsel the recruit yourself?''

''Yes, Sergeant Major.''

''Did you try to see anyone else?''

''Slate and Deale.''

''A nitwit and an asshole. All right, why did you assign Jones to weapons' guard this morning?''

''He asked to be assigned; said he wasn't hungry.'' Terry lit a cigarette.

''Anything else, Sergeant?''

"Yes. I want the Medical Examiner to see if Jones has been . . . to see if Jones might have had anal sex last night."

"*What?!*" the Sergeant Major's question was a harsh whisper in the predawn.

Terry told him of his suspicions. The Sergeant Major's face was pale and hard. "This could get sticky, Terry. Very sticky. We might have all kinds of flack over this. I know the M.E.; I'll have him do this on the Q.T. God! That's disgusting!"

Captain Young and the Military Police arrived, along with a member of the Provost Marshall's office, all within seconds of each other. Pictures were taken and questions were asked, over and over. The Commanding General of the base arrived, looked around, shook his head in sorrow and disbelief, then went back home.

A blanket was tossed over what was left of Private Jones, Edward P.

For the first time, all present—except for Jones—realized they had an audience. Every window of the barracks was full of young faces, looking out at them, at death, now covered with a blanket, one fist protruding from under the wool.

"Sergeant Kovak," Captain Young told him, "tell those men to occupy themselves in some other manner."

"Yes, sir." Within seconds after Terry entered the building, the windows were empty, blank rectangles of light staring at nothing through sightless eyes of reflection.

Terry returned to the snow and the cold and the blood and bits of bone and gray matter and squatted down beside the cooling flesh of Jones. Terry knew he had to keep his shit together; had to play down what he suspected was true.

"The Dear John letter," he said aloud. "From the bitch up in Pennsylvania." He or Terrian would deal with Jordan.

"What's that, Sergeant?" an MP asked.

"Like I told the Lieutenant, his girl back home got herself pregnant and married and sent Jones a Dear John, 'keep the saddle' letter."

"Guess that's why he zapped himself," the MP said.

Later, Terry told his story a dozen times, leaving out only one part: Jordan.

The body was gone, the area cleaned. The sky began to spit snow, light at first, then coming down like a white spotted sheet. The whiteness covered the smudged outline of Jones's death scene and the bootprints surrounding it. The slug that tore the life from Jones had been found embedded in the wall of the barracks. A white chalk mark circled the spot, standing out in the dim light.

A Colonel asked Terry—since it was his platoon—what he had planned for that day.

"I'm going to march them," Terry said bluntly. "March them until they're too tired to think about anything other than their sore feet." As he talked, he looked at Captain Young, waiting for him to contradict the orders.

The Captain looked at First Sergeant Deale, who was standing around looking very uncomfortable. "Turn the Company out, Sergeant Deale. And change out of those Class-A's and into fatigues—you're going with us."

Deale made five miles with the Company, then dropped out, complaining of a bad head cold. Sergeant Major Terrian, working with Young's Company that week, looked at Deale in disgust.

"Lard-ass!" he muttered, while the men took a break. He turned to Terry. "If the M.E.'s report confirms what you told me, you really think it was Jordan?"

"Yes."

Late that afternoon, the M.E.'s report was quietly handed to Terrian. The Sergeant Major came to see Terry. "Jordan," he said. "Break him!"

Jordan slipped in the snow during the second five miles of the march and Terry was on him with the speed and fury of a pit viper.

"Pick up that weapon and clean it!" he barked. "Then give me twenty push-ups for your fumble-butted efforts at being a soldier.'' He turned to his Platoon Guide. ''Take the men on. I'm staying here with Jordan.''

Jordan did his twenty, rose to his feet, and faced Terry. ''I can take anything you can dish out, Kovak.''

Terry smiled. ''Sure you can, Jordan.''

Three days later, Jordan had just about reached his breaking point. It was night, and Terry had him digging holes in the hard, rocky Kentucky earth. Digging them with a small entrenching tool.

''I want it six by six by six, Jordan,'' Terry told him. ''And that's feet, not inches.''

Jordan looked up from the hole. ''You can't do this to me. It's not legal. I'm going to report you.''

''I'm doing it, hot-shot. If you don't like it, you can crawl out of that hole and come at me.''

''Can I talk off the record?''

''You can say any goddamned thing you want to say, Jordan.''

''I'm going to kill you, Kovak. I swear to God; I swear on my mother's picture—I'm gonna kill you.''

Terry laughed. ''When you make your play, Jordan, do me one favor.''

''What, bastard?''

''Do it in front of witnesses. That way I can stomp you legally.''

''I didn't do nothing that Jones didn't like—he was a queer. He liked it when I was doing it to him.''

''You're a sorry son of a bitch, Jordan!''

Seven days after Jones's death, Jordan broke under the pressure from Terry, Captain Young, and Sergeant Major Terrian.

Terry had singled Jordan out and was having him do close-order drill in the street in front of the barracks, while the others in the Company stood in loose formation, laughing at him, as Terry barked commands so fast Jordan finally tripped over his boots and sprawled on his face.

Jordan slowly picked himself up, looking at Sergeant Major

Terrian. Terrian stood smiling at him. Then Jordan made the biggest mistake of his life. A soldier may curse God if he so desires. A soldier may lose his cool and take a swing at his CO—that will cost him a little time in the stockade. But a soldier must never, ever, get a Sergeant Major down on his case. To make matters worse, Terrian was a Command Sergeant Major, and a Command Sergeant Major sits directly by the feet of God. A CSM has friends of all ranks, all services, all over the world. One will never, ever, escape the wrath of a CSM.

"You goddamn motherfucker!" Jordan cursed Terrian.

Captain Young visibly paled. Second Lieutenant Slate—who was deathly afraid of CSM Terrian—doubled up and ran into the barracks and into the latrine, where he lost his lunch. First Sergeant Deale, who had about as much chance of making CSM as Andy Gump did of becoming President of the United States, walked back to his office and said a very short and sincere prayer for the ass of Private Jordan—for it now belonged to Terrian.

Jordan wouldn't shut up. "Son of a bitch!" he screamed "I'm gonna tear those pretty stripes off your jacket and shove 'em up your ass!"

Terrian's expression did not change; only a slight narrowing of his eyes indicated he even heard Jordan. He slowly field-stripped his cigarette and scattered the tobacco, putting the balled-up paper in his pocket.

No one heard Terrian when he muttered, "You belong to me, Jordan." He spun on his heel and walked away.

Terry smiled, knowing he could now ease up on Jock Jordan for Jordan was through. When Jordan completed basic training he would have twenty-two months left in the Army, and they would be the most miserable months he would ever spend— if he lived through them. The papers assigning him to radio school would vanish. Jordan would go on to Infantry School then, in all probability, to a Line Outfit. There, he would draw every shit-detail known to man. He would never make any rank. Or, if Terrian was feeling especially ornery, Jordan would be sent to Guam or Wake Island, where he could spend his time cleaning Gooney Bird shit off the runways. Or, as i eventually happened, he would be sent to the rugged country around Vicenza, Italy, where a small detachment of Army Rangers are stationed. CSM Terrian was one of Colonel Darby's original Rangers.

Terry was still smiling as he walked up to Jordan. The recruit's face was still white with anger. "Now, Jordan, you'll pay for what you did to Jones."

"I didn't kill him!" Jordan snarled.

"You didn't pull the trigger," Terry corrected.

Months later, Jordan fell out of a helicopter, falling fifteen hundred feet to his death.

"How regrettable," Terry said.

In the years to come, Terry would look back and wonder: If I hadn't put Jones on weapons' guard, would he still be alive?

Twelve

"Interesting scar you picked up, Sally," Terry ran his fingers over her belly to touch the puckered scar that marred the skin on her left side. "Little bit more to the center and you wouldn't be here." His fingers left small traces in the sweat on her body.

"I turned just as the dude pulled the trigger—lucky for me. The bullet bounced off my hipbone and knocked me flat on the ground. I really thought I was gut-shot."

"Did you get him?" Terry lit two cigarettes and handed one to Sally.

"I got him," she replied nonchalantly. "With the second shot. God, I hate those hammerless .38's!"

The sounds of Saigon drifted up to them: the jingling bells of bicycles and the noisy horns of small cars. The street vendors calling out their wares. A not-unpleasant mixture of smells and sounds from a country soon to be ripped apart by a full-scale war; a country already war-weary from years of bloody guerrilla war.

The sweat cooled and dried on their bodies; the warm air blowing in through the open window fanned them as day began to separate from dusk and night gently covered the city.

"Funny we should meet here in Nam," she said. "I heard

you were in Germany. Something to do with knocking off some double agent.'' She ran her hand along his leg, touching an old bullet scar on his thigh. When Terry did not reply, she said, ''I want out, Terry. I've had enough.''

''Take it up with Colonel Perret.''

''I did. He said to take a few weeks off and think about it. I took a few weeks off. I thought about it. But I still want out and I told him so. That's when he sent me over here. Now I meet you.''

A chill moved over Terry, the unfriendly sensation ignoring the warmth of the climate. ''Have you met some guy? Are you in love, Sally?''

She hesitated, then said, ''Yes. He's an insurance man from Michigan. We've been seeing each other for about a year.'' She rose from the damp, rumpled sheets of the bed, pulled on her panties, and struggled into her bra. ''He loves me, wants to make an honest woman of me.'' She laughed, a short bitter bark. ''Isn't that a kick for you?''

''Have you told this dude anything about who you work for or what we do?''

The slight pause on her part told Terry what he wanted to know, and it sickened him: she had blabbed.

''Of course not,'' she said, avoiding his eyes. ''I know better than that.'' She slipped into her blouse and skirt, then slid bare feet into local sandals. ''We'd better report to the AID office separately,'' she changed the subject. ''At least a half hour apart. You know the rules.'' She moved toward the door. A graceful, pretty young woman. ''Maybe I'll see you over there?''

''Yeah, maybe. I still don't know what my assignment is.'' But Terry had a hunch.

The hotel was Agency-run, the phones as clean as they could be in a foreign country. In five minutes, Terry had Colonel Perret on the line.

''It's scrambled on both ends,'' Perret said. ''So we can talk. She's gone over to the other side, Terry. We've had that so-called 'insurance man' under surveillance for months. He's a peacenik, self-proclaimed; totally opposed to our involvement in Southeast Asia. He may be right about that; I suspect he is, considering the fact that Congress is going to run the war, when and if it happens, instead of allowing the military to handle it, but that's neither here nor there. This guy's political leanings place him hard left, and he's been seen many times with Red agents. Sally has been passing info to him for months. When we picked up on that, we only gave her info we wanted her to pass. There is not a doubt: she's a traitor. I gather by now you're beginning to realize your being in Saigon is no accident?''

"The thought occurred to me about twenty minutes ago." Terry's reply was terse.

"In a matter of hours," Perret said, thousands of miles away in Fort Bragg, N.C., "her 'insurance man' will have met with a very unfortunate accident. I expect you to handle your end with equal expertise."

"I just made love to her, Colonel."

"I warned you about getting involved with agents, Terry. I warned you years ago. This is not the first time, nor will it be the last, that an agent turned traitor. We can't afford the luxury of a public trial—you know that. Postcoital depression can lead to all sorts of things, Sergeant. Do I make myself clear?''

"Very clear, sir."

"Good. You have your orders. Carry them out."

The line went dead, and Terry was left with a buzzing receiver in his hands. There was a sick feeling in his guts.

"The countryside is so beautiful," Sally said. "It's hard to imagine a guerrilla war is all around us. Don't you feel that way, Terry?''

It was early morning, and they were driving toward what Sally believed was a meet with a Special Forces detachment a hundred miles from Saigon.

Terry knew perfectly well there was a war around them: a Thompson SMG lay on the back seat, a dozen full clips in a pouch beside the weapon. The top was down on the small rental car; cool air, scented from the fragrance of hundreds of flowers, blew around the man and the woman.

While Sally had gone to the restroom of the small cafe at the hotel, Terry had prowled through her purse, unloading her pistol and removing her cyanide pill: standard issue for all of Perret's people, to be used if capture was inevitable. Terry had long ago thrown his pill away. He was far too certain of himself for that.

He did not reply to her question, and she looked at him, eyes large and wary in her face. "You said yesterday you didn't know why you were sent to Saigon. I guess you know now. Right?"

Terry did not look at her as he said, "Yeah. I talked with Perret after you left."

She seemed resigned to her fate as several miles hummed by in silence. "I guess if it had to be anyone, I'm glad it's you, Terry. At least you won't make me suffer like some of the others would."

"Why did you do it, Sally?"

She looked at the passing landscape for a moment, knowing that unless a miracle came to pass, her time for viewing beauty on this earth was at a premium. "I'm sick of it all: the secrets, the killings, the living with fear of being caught. No government is worth what we do, Terry. It's all wrong—what we're doing, I mean."

"And Communism is right? Don't hand me that line of crap, Sally—you're far too intelligent to believe that."

"Thank you for the compliment. But it isn't all a belief in Communism, although that form of government makes as much sense as Democracy, at least to me, at this point in my life. I just want out, Terry! You don't understand, do you?"

"Hell, no!" Terry suppressed a strong sense of rage building in him. "I have to ask, Sally; have to confirm what Colonel Perret said: have you been passing secrets?"

"Trying to make your shitty job a little easier?" she spat the question at him.

"Maybe."

Her words were barely audible over the rush of wind in the open car. "Yes, I have."

And that was to be the beginning of the end of Perret's Dog Teams.

His anger boiled, spilling over. "Goddamnit, Sally! Why did you do it?"

"I was a scared kid, Terry—a long time ago. I'd done something wrong, got in a little trouble with the law. I told you all this. Then Perret stepped in, all smiles and cordiality, telling me everything was going to be all right. His words sounded good to me then—now they stink. He's done the same to you. Blackmailed you."

"No," Terry shook his head, "that's not true. I got out for a time. He didn't try to stop me. You could have done the same thing," he cut his eyes to her, "before you turned traitor, that is."

She grabbed at her purse on the seat and jerked out her pistol, pointing it at Terry. She could not understand his slight smile. "I'll kill you, Terry. I don't want to, but I will. Please don't make me do that. What I'm doing is right—working for peace. What you're doing is wrong. I'm telling it all, Terry. Now, stop the car."

Whatever feelings he had for her vanished. He felt no pity, not one second of sorrow for what he had to do. Terry could not tolerate disloyalty. His dossier read that he was an arch-patriot. His dossier was correct.

At her instructions, Terry turned off the highway and down a rutted, bumpy dirt road. A mile farther he pulled over, cut the engine, and pocketed the keys. He got out to stand by the side of the car.

"Now what, Sally?"

"Give me the keys, Terry. Give me the keys and some time. I'll let you live. I promise."

"Sure you will, Sally," he said dryly. "And the moon is made of green cheese."

She pulled the trigger, the hammer falling on an empty chamber. Again and again, she pulled the trigger to the sound of clicks. She cursed Terry. "Son of a bitch!" She threw the pistol at him. Terry caught the .38 in his left hand and shoved it in his belt.

He reached into his pocket and held out the cyanide pill. ''You want it this way?''

The thought of physically taking Terry only briefly entered her mind. She knew no one had ever taken Terry Kovak. Not even Perret could do that, not anymore. With tears running down her face, she begged, ''Give me a break, Terry. Please!?''

His silence wrote the final chapter on Sally Malone, girl who had it all from Binghamton, NY. Her shoulders slumped in surrender.

''There's still the man in Michigan,'' she tried one more ploy. ''He'll tell it all.''

''He's dead,'' Terry informed her.

''Yes, I suspected as much. But part of what the Dog Teams have done is carefully detailed and tucked away. Perret will be able to squash most of it, but a little will leak out.''

''It's happened before, Sally. You know that. Perret will just change the names and keep going. He might be forced into retirement, but someone else will take over. We'll always be around.''

She took the pill from his outstretched hand and looked at it. ''Kiss me goodbye, Terry?''

''No! I have no sympathy for traitors.''

She slipped out of her blouse and skirt, standing before him in bra and panties. ''One more time for good luck, Terry?''

His eyes held only disgust.

Sally shrugged, popped the pill in her mouth, and swallowed it. She sat down on the marshy ground. A few moments later she was dead, her face contorted in agony as the cyanide stopped all vital functions.

Terry picked her up, while a water buffalo watched through mean eyes, and carried her to the car, dumping her in the trunk. He drove back to Saigon, parked the car behind the hotel, where other agents would dispose of the body. Five hours later he was on a MATS plane, heading back to the United States. Back to Colonel Perret. To another assignment.

Jill

An invisible force moved between them as their eyes met, shifted away, returned, and locked. The force whizzed between them, back and forth, attempting to stir one or the other to action.

The St. Louis bar was crowded with people: laughing, talking, ordering more booze, singing and shouting in and out of time with the overworked and most of the time too-loud band. But, for the soldier with the hard pale eyes and the young woman with the dark hair and sexy mouth, seated several stools apart around the curving bar, they were the only two people left in the world, as they looked at each other, oblivious to the happy chaos roaring about them.

Terry smiled, the smile momentarily warming his pale eyes, and raised his glass to her. She returned the smile and raised her own glass in a taunting mock salute.

Terry had been in the States less than twenty-four hours, having flown in from Germany. He had had thirty days' leave time coming, and he took it all, deciding to wander around the country, having no desire at all to return to Bishop, Georgia.

He left his bar stool and walked to the woman's side. She laughed, raised her hands, and said, ''I surrender, sir. But, I remind you, under the rules of the Geneva Convention, I am required only to give you my name, rank, and serial number—nothing more.''

His eyes inspected her more closely. ''I'm a Sergeant, not a Sir, and I'll settle for your name.''

''Very well, Sergeant.'' She patted the empty stool beside her. Terry sat. ''Jill Slane. Schoolteacher *extraordinaire,* attempting to enjoy her Christmas vacation, away from what, during the final week, appeared to be millions of screaming little monsters, and the rather drab Illinois countryside. I'm also a little bit drunk. Now that you know my entire boring life history, tell me, what is your name?''

''Kovak. Terry Kovak.''

''And your home, Terry Kovak?''

He waved his hand. ''Where the Army sends me. St. Louis, for the moment.''

''And tomorrow, the world,'' she breathed the words with a mischievous smile. She looked him up and down, put a small hand on his shoulder, and said, ''You look as though you can be trusted, Sergeant, so how would you like to buy a lady a steak dinner?''

''My pleasure, ma'am.''

''Good Lord! Do I detect the subtle phrasings of a Southern Gentleman?''

He grinned. ''That depends upon your interpretation of the word *'Gentleman,'* ma'am.''

She winked at him, leaned forward, and almost fell off the stool. Terry caught her, strong hands on slender shoulders. ''That's an old joke, Sergeant.'' She straightened up, composing herself, slightly embarrassed by her clumsiness. ''And a crude one, at that. However, I shall not take offense. Let's get out of here.''

She ate like a starving cannibal, through a huge salad, a baked potato with butter and sour cream, and a twenty-ounce steak, rare and bloody. She occasionally brushed back a strand of black hair; a worrisome lock that kept falling over one eye.

After coffee was served, she asked, "What are those little silver things on your chest?" she pointed.

"Wings. Paratrooper wings. Jump out of airplanes. Geronimo, and all that."

"Aren't you afraid the thing won't open?"

"That thought has occurred to me from time to time, but we wear a belly pack, too."

"A spare parachute?"

"Right."

"And if that doesn't open?"

"Then the medics will have something to do."

She grimaced, rolling her eyes in dismay. "Fatalistic sort, aren't you?" She cocked her head to look at the patches on his shoulders. "I thought Rangers took care of trees in National Parks."

Terry put his head in his hands and feigned great pain. "Oh, my God!" he moaned, then laughed at her.

"Really, I did!" she said.

Terry asked if she'd like to take a walk and let dinner settle?

"In St. Louis at midnight? You've got to be kidding! Or making bad jokes. You want to get rolled, or something?"

Terry smiled at her last question, wanting to say he'd very much like to see the punk who could roll him, but, instead, he asked, "Got any suggestions of your own?"

She looked at him, her gray eyes startlingly vivid in their frame of smooth face and black hair. She placed both hands on the table and felt a delicious shivering in her loins as she gazed at the man sitting across from her. She was aware of a quickening of her heartbeat. "What are you trying to say, Sergeant?"

He looked down at his coffee cup, then brought his eyes up to meet hers, conscious of the fact that he felt a strong . . . something for this almost-stranger. "Maybe I don't want the evening to end?"

Jill was almost flip with her reply, then realized she was very much drawn to this young soldier, and sauciness might be the wrong way to further their relationship, and she knew she wanted their relationship to go much further. She studied him. He was young in years, surely no more than twenty-five, but his eyes—when she could read them—were very old, wise; as ancient as time. Strong hands, with tiny scars on the knuckles. Very blond hair, cut short. His face tanned a deep bronze. She knew this soldier spent very little time in an office.

She blurted, "Do you want to sleep with me, Terry?" then railed silently at herself for saying it.

She had known sex with two men in her twenty-two years, and was famous as a notorious flirt and a lot of fun. But during her college years it was said of Jill Slane: "Lots of fun, but no screwing."

Terry did not reply, maintaining his steady gaze with pale eyes that gave away nothing.

Jill realized that, with her question, she had lost ground, and she wanted—for some reason as yet unknown to her—to regain it. "I'm not a tart," she said. "I'm not the kind of woman to sleep around with strangers."

"Then why did you say it?" Terry was suddenly irritated with her and didn't know why he should be. Hell, he'd just met her. There was nothing between them. But he wanted something to be between them, and that thought confused him. Everything was happening too quickly.

She touched the back of his hand with cool fingertips. "Forgive me, Terry. I sometimes say things I instantly regret. It's a defense mechanism with me. Protective coloration, that's all."

His anger cooled, to be replaced with calmness and a question. "I don't have a room as yet—all my gear is still in my car. I have thirty days to kill." He wondered why he used the word "kill?" "Jill, you want to spend some time with me?"

"Yes, I would," she quickly replied. "But where?"

He shrugged. "How about Canada?"

She didn't believe she'd heard him right. She blinked twice, then asked, "Canada?! Like the country? Mounties and Lake Louise and all that kind of stuff. Canada?" *This is insane! I just met the man.*

"Yeah. Right. Why not? Do you have enough time to make the trip?"

"I . . . have seventeen days."

"Well?" He didn't know why he'd picked Canada, or why he'd asked a woman he didn't know to travel with him. Was she one of Perret's plants? He did that from time to time, testing his people, to see if they would open their mouths and talk about the Teams. No, she wasn't a plant, Terry concluded.

My God! Jill thought: this man might be a murderer on the loose. A rapist, or worse.

Canada? "Let's go," she heard herself say.

They drove as far as Chicago. There—with unspoken, silent agreement—they checked into a motel, and spent the next ten days together in the Windy City, falling more in love with each other as the hours passed in a dizzying blur. Jill told him her life's story, hoking it up, making her life seem more mundane than it really was. Terry told her about himself, lying a great deal to fill in the many gaps of secrecy. They walked a lot, holding hands. They spoke of their hopes, plans, dreams, as they strolled along the cold shoreline of Lake Michigan. They laughed at things that would not have amused either of them singly. And they made the sweetest of love at odd hours of the night and day; for them, the clock had stopped. She touched and kissed each scar on his body, questioning their presence, usually receiving an answer that did not satisfy her, but spoken in such a manner as to suggest that any further discussion would be pointless, and to leave the unknown where it belonged, in limbo.

She was everything he had ever envisioned in a woman. Beautiful and perfect in every way—in his eyes. Intelligent, possessing a dry, cutting wit. Jill spoke almost perfect, grammatically correct German, speaking it with such a flat, Midwestern twang that Terry could not understand a word of it.

He was everything she had looked for in a man. An incredibly powerful man, but one who did not strut about, flexing his muscles, boasting of his power. He had the grace and quickness of an athlete, but sports held zero interest for him. She had asked him, once, about that.

"I don't see the point," he had replied, and she dropped the subject.

He had never told her, but she sensed he could very probably kill with his hands; hands that were so wonderfully gentle as they stroked her skin. He was very intelligent, but usually kept his mental alertness hidden, except, she suspected, from those he trusted. Which, she felt, numbered very few.

Several young thugs followed them one night, as they strolled back to their motel. The punks made several suggestions as to what they would like to do to Jill, and what they would do to Terry if he didn't give them his money and if he tried to interfere in their taking of the woman.

Jill had the brassy taste of fear in her mouth, but to her amazement, Terry was smiling, calm, almost as if he were looking forward to any move the punks might make.

When the thugs made their move toward them, Jill did not see the hands that struck so quickly; the feet that kicked as high as a ballet dancer's; and the eyes that held no emotion, that were as cold as snake's eyes.

It was over so quickly—as violence usually is. Two of the punks lay on the sidewalk, one with blood pouring from his nose, mouth, and eyes. One eye was gone. The second thug had no lower chin intact, for Terry had kicked it several inches to the right. The third punk was on his knees, holding his groin area, vomiting in the gutter.

Taking her elbow, Terry walked Jill away from the scene. His face had not changed expression.

Later, in bed, she asked, "Terry? If I had not been with you tonight: what would you have done with those . . . animals?"

"I would have killed them."

"Was that karate you used?"

"Only part of it, a form of karate." He spoke softly, for the incident was forgotten in his mind. "But it's a form you'll never see taught in any civilian defense school."

"Why?"

"Because the judges in this country don't want the law-abiding citizen to be able to protect himself. The law is on the side of the animals in the streets."

"Some might call you an animal for what you did tonight?"

"That's what I mean, honey."

She dropped the subject.

Jill was not experienced in bed, but she was curious and sometimes demanding as they moved from position to position, testing and exploring, wanting each second to last an hour, the hour finally exploding in tangled sheets and pounding hearts.

On the tenth day, Terry asked her to marry him.

"Yes," she said, with no hesitation.

Thirteen

Butler, Illinois, looked very much like a picture post card, with its cover of snow, steepled churches, homes that somehow all looked alike, and small-town main street. Butler depressed Terry.

"They've resigned themselves to it, I suppose," Jill said, her hand resting lightly on Terry's leg. They drove through the snowy streets to Jill's home. "Mother cried a lot and for the first time in my life I heard my father say a really vulgar word." She smiled. "I hope you brought the blood test report."

"It's in my gear. Jesus, you should have heard my commanding officer cuss when I told him I was getting married. My Colonel really let the hammer down on me. He likes his personnel free of entanglements."

"I never heard of such a thing," Jill said indignantly. "A grown man having to ask permission to get married."

Terry grinned. "That's the Army for you. Rules and regulations."

"Stupid!" Jill looked out the window. "Turn here. It's the third house on the right. The one with that silly-looking pink flamingo in the front yard."

"I didn't feel this queasy when I made my first jump," Terry pulled into the drive. "My God, look at all the cars and trucks. Your entire family must be here."

"Oh, shit!" Jill cursed, and Terry laughed at her.

There was a solid wall of hostility against him. Terry could sense it and see it in the eyes of the Slane family. They resented him, and made little effort to hide that resentment. There wasn't an ashtray in sight when Terry lit a cigarette. He knew it, and took pleasure in it. When no one got up to get him an ashtray, he placed his coffee cup on the arm table and used his saucer.

"No one smokes in this family," Mr. Slane said smugly.

"I do," Terry replied.

Jill got up from the couch, fighting to hide a grin, and got Terry an ashtray. She sat down on the arm of his chair and put her hand on his shoulder.

"How long have you been in the Army, Sergeant?" Jill's older brother asked. Larry Slane, a farmer, one of several pillars of the community, an every-time-the-doors-open churchgoer, and, Terry suspected, a one hundred percent hypocrite.

"Oh, 'bout eight years, counting Guard time."

"Make good money?"

Terry started to tell him it wasn't any of his goddamned business, but held his tongue. "A living."

Larry Slane grunted. "Guess you and Jill will be traveling around a lot, mixing in with all those foreigners?"

Terry allowed the slur on his Mother Country to slide. "Not really. My permanent base is Fort Bragg." He met Larry's stare with a hard grin. "That's in North Carolina—America."

Larry flushed and kept his mouth shut.

"Well, as far as I'm concerned," Jill's father said, "you two should get to know each other a little bit better. Two weeks is not much time in which to build any kind of lasting relationship."

Terry surprised the father by agreeing, then angered him by saying: "But if we make a mistake, there's always the divorce courts . . . right?"

Jill laughed at her father's expression. "Believe me, Dad, we know each other well enough."

"I imagine that is quite true in one respect," her father replied, blunt and unfeeling accusation in his tone. "However, that is not what I meant."

Jill flushed in anger, then blushed as her mother began to weep.

"Let's get the hell out of here!" Terry stood up.

"Are you calling the wedding off?" Jill's uncle asked.

"Hell, no," Terry said. "We're going to find a judge."

An hour later, Terry and wife were heading for Bishop, Georgia.

Their reception at the Kovak house was, as Terry knew it would be, very different from that at the Slane home. The newlyweds were fed, pampered, petted, and congratulated. Terry and Jill spent two days in Bishop, then, with time running out, left for Fort Bragg.

There is a camaraderie among career military personnel seldom found in civilian life, prevailing among the women as well as the men. Within minutes of the van full of new furniture pulling into the drive of their new quarters at Fort Bragg, a dozen Sergeants and wives were standing by to help the newlyweds settle in. Two dozen hands were eager to put up curtains and drapes, move furniture, sort out and carefully put away dishes. By six o'clock that evening, their quarters were ready to be lived in, and dinner was prepared for them and on the table. It was then that Terry and Jill looked around and realized they were alone: their neighbors had quietly slipped away.

"It isn't this way on the outside," Jill observed, already picking up the Army jargon.

"No," Terry swallowed a mouthful of roast beef, "it isn't. A military unit is like a close-knit family—we hang together."

She touched the back of his hand with gentle fingertips. "We're going to make it, aren't we, Terry?"

"If we try," he said soberly. "And if we have the time."

Jill found a job teaching school in a nearby town—substituting at first, then becoming a regular—and their lives rocked along well for several months, while Terry trained with a Special Forces group. Things were heating up in Southeast Asia, with that part of the world coming up often in discussions.

On Saturday afternoon, there was a shower for Sergeant Topper's wife, Alice, and after the presents were opened and admired, the ladies sat sipping coffee and talking. Army wives often know as much, and sometimes more, than their husbands do concerning military affairs.

"Al's going to Vietnam next month," Alice said softly. "Several 'A' Teams are shipping out. It's all supposed to be hush-hush, but I know all the signs. Al's out looking for quarters off base, now."

Al Topper was a Master Sergeant with Special Forces, a demolition expert cross-trained in light weapons. Al was team Sergeant of his detachment: a quiet, studious man whom Jill had gotten to know well through her friendship with Alice. It had surprised Jill to learn that Al was just a few hours away from having a degree in History, but had chosen to serve his country rather than pursue a teaching career. This was to be their third child.

Alice studied Jill over the rim of her cup. After fifteen years as a military wife, she could spot, with but a glance, all the signs that Terry was keeping the news of his departure from his wife.

"Terry hasn't told you yet, has he?" she asked, and all eyes in the room shifted.

Jill experienced a sick feeling in the pit of her stomach. "I know he's been training with an 'A' Team. Is he shipping out, too, Alice?"

"Yes," Alice leveled with her. "He's with Al this afternoon, looking for quarters off base."

Every woman present was the wife of a Ranger or SF man. Jill looked at each of them for several seconds. "They're all going, aren't they?"

"Sixty of them," the Sergeant Major's wife said. "That's still highly classified, honey, so sit on it, will you?" She smiled reassuringly at Jill.

"For . . . how long?" Jill said numbly.

"A year," an SF wife said.

Jill's hand trembled as she raised the cup to her lips, and drops of coffee spilled into the saucer. She gave it up and carefully placed the cup into the saucer. "What are we supposed to do while they're gone?"

"Wait!" a Sergeant Major's wife said bluntly. "I waited for Oren during World War Two. I waited for him during Korea when he was with UNPIK, so I guess I can wait for him during this one, too. Guess, hell! I have to—we all have to." She laughed aloud. "One thing about it, though: Oren's almost fifty; he won't be chasing so much poon this time around. When he gets in from days of stomping around the jungle, it'll take a block and tackle to get it up."

The older wives laughed; the younger ones shook their heads and smiled: all of them knowing Mrs. Masterson was just putting up a brave front for the other wives. It was expected of her; part of her role as the wife of a Command Sergeant Major. Part of her many duties.

"A year," Jill said. "One whole year."

"Six months," Mrs. Masterson corrected. "There's a good chance they'll get R & R in Japan. We can fly MATS over to them for a few days." She stood up and walked across the room to sit by Jill. She patted the young wife on the arm. "Hang in there, babe; you're Army now. It's tough to be an Army wife. And it gets tougher when the bed seems to get bigger and emptier and you're worrying about your man stopping one in some Godforsaken part of the world.

"Honey, our men don't get near the credit due them, and it's a shame, 'cause without the men who fight the lonely wars, we wouldn't have a country." She looked at the other wives. "When our men ship out, we'll all try to get together a couple of times a week, compare letters, try to read between the lines." She grinned. "You can censor out the mushy parts. And we've got to keep the young studs away from the young gals. I hate to be crude, ladies, but you girls are going to have to keep your legs crossed for six months at a whack, so get lots of lovin' before your men leave."

*   *   *

Jill would share a house in Rockingham with Marianne Price and her young son. There, they would wait for their men to return—if they returned.

The couple clung together in bed, the last night before Terry shipped out. Jill's brave front had crumpled and she was crying in his arms. Terry suspected fifty-nine other wives—for most Special Forces men were married—were doing the same thing in beds in and around Fort Bragg, including Mrs. Masterson.

The airfield at Bragg, 0500 on a June morning, just breaking light in the East. Sixty Forcemen and Rangers and their wives. One more touch; one more kiss; one more comforting word. Look after the kids, honey, and I'll write to you once a week, I promise. But if you don't hear from me, please don't panic, 'cause the mail service is gonna be lousy, and we may be 'way to hell and gone back in the boonies. I won't need more than a few bucks a week where we'll be, so you ought to be able to make it okay. If you get in any kind of jam, baby, call the folks—they'd want you to do that. Just remember one thing, honey: I'll be back.

I love you.

I love you, too.

The women watched the transport roar down the runway and slide into the air, carrying hopes and dreams and a cargo of limp peckers from the night before.

Terry watched the ground disappear into the clouds and his thoughts were of Jill and Colonel Perret; confusing thoughts of both people. Jill, because she loved him and he loved her, and Terry did not understand the emotion. Perret, because he had not refused Terry's request to transfer to SF.

"I don't blame you, Terry," Perret said. "Special Forces is the Glamor-Boy Outfit. Don't misunderstand my words; I'm sure as hell not knocking them—not at all. They're triple-A number-one soldiers, every one of them. But Congress and those chairborne blockheads in the Pentagon will never really turn SF loose to perform to their full maximum. You'll discover that yourself. God, just once I'd like to see a war run from the battlefield instead of from Washington.''

"You really believe we'll get into this war full steam, Colonel?''

"Hell, yes. And we'll lose it, too, unless we're allowed to fight just as dirty and savage as Uncle Ho's boys. Unless you guys can perform just as rough and mean as you're trained to do—and I hope to the Gods of War you men do just that.'' He held out his hand. "Good luck, Sergeant.''

Terry had not seen Perret since.

"It's not fair, Terry,'' Jill had cried onto his shoulder. "I've never even heard of Vietnam. What do I care what happens over there?''

Terry considered giving her a lecture on world politics, but decided against it. He believed in freedom, hated Communism, and was a soldier doing his duty. And that was that.

He said, "I'll come out of it, honey. A year is not that long.''

She had looked at him, eyes serious and not really comprehending. She had been suddenly thrust into a world of blood, sweat, and solid, uncompromising, unyielding patriotism, and she did not understand what motivated these men; these fighting men. The men she had known who had served in the military were not like these men.

She said, "I'll wait for you, Terry. I promise you. I'll be here when you need me.''

Fourteen

Terry did not trust his Vietnamese counterpart—Sergeant Dang—and he told Captain Parley of his distrust. "The son of a bitch is a shirker, sir. He's a coward to boot. He doesn't know his ass from a can of C ration."

"His father was an in-tight buddy of Big Minh, Sergeant. Dang was too stupid to get through the Vietnamese version of OCS, so they made him a Sergeant."

"Reminds me of home," Terry said dryly.

Sergeant Major Masterson was only slightly less diplomatic. "The little bastard is in cahoots with some of these lazy VC sympathizers we're always running off from here. Personally, I'd like to shoot him."

Captain Parley poured them all a drink of sour mash. "Ours is not to reason why," he grinned, tossing off the whiskey neat. It was his last drink. Hours later, on a night patrol, he was shot in the head. Parley left a wife and two children back in Virginia.

"You'd better be careful, Jill," Marianne cautioned her friend. "Mrs. Masterson is getting kind of grim-looking about your accepting rides home from school with that teacher. Jill," she touched her arm, "it doesn't look very good."

Jill sluffed off the criticism. The overprotectiveness of the other wives was beginning to rub her wrong. "He's just a friend, Marianne; he's never made any kind of off-color remark to me."

"It doesn't look right, Jill, and you know it. Terry's got his butt in the grass for his country and you're playing footsie with an English teacher."

"We're not playing footsie!" Jill retorted, becoming angry. "Can't a woman have a male friend around here? Lee is a nice guy, easy to talk with. With my car in the shop, what am I supposed to do? Walk ten miles?"

"I'll be happy to give you a ride to and from school," Marianne offered.

Jill did not reply and would not look at her friend. She knew that what she was doing was wrong—sort of—but she felt she couldn't help herself; didn't want to help herself. She was lonely, and Terry was eight thousand miles away, fighting in a stinking little war Lee said was wrong—immoral—and he talked openly against it. And although Lee had never served anywhere, Jill believed him.

Of the sixty men in Terry's group that were sent to Asia, eight had been killed in action and a dozen more were sent back Stateside because of their wounds. Their replacements brought news from Bragg. The Sergeant Major went to the Captain with some of that news.

"Got some wives fucking around back home," Masterson said. "Lieutenant Black's old lady, Captain Hunt's wife, and Sergeants Kovak's and Burgos's wives. This is gonna tear morale all to hell and gone."

"If we let it, Oren," the Captain said. "Oren, do you believe in the double standard system?"

"What do you mean, sir?"

"That it's okay for the man to dick around, but not the wife."

"All those guys aren't chasin' pussy, Captain. I know that for a fact."

"Black and Burgos are. Not Hunt or Kovak, though."

Masterson took a drag from his cigarette. "Sir, you know what Kovak was before he joined us in Bragg. He'll kill that damned schoolteacher."

"Rumors, Oren, just rumors about that mythical death squad. What are they called: Dog Teams? No, just rumors."

The young Captain and the much older Sergeant Major locked eyes. The Captain backed down. He sighed. "You were with Wild Bill during the Second World War, weren't you, Oren?"

"Yes, sir."

"Is it rumor, Oren?"

"Just between you and me? No."

"Well, then, we keep Terry from finding out about his wife. That's all we can do."

"Good luck to both of us, sir."

"We'll get R & R in a couple of months—maybe. Terry can square things with his wife then."

"Yes, sir." But his tone held no conviction.

"I shouldn't be seen with you, Lee," Jill said. "Much less holding hands in public."

"No one knows us here in Charlotte," Lee smiled. "Besides, I think it's reasonable to assume that Terry hasn't been living the life of a monk in Vietnam. Those Army people are such savages—they have to be, honey. Why would they enjoy combat if they weren't?"

"Yes. I think you're right about that."

Lee had been working on her mind for months, slowly poisoning her toward the Army and Terry.

At lunch he kissed her and she did not resist. They sat in a booth, in the rear of the cafe, away from other eyes. Jill could not remove from her mind the picture of Terry making love to some small brown Vietnamese girl. The make-believe scene enraged her, and she rather enjoyed the anger: it would make what she was going to do much easier to live with. She imagined them in some sort of primitive hut, sweaty and moaning as they lunged at each other.

Jill leaned close to Lee and kissed him, pushing her tongue between his lips, her hand rubbing his leg. She was very lonely, and Lee had been very persuasive.

His voice husky, he asked, "What do you want me to do, Jill?"

"Make love to me," she said.

"Goddamn, get it off me!" The American AID man shuddered. The leech on his leg had swelled to more than five inches long, puffed and swollen on his blood.

"Take it easy," Terry said, holding the lighted end of a cigarette to the leech. "It's no big deal. This will get it off."

The purple creature fought the heat, then dropped to the earth, leaving an ugly mark on the man's leg. A medic wiped the leg clean and applied salve to the tenderness.

"Why in God's name did we ever get involved in a place like this?" the AID man questioned, his remark directed at no one in particular. "Nasty, filthy, stinking place. God!"

"You ought to pull some time down in the Panama Canal Zone," Terry grinned. "And have a three-pound bumble bee land on your head."

Sergeant Burgos smiled. "Now, Mr. Harrison, you're going to have us thinking you don't like Vietnam, with all its friendly people and quaint French-colonial charm."

"Mere words cannot begin to express my true sentiments about this part of the world," Harrison said, rolling down his pants leg.

Sergeant Burgos laughed and stood up, adjusting the straps on his pack. His neck brushed against the side of a vine that was hanging down. The SF Sergeant screamed once and fell writhing to the ground, a snake around his neck, biting at his throat.

Terry jabbed at the viper with the barrel of his Thompson SMG, unable to fire for fear of hitting Burgos. The snake finally ceased its biting and crawled onto the path. Terry stepped on its head, grinding it into the dirt.

"My God!" Harrison from AID said, unable to take his eyes from Burgos. "Do something for him."

Captain Thornly stood up from Burgos's still form. "It's too late to do anything. He's dead. That was a seven-stepper that got him."

"Seven-stepper?!"

"Yeah," an SF Sergeant said. "You got time for about seven steps after you're bitten—then you fall down dead."

Harrison from AID doubled over and vomited on the ground. "I hate this fucking place," he said, wiping his mouth.

"Call a dust-off," Captain Thornly said to the radio man. "Tell the chopper pilot we'll smoke him in." He shook his head. "I'm not looking forward to writing Carolyn."

"Who is Carolyn?" Harrison said.

"Burgos's wife," Terry said.

"She ain't gonna give a big shit!" Sergeant Hamilton quietly ventured.

"Burgos liked his pussy." Captain Thornly ended the conversation.

Carolyn Burgos whispered obscenities to the man above her, thrusting inside her. Her legs locked around his waist, her hips meeting him with equal passion.

When she returned home late that afternoon, several of her friends were waiting for her, Mrs. Masterson among them.

"Colonel Jackson's been trying to get in touch with you all afternoon," the Sergeant Major's wife said, her eyes cool. "He tried this morning, and last evening. I told him you were probably spending the night with a friend."

Carolyn flushed. "What I do with my time is my business."

Mrs. Masterson slapped the words at her. "Your husband was killed in Nam."

Carolyn's face flushed, then went deathly white. She put out a hand to steady herself, grasping the edge of a table. "He's . . . what?"

"Sergeant Burgos was killed in Vietnam," Mrs. Masterson repeated. "Now you can go screw your lover with a clear conscience. You're no longer a married . . . lady."

Carolyn collapsed on the living room floor, her head bouncing off the carpet.

"Get me a wet cloth," Mrs. Masterson said, kneeling down. "I may not like her very much, but we're all in this together."

Terry escorted the body of Sergeant First Class Randolph Burgos back to Fort Bragg. The orders came as a surprise for him, and, as it turned out, quite a surprise for Jill.

Jill Slane Kovak's butt bounced off the floor for the second time in fifteen seconds. Her mouth was bleeding where Terry had slapped her. She crawled behind a sofa and Terry kicked her in the butt with a highly polished Jump Boot. She screamed out in pain and fright as the front door splintered open under the shoulder of an SF Sergeant. The Sergeant grabbed Terry— very carefully—and spun him around. He stepped back, ready to fight off Terry's attack, if one came.

"Ease off, Terry!" he shouted. "Don't kill the bitch, she's not worth it."

In his rage, Terry moved toward the Sergeant just as the room filled with soldiers. Several hands grabbed Terry, wrestling him to the floor, holding him hard against the carpet.

"I CAUGHT HER FUCKIN' THE SON OF A BITCH!" Terry yelled, trying to fight against the hands that pinned him to the floor. His fight proved unsuccessful for, even in his rage, he would use no killing or crippling blows against these men.

"Oh, Jesus," a Sergeant said. "Dan, go check the bedroom, Kovak may have killed the dude."

"Let me up," Terry said, calming down. His voice was steady. "I didn't kill the bastard. He jumped out the window and ran off down the alley. All he's wearing is his socks and skivvies."

"Go find the shithead," an SF man told a young Buck Sergeant. "Lean on him some. But," he warned, "do it in private. Don't kill him, just mark him some."

"Don't you dare hurt Lee!" Jill hollered from behind the sofa. "He's a good, gentle person, and I love him. I think I'm pregnant, too, and it's his baby, damn you!" She began to cry. "You had no right to go off and leave me. It wasn't fair."

The Forcemen let Terry get to his feet—very carefully. Three Green Berets and two Rangers stood between Terry and his wife.

Terry slowly turned to look at Jill. "Well, honey, you can damn sure have him. And I hope I never have to look at your two-timing face again."

Jill crawled from behind the sofa to glare at her husband. Her face was ugly with rage and hate. She held an afghan, covering her nakedness. A trickle of blood leaked from a corner of her mouth.

Two civilian policemen jumped out of a squad car and were met by two MP's from Fort Bragg. The foursome stood on the sidewalk in front of the home.

"It's all taken care of," an MP told a cop. "We'd appreciate it if you guys let us handle this."

"All you goddamn soldiers do is fuck up!" a local cop said. "If it wasn't for you guys our jobs would be a hell of a lot easier."

A very large MP looked at him. "How'd you like to meet me after work? Without your badge and gun. Just you and me, partner."

The civilian cop flushed, started to speak, and his buddy stuck an elbow in his ribs. "Don't let your ass overload your mouth, Jimmy."

The two civilian cops turned, got in their squad car, and drove away.

In the house, Jill said, "I suppose you want me to believe you never got any of that gook pussy over there?"

Terry's voice was calm. "No, Jill, I didn't. I wanted to, I'll admit that, and it wasn't easy for me. But I fought back, and won over my feelings."

"Then you're a damned fool!" she shouted. "Or a damned liar!"

"How about a person who takes his marriage vows seriously?'' Terry countered, fighting to keep his temper under control.

"Go to hell!'' she spat at him, the saliva running down his cheek.

Jill suddenly knew she was throwing her life away, knew she was making a big mistake, lousing up Terry's life, and probably her own. She began to cry, feeling sorry for herself.

"Me?'' Terry laughed. "Go to Hell? Baby, I got a room reserved.''

Three weeks later, he was back in Nam.

Fifteen
Terry

1964

A blue, powder-puff sky floated lazily above him. The silence surrounding him was almost loud in the absence of noise. Terry knew he was hard hit and wondered if he was going to die. He couldn't make his left leg work, and the side of his face was numb and sticky with blood. His left arm wouldn't obey commands from his brain. How long had he been here? Terry remembered the brutal firefight with the VC: they had come at them in the night, first outside, then inside the Special Forces compound. The fight had lasted all night. But how long ago was that?

Terry moved his head, looking around the shattered compound. Sergeant Major Masterson was dead, a few feet from him, chopped to bits, half his head gone. One eye remained open in death.

The compound was in ruins, smoking from small fires. Bodies lay all around the area. The VC must have been battalion-sized when they hit them. The Cong had won the fight, but in doing so had taken a terrible toll on themselves.

Terry moved his head in the other direction and looked into

the dark eyes of a wounded VC, lying just a few feet from him. The Cong was hard hit, his black shirt stained with blood.

"Help me," he said in English.

Terry clawed a .45 out of his holster. "Fuck you!" he answered, then he blew a hole in the VC's head.

Just before Terry slipped into blackness, he heard the sounds of incoming helicopters, their great props battering the hot air.

Christmas, 1964

"It's not his physical wounds that concern me," the doctor said. "He's completely recovered from those. But . . . he was Dog Team for a good many years."

The military psychiatrist arched an eyebrow. "I thought all that was rumor." He was very interested in speaking with Sergeant Kovak.

The doctor shook his head. "We wish. Thank God, most of them are dead, and the Teams have been disbanded. I'd hate to think we had several thousand of those people running around the country."

"Tell me about them." The psychiatrist leaned forward, eager to learn more about this mysterious group of men and women. Twenty years in the Army and he had never met a Dog Team member.

Or, he thought, at least I don't believe I have.

"We are discharging Sergeant Kovak from the hospital at Carson tomorrow. He'll be flown in here and assigned to your section. It's going to be up to you people to down-train him."

"Is he going to level with me?"

"I ordered him to tell the truth," the doctor smiled.

"What was his reply?"

"He told me to stick it in my ear."

All his possessions were in one footlocker and two duffle bags. In the footlocker, buried among rolled socks and shorts, were the boxes that contained his tributes for the years he had served his country: several Bronze Stars with V for valor. A Silver Star with V. DSC. The Congressional Medal of Honor. Six Purple Hearts. A dozen other awards from America and Vietnam.

Cold by the side of the runway. Cold and lonely. The wind whistled around the dark hangars. The car that was to meet him was late. That did not surprise Terry.

His legs still ached occasionally from the operations to remove the shrapnel and other assorted metal and lead. A scar ran down from his hairline to just below his ear. Terry reflected on his new position. He was out of the Army, with no place to go. Or rather, he would soon be out of the Army. He was to meet with the shrinks at Letterman the next morning to begin many weeks of down-training but, technically, he was out of the Army.

Terry chuckled, rather bitterly. He had all his medals, and if he added fifteen cents to them, he could buy a cup of coffee. Plus tax. If some civilian ever asked him about his service career, he was to lie: look the civilian square in the eyes and lie. Naturally, he had to lie. Terry had a quick mental picture of himself strolling into Snelling & Snelling and telling some nice job counselor: "What did I do in the Army? Hell, lady, I killed people! I killed lots of people who were passing secrets, acting as double agents, and doing all sorts of things you never heard of—could never even dream of in your worst nightmare. I tortured, maimed, murdered, kidnapped—you name it, I did it—all for my Uncle Sammy. Now, then, what can I do in civilian life?"

After the nice job counselor picked herself up off the floor, where she would have fallen in a hot faint, slobbering and screaming on the way down, she would pick up the phone, call the cops, and they would come get him and drag him off to the nearest nuthouse, where Terry could spend the rest of his days, making pretty little baskets and attempting to shove square pegs into round holes.

Terry laughed at his bitterness and his loneliness. "Hell," he said aloud, "you knew what you were getting into. Don't blame anyone else for it."

He sat on his footlocker and waited for the car to come get him; to get this soldier coming home.

Somewhere in the distance, coming from one of the hangars, whispered the muted voice of a DJ, and then the lonely sounds of Acker Bilk and *Stranger On The Shore*.

"I'm going to give you a word association test, Sergeant," the psychiatrist said, when Terry was comfortable in the chair. "When I say a word, you tell me the first word that pops in your mind."

"You may fire when ready, Gridley," Terry said, his tone that of a man about to do something he found very distasteful.

The psychiatrist opened his notebook, clicked his ballpoint pen, and said, "Home."

"Defend."

The doctor's eyebrows raised a bit. "Enemy."

"Kill."

"Airplane."

"Jump."

"Snake."

"Eat."

"What?"

Terry glanced at the shrink. "Am I supposed to reply to that?"

"What? No. No! Why did you say eat?"

"Because it's good to eat. I've eaten a lot of snake in the jungles and in training. Dog and cat, too. Dog is better than cat. Monkey, too. But you've really got to boil a monkey to get the worms out."

The psychiatrist shuddered and looked ill for a moment. "Please, Sergeant—if you don't mind? Thank you. Now, let's continue. Ready?"

"On the right."

"*What?*"

"You said 'ready,' I said 'on the right.'"

The psychiatrist sighed. "No, Sergeant, I meant: were you ready to continue?"

"Oh, yeah. Sure."

"Very well. Wife."

"Dishonor."

"Fight."

"Kill."

"Army."

"Home."

The psychiatrist scribbled a few sentences in his pad, paused, then wrote a few more words. He said, "Duty."

"Country."

"God."

"Duty."

"Apple pie."

"The girl next door."

The doctor closed his notebook. "All right, Sergeant, that will be all for today."

After two weeks of testing, Terry was called into the Chief Psychiatrist's office and was motioned to a chair.

"Would you like to hear my doctor's reports on you, Terry?"

Terry shrugged. He did not like this place at all. He had not been trained to cope with anything like this. "Is it going to make any difference one way or the other, Colonel?"

The chief shrink hid a smile. He knew no amount of testing and prying would ever break down the barriers around Kovak, but it was his job to try. "It might. Everything depends on your attitude and answers."

"Let's have it."

"Captain Moore does not believe you should be returned to civilian status in your . . . present mental state. He believes shock treatments are in order."

"Colonel?"

"Yes, Sergeant?"

"Fuck you!"

"I really don't care for your attitude, Terry. We're trying to help you here."

"I didn't ask for any help. And I will *not* undergo shock treatments."

"Perhaps you don't have a choice, Terry."

"Oh, I have a choice, Colonel," he smiled. "Believe me, I do. I don't think you're that anxious to die."

The Colonel realized he was one step away from very dark, deep waters. "What do you mean, Sergeant?"

"You punch a button to have guys come in here after me, sir, and I'll take you out first. You'll be dead five seconds after I hear footsteps in the hall."

The two men stared at one another for a full minute. Finally, the Colonel nodded. "All right, Terry." He stood up, pouring them coffee from the pot on a stand by his desk. "Terry, you've got to understand something: you're dangerous; we've got to help you." He jerked his thumb toward the outside. "Those are civilians out there, Terry. They are not warriors—they won't, can't, accept you the way you are. You won't be able to relate to them, nor will they to you. You walk out of here thinking the way you do, and you'll never be able to make a living out there. I've got to make you see that."

"In so many words, then: I'm an animal?"

"I didn't say that. You've been highly trained, programmed to kill, to defend yourself at any cost. But civilian judges and lawyers won't accept that. Oh, it's fine in the movies, Terry. But not in real life. I've got to somehow make you see that."

"I see it, Colonel; I'm not stupid. And I'll work with you, but I won't accept shock treatments."

The Colonel closed the file folder. "All right, Terry. Have it your way. You will allow us to attempt to down-train you through conversation sessions? Good."

"Is it okay to leave here for a few days, Colonel?" Just wander around the city?"

"I don't run a prison here, Terry. Of course, you can. Yes, by all means, do just that. Mix among the hippies and the peace and love crew. It will be interesting to see your reaction."

Terry's reaction was one of disgust. Hairy, dirty people walking around with the American flag sewn to the seat of their pants. He couldn't believe people would have so little respect for their country.

Then, in a small bar, a hippie made a comment about the Vietnam war and the American assholes in the military—career types—fighting it. Uniform lovers. The hippie had several male buddies with him: with beads and beards and ponytails. They made a few remarks about the oppression of youth and the draft and how great LSD was, man.

Terry rose to leave. The hippie grabbed his arm. "Hey, man, don't you like the conversation?"

"Take your hand off my arm."

"Don't get bossy, man."

"Remove it, or lose it," Terry warned him, cold menace in his voice.

The hippie's eyes took in Terry's close-cropped hair. "I bet you're military, man. Hey, guys: dig the white-wall haircut."

And they all laughed.

All except Terry.

Terry tried to pull away from the hippie's grasp, but the young man refused to let go. Terry broke the hippie's arm. His friends jumped into the fray. One would never walk again, and the other would be paralyzed from the neck down. Terry slipped out the back door as the bartender was calling the police. The entire fight had taken less than a minute.

Two hours later, Terry was back in the hospital. "Are you going to call the police?" he asked the Colonel.

"Certainly not! You know that in cases such as these—if we can possibly do it—the military cares for its own. But you see now, Terry: you're overtrained."

"If you say so, sir. When do you want to start on me?"

"In the morning," he smiled. "We held your room for you, Terry. I knew you'd be back. Get something to eat and then get a good night's sleep."

"We may have helped him some," Captain Moore said. "I think we did, in certain areas. He's not nearly as hostile as before, but he's still one of the most dangerous men I've ever dealt with. I . . . I have a guilty conscience about this, Colonel. We—the military—trained him to be what he is. Oh, the potential was there, but we took it and shaped it, molded it, gave it finesse. Obviously, Kovak served his country well. He's a hero, or rather, perhaps, an antihero; that term always confuses me. But now, what do we do?''

''We take a deep breath and release him into the bosom of society,'' the Colonel smiled. A tight smile, without humor. ''Into the arms of those civilians who look down their sanctimonious noses at men who serve their country.''

''Begging the Colonel's pardon, but that isn't very professional. And it doesn't help Terry Kovak. Not at all.''

''What do you suggest, Captain?''

Moore rubbed his hands, pinched at his nose, then frowned. He looked at his chief, grimaced, and said, ''Surgery.''

''What kind of surgery, Captain?''

''You . . . know the type I'm suggesting, sir.''

''You would have a frontal lobotomy performed on a man who has given more than ten years of his life for his country? Who has worked in some of the most difficult areas of shadow warfare, risking his life dozens of times?''

Moore rose to his feet. ''Kovak is dangerous, sir! He's been overtrained. Good Lord, sir, just a few weeks ago Kovak crippled three young men in a bar. . . .''

''No,'' the Colonel cut him short. ''No surgery on Kovak.''

''Then what do we do?''

''Turn him loose. I've signed the papers; he's being processed now.''

''Sir, Kovak can be turned into a useful, productive citizen—it isn't too late.''

The Colonel sighed. ''I have this fading dream of someday meeting a young psychiatrist who isn't an idealist. Kovak has killed many times for his country, Captain. And if he kills out there,'' he jerked his thumb to the outside, ''I'll bet a year's pay he won't get caught. He's a professional.''

''*If he kills out there?*''

''You don't believe some people need killing, Captain?'' the Colonel smiled.

''God, no!''

''Dismissed, Captain.''

Sixteen

"Relax, Mr. Kovak," the VA psychiatrist said, trying to put Terry at ease. "Talk to me."

"Screw you."

"Why are you so hostile today? I thought you were happy with your new job."

"The guy I work for is a prick. A jerk. An idiot. A pompous strutting ass!"

"I gather you don't care for your new employer."

Terry glared at him.

"Why don't you seek other employment, if you feel you can't adjust to your present job?"

"Yeah, I'm gonna do that. Just as soon as I punch this dude out."

"Don't do that, Terry. You've got to learn to control your hostility. You're a civilian now."

"Yeah. Sure. Tell me about it, will you?"

"Mr. Kovak," the job counselor said, "I'm sorry, but I just don't have anything for you. I . . . we can't help you. You're just not qualified for any opening we have. Look, the VA will train you; go back to school.''

"I tried that. It didn't work." Anybody want to hire a used assassin? Comes highly recommended . . .

"I'm sorry, Mr. Kovak."

"It's okay," Terry said. He was getting used to being turned down for jobs. "It's not your fault."

But whose fault was it?

Standing outside the employment office, Terry lit a cigarette and wondered what to do next. He was almost out of money.

"Kovak?" A voice spoke behind him, a somehow familiar voice from his past.

Terry turned. "Yeah?"

Master Sergeant Tate, in civilian clothes. He was grayer, and a bit heavier, but still looked in good shape. Terry grinned, holding out his hand. "Hey, Tate! Damn, it's good to see you."

The two men shook hands. "I've been trying to track you down for two months, Terry. Finally a guy in the Agency said you were spotted down in New Orleans." He grinned. "You gave the Agency people the slip—really pissed certain people off.''

"Yeah, that dude wasn't very good at his job. I got word I was going to be followed from time to time." He shrugged. "I guess certain folks in High Places want to see I stay out of trouble."

"Certain folks in High Places want to see we all stay out of trouble, Terry. I think those certain people wish we'd all fall down dead."

"Colonel Perret?"

Tate shook his head. "He's in rough shape. When he was forced into retirement he lost his guts—or so it seems. Drinks a lot, now. Thinks he might write a book about Dog Teams. Word is he's gonna get zapped if he isn't careful."

"Let's get a drink and talk about this. I don't believe you tracked me down for old time's sake."

Tate grinned. "Now you're talking."

* * *

"So they forced you out, too," Terry swallowed the last of his beer and waved for another round. "What's going on in today's Army, Tate?"

"Politics, buddy—it's the New Army. Oh, there's still some rough units around, but guys like us—no."

"What's on your mind?"

"You're not working?"

"That's right."

"What have you been doing to stay alive?"

"Odd jobs, scut work."

"Can you make it on your disability?"

"If I live in an alley in a cardboard box."

"Any job prospects in sight?"

"Not a one. You?"

"No," Tate sighed. "Hell, what are we qualified to do?"

"I guess we could join the Mafia," Terry smiled.

Tate returned the smile. "Where do we apply?"

The two men sat in silence for a moment as the waitress placed fresh bottles of beer in front of them. "So," Terry said, "what do you have on your mind?"

"Let's go to North Carolina and look up Perret. Let's see if the three of us can't get back into soldiering."

"Hell, man, where?"

Tate swallowed a mouthful of beer and very carefully placed the bottle on the table. "Africa."

"As advisors?"

"As mercenaries, Terry. Do we have any other options?"

Terry drained his beer. He thought briefly of Bishop, Georgia, and his parents. Jill entered his mind and bitterness swept over him. Paula pushed Jill out of the way and finally Sally stood before his eyes. He sighed. "Let's go."

Colonel William Perret (Ret.) looked at his uninvited guests through eyes that were red-rimmed from too much drinking and not enough sleep or food. "You fuckin' guys are nuts!

Africa?'' He held out his hands. ''Look at me. I got the shakes from too much booze and you guys want me to go back into combat? Get out of here, you yoyos!''

''Where's your wife, Colonel?'' Terry asked.

''None of your damned business. Gone shopping.''

She was gone, but not shopping. The house was a mess, dirty clothes tossed about the room. ''She left you, didn't she?'' Terry asked, memories of Jill in his mind.

Perret put his face in his hands and openly wept. Tate and Terry went outside to let the Colonel get it out of his system. The two men sat in the back yard of the secluded country home for more than an hour, talking of old times and wars fought, of friends long dead, dying in some dirty and nasty corner of the world: for their country and its citizens, who, for the most part, did not appreciate their sacrifice. Then Perret appeared in the yard, dressed in old, faded field clothes.

''All right, Sergeants, put me back in shape. Then we'll talk of the Dark Continent.''

''We'll get something to eat,'' Tate said. ''Then we've all got to get back in shape.''

It was April, 1965, when the three men landed at Orly Airport in Paris. Following instructions, they made contact with the Merc recruiter in a quiet bar on a side street, and received their orders and travel money.

''It's a real potboiler over there,'' the man known only as Cricket said. Put your finger on any spot of the map, and there's fighting. Coup after coup. General Happy Jack DeLury said he'd be glad to have you men. I assume you'd like to work together?''

''If at all possible,'' Perret said.

''It's all been arranged,'' Cricket said. ''You will be met in Durban.'' He shook their hands. ''Good luck.''

The men were of many nationalities: French, Belgian, British, South African, American, Portuguese, and others. They were all combat vets of many, many wars, and it would be unfair to call them mercenaries in the literal sense of the word. Soldiers of Fortune; Professional Adventurers. Perhaps they were men who had served their country, gotten out of the military, for whatever reason, and then could not find work. Or simply would not take a lot of guff from a loud-mouthed boss, whose nearest experience to combat was when his wife hit him with a frying pan.

Perhaps the men enjoyed the gut-wrenching impact of combat; for man hunting man is the most challenging hunt of all: the Ultimate High. Mercenaries are not savages—not all of them, perhaps not even most of them. There are many people earning a living in much less honorable ways: a browbeating boss; a shifty used-car salesman; a politician who votes against a bill he knows would be good for the whole country, but who votes against it because it came from the opposition; or a sue-happy lawyer . . . to name a few less honorable occupations.

The men are Ranger and Special Forces trained; Marine and Marine Force Recon; Commandoes; Paratroopers; Special Air Service; French Foreign Legionnaires; Pathfinders; SEALs; Grunts. Many have had no military experience at all: sometimes those make the best mercenaries.

The men had been reared in half-million-dollar mansions and in slums around the world. They are married, single, divorced. There is no such thing as the stereotyped Mercenary. Some are just literate, others have Ph.D's. Some speak one language, others speak half a dozen. They are defrocked priests and homicidal maniacs. But they share one common thought: they know how to fight, and they like it. For the most part, Mercs will stand shoulder to shoulder and not back down. After the fight is over . . . well, that's something else.

Most Mercs will fight against Communism, but some will fight for whatever side picks up the tab. Friend will meet friend in open combat; friend will kill friend in open combat. It doesn't happen often, but it happens.

Mercs are usually left where they fall. Burial is a waste of time. In the bush, wild dogs or hyenas will almost always dig up the corpse and eat it. Sometimes insurance is provided for the Merc—sometimes not.

After a year in Africa, Perret was the first of the three to go. His scout car hit a land mine and blew the Colonel and his driver to blood and shattered bone. Colonel William Perret drifted quietly into Valhalla, to join the centuries of other warriors, and to meet his friends and await the others surely to follow.

It was not a long wait.

Tate took a bullet above the left eyebrow and died without making a sound, going the way warriors and true heroes wish to go, fighting all the way into the foggy unknown.

For nine years, off and on, Terry fought all over Africa: from small teams of Recon to the famed, or infamous, Five and Six Commandoes. Terry moved around, working in Ethiopia, finally drifting to Southern Africa. He no longer possessed any dreams of ever being any more than what he now was: a mercenary. Although only in his mid-thirties, Terry was graying, and his face was lined. It seemed to him he had been a soldier for a thousand years.

Slowly they had been beaten back, fighting impossible odds, taking heavy casualties as they retreated. The Mercs, led by Happy Jack DeLury, had stuck their contracted noses into another civil war and were getting the crap kicked out of them— Terry right in the middle of it.

There had been three teams of Mercs, and Terry was Team Leader of his men. The other teams had split off, heading across country to the airstrip some sixty miles away. But the Rebels controlled the countryside, and Terry had asked the other team not to split up; they didn't stand a chance out there. They had gone ahead, heading across the plains.

None of the forty men would ever be seen again.

Terry's team was resting on the side of the road, waiting for Terry's order to head them out to the airstrip where, hopefully, transport of some kind would be waiting to fly them out. Hopefully.

"Team Leader Kovak!" the voice was full of surprise, horror, and a little fright. "Sarge! Come on, hurry!"

Terry pulled himself wearily to his feet and walked to the young merc standing by the side of the road, pointing into the ditch at an object wrapped in a dirty blanket. "Look, Sarge—what the hell is it?"

Terry looked, blinked, looked again. He could not believe his eyes. The blanket-wrapped object let out a thin, mewing cry; a tiny hand protruded from under the dirty blanket.

"Goddamn!" Terry whispered. "It's a baby!"

He handed his AK47 to the young merc and gently eased into the ditch, being careful where he placed his boots. It could be a trap: the ditch filled with mines.

Nothing happened; the ditch was clean. The little baby was real—Terry could smell the stench of him, or her—where it had fouled itself. He picked the little thing up in his arms and pushed back the blanket from its face. A white baby, about a year old, Terry guessed. Filthy and hungry, almost too weak to cry. Terry stepped back on the road.

"Get the men together and see if we can't come up with a clean T-shirt to wrap this kid in. Somebody find something to eat; mash up some rations and heat it. Somebody heat some water. She . . . him . . . whatever it is, it's got to have a bath."

A huge German merc with a scarred face stepped forward. "Is it really a little baby?" he asked.

"Yeah, Fettermann, it's a little kid."

"I've never held a little baby before," the German said, slinging his weapon. "May I?" he held out his hands.

"Hey, Kraut!" a merc called. "You're too damn ugly to fool with a kid. What are you tryin' to do, give the kid nightmares?"

"Shut up, Lenny," Terry ordered, handing the baby to the huge merc.

"I have a clean undershirt," Fettermann said, smiling at the baby, oblivious to the odors of the child. "I would be honored to let the infant wear it."

"Fine, but first let's bathe it."

Fettermann looked pained. "But what if it's a . . . female?"

"So what? Male or female, it's got to have a bath, doesn't it?"

"I don't think that would be decent if it is a girl."

"Well, hell!" Terry said, a little disgusted. "I'm not going to assault the kid, Fettermann."

Terry took the baby from the German and unwrapped the blanket. Its diapers were filthy and Terry tossed them in the ditch, then wrapped the child in a slightly dirty field shirt.

"It's a girl," Terry said. "Let me think. I seem to remember something about being careful when bathing a little baby girl."

"Why?" a merc asked.

"Well . . . you know . . . it's just different, that's all. I guess that's it."

"I think that is disgusting!" Fettermann said. "Men shouldn't be allowed to view a young female. Terry Kovak, when you bathe the child, we will form a circle, with our backs to you and the girl, and no one will look!" His voice rang with finality.

Terry shook his head and joined the others in laughter. "Whatever you say, Fettermann."

The bathing of the child was quite an event; it was a spit bath at best, using water from the men's canteens. There is something about a small child that calms men—even tough, profane, ornery mercenaries. It was a sight to see. Heavily armed men, with knives, bandoleers of ammo, pistols, and grenades hanging from their web belts, all standing in a circle with their backs to Terry and the kid, Fettermann stating every few seconds, "Don't peek! Don't peek!"

The bath took longer than it should have, because one of the men looked around at the baby and the German boxed him on the side of the head with a huge hand. The blow knocked the merc flat on his back in the middle of the dusty plain.

"Jesus, Fettermann! I was just lookin' at the kid, that's all."

"Animal!" the German growled.

One of the men fixed a bowl of dehydrated field rations and another came up with a can of condensed milk from his pack.

"I like cream with my coffee," he confessed, holding out the can.

"You asshole!" a merc snarled at him.

"That's enough of that!" Fettermann warned. "There will be no profanity around the child."

"That means half the men won't be able to talk," a merc grinned.

"Mother Fettermann," Lenny whispered to Terry. "I hope Happy Jack don't come through here and see this. He'd have us all shot for insanity."

Bathed and fed—after a fashion—loved, and burped, held in the strong arms of the German, the baby—named Abby by the mercs—slept as they marched. That night, Abby slept beside Fetterman.

"No child ever liked me before this," he said. "My scarred face always frightened them."

"Babies don't know what is ugly or beautiful or whatever," Terry said. "They know only gentleness and love. To her, Fettermann, you're a handsome person."

"Das' gut," the German smiled, and patted the baby.

"You're quite a philosopher, Team Leader," a merc said. This merc rarely spoke, and no one knew if Charles was his first or last name, or, really, any part of his name. He never said, and it wasn't a polite question to ask, since many mercs use code names.

"Philosopher?" Terry looked up from his field rations. He shook his head. "I've been called a lot of things, Charles, but never that."

The quiet merc sat down beside Terry and opened a can of field ration. "What's going to happen to Abby, Terry? That is, if we get out of this mess?"

Terry grinned. "Well, if I can get her away from Fettermann, I'll try to turn her over to some church group—maybe the Red Cross. I don't know, really."

"What do you suppose happened to the girl's parents?" Charles looked at the green scrambled eggs in his can, shuddered, then plunged his spoon into the mess and took a bite.

"Killed," Terry chewed his food. "How she got where we found her is anybody's guess. She's just lucky she wasn't raped by the Rebels."

"They would rape a year-old child?"

Lenny laughed. Terry said, "Charles, I've seen four- and five-year-old girls raped—to death. Buggered. You're new to this war; you haven't seen what these Rebels can do—are capable of doing."

"Yeah," Lenny said. "Remember last year, Terry? Or was it two years ago? Whatever. We came up on this farmhouse just after the Commie-backed Rebels hit it. They had whacked off the head of the youngest boy—'bout twelve years old, I guess. Then they tortured the farmer to death, after making him watch about twenty of them rape his wife and daughter—rape, among other things. They took the young girl—'bout sixteen, I guess—out back, shoved a rat up her pussy, tied the lips of her cunt together, and the rat chewed its way out her belly. In the house, they tied the woman up by her wrists, hanging from rafters. They cut off her husband's pecker and balls, shoved his balls up her cunt and tied the lips; shoved his pecker in her mouth, used twine to tie her lips, then killed a stallion in the barn, cut off its pecker, and shoved that up her asshole. They're real nice people, Charles, these Rebels. To hear the American press tell it, they're just fighting for independence." He spat on the ground. "Yeah, sure."

Charles put down his can of ration. "What happened to the woman?"

"She went nuts. Oh, I forgot: they cut off her tits, too."

The mercs rested for a few minutes by the side of the road, under a huge baobab tree, oblivious to the African belief that spirits dwell in the branches. Most of them watched Fettermann, amused at his playing with the baby. A veteran of countless battles, sitting with the baby in his lap, mouthing: "Goo, goo—Da, da," and singing German lullabies to the baby.

At first it was only a buzzing in the sky, then the buzzing became a high whine. The attack came without warning, the jets screaming from the sky, blasting the area with machine gun and rocket fire. A half dozen men were killed in the first run, chopped to bloody meat by the strafing. The mercs ran for the limited cover, Fettermann holding Abby close to his barrel chest.

"Get behind the tree!" Terry yelled at the German. "Watch out for that kid!"

Before the German could make it to the huge tree, a rocket hit some fifty feet to his left, the concussion flipping him like a rag doll, Abby sailing from his arms. Lenny—the sarcastic merc—caught the baby in his arms just as a third jet came roaring past, its guns rattling and pounding. Lenny was a half step too slow in making the tree, and the merc and the kid were cut apart by cannon fire, tossed to the ground in chunks.

The jets screamed away to the East, their damage done. The plains were quiet.

Ten dead, including Lenny. Half of Terry's team. Three wounded, none seriously. Fetterman was stunned, but not hurt. Abby was dead.

"Goddamnit!" a merc cursed. "Why her? She never done nothing to hurt nobody."

Terry looked at the now empty sky. "I think it was Freud who said something like: 'If I ever meet God, I am going to show Him the bone of a child who died of cancer. I will say: Explain this, Sir.' I think it was Freud."

Charles smiled. "Now, how did you know that, Team Leader?"

"I read a lot," Terry replied.

The mercs gathered around what was once Abby. More than one had tears in his eyes. Fettermann picked up the bloody pieces of her and carefully wrapped them in a T-shirt given him by a merc.

"Probably won't do a bit of good," a merc said. "But I'll dig a hole. Maybe if we pack enough rocks around it the dogs won't get her." He walked away, cursing an enemy who would kill a child. As he walked to get an entrenching tool, the merc wondered if, of all the grenades he'd thrown, all the bullets he'd fired, all the bombs he'd set, he had ever killed a child.

The hole dug, Abby placed gently in it by Fettermann, the mercs gathered around, not knowing what to say or do next. The silence grew about them.

"Somebody ought to pray!" a merc blurted, the words odd on his tongue. "Or do something. Don't you-all think?"

Everybody looked at him, astonishment in their war-hardened eyes. *Pray! Yeah, sure, that's right, but you do it.* All but one merc had a funny look in his eyes.

"I don't know no prayers," a Canadian merc mumbled. "Except the one my momma used to say . . . when I was a kid." He shook his head, embarrassed. "I don't remember all of it."

"Team Leader?" the young merc who first discovered Abby said. "Do you believe God hears the prayers of a mercenary? I mean, well, you know, do you?"

Terry shifted his booted feet and looked at the ground, uncomfortable in this new role. "Hell, I don't . . . I don't know! We wouldn't be praying for ourselves—it would be for the baby—right?"

"I'll say a prayer," Charles said quietly, slinging his weapon.

"How come you know a prayer and the rest of us don't?" a merc asked, his tone accusatory, as if being slighted for his lack of a prayer for every occasion.

"Because I used to be a minister," Charles said.

"You used to be a *what?*" Fettermann blurted.

"What in the hell are you doing out here?" another merc popped. "Good Christ!"

"I sinned," Charles said. "I broke my vows to my church and to God, and to my congregation."

"What does that mean?" a merc asked.

"Means he probably fucked the piano player after choir practice."

"Crude, but reasonably accurate," Charles said, removing his beret. "Now let us all bow our heads and ask God to let this child enter Heaven."

Seventeen

1974

Terry looked at his passport: at the word stamped on the inside. REVOKED. The State Department had finally caught up with him.

He had just left the office of the Under Secretary of State. He stood on the sidewalk and looked across the street, first at the Navy Dispensary, then at the building behind that. CIA people used the second building.

"Justice says they are not going to prosecute, Mr. Kovak." He smiled his words with all the charm of the career diplomat. "Because of your fine record in the Army."

"Bullshit!" Terry returned the smile. "You're not going to prosecute me because I know where the bodies are buried, and you realize that, partner."

The Under Secretary's smile faded. "Don't push your luck, Mr. Kovak."

Terry laughed at him.

"Stay out of trouble, Kovak, and in four or five years you may reapply for a visa."

"Partner," Terry spoke his words very slowly, clearly, distinctly, as to leave no doubts, "if I ever want to go back to Africa to fight, I'll just go, and you can stick your visa in your ear. Or in or up any other part of your anatomy."

"Good day, Mr. Kovak. You may let yourself out. Turn in your pass to the guard."

Terry decided to go home. It had been years.

When the door closed behind him, the Under Secretary punched a button on his desk and picked up a phone. "Get me ASA," he said.

Twenty minutes later, a young woman from the Army Security Agency walked in, dressed in civilian clothes. "Yes, sir."

"Kovak," he said. "Terrance Samuel." He handed her a folder.

"I know of him. He was part of those Dog Teams some years back."

A quick grimace of distaste passed over the man's face. "Please, Lieutenant, don't speak those words aloud. Don't even think them. God! If the press ever learned of their existence . . . well, the country has enough troubles without dragging . . . people up again."

"Yes, sir. Whatever you say, sir. My assignment?"

"Keep an eye on Kovak. I've already spoken to your CO— you're now with us for a time. Take as many people as you need. Kovak is one of the last of . . . those men and women in that . . . thing, that organization. Watch him."

"Yes, sir."

"There can't be more than forty or fifty of those people left alive. God, I wish they would all fall down dead."

"They were doing a job for their country, sir," Lt. Joyce Flexner reminded the man.

"A very odious job, Lieutenant, and one we *don't* want to see revived. Understood?"

"Perfectly, sir," she said, thinking: *You ass-kissing bureaucrat. You wouldn't know a real man if one fell on you!*

"Oh, Terry," Momma Kovak kissed her son for the twentieth time in a minute. "Poppa's gone away."

"Gone? Gone where?" Terry disengaged himself from her.

"He's dead, son," the old woman said. "Died almost three years ago. We tried to get in touch with you, but we didn't know where or how. We haven't heard from you in months. You sent money we didn't need, but no letters in all that time."

"Dead!" Terry sat down in an overstuffed chair in the living room of his mother's new home. Their old house was gone; a shopping center covered the entire block.

"How . . . did it happen?"

Mother Kovak looked at her youngest son. He was bigger, rougher-looking, his tan burned deep into his skin. Terry looked mean, even a little cruel, she thought. She poured them coffee. "Heart attack," she said. "The doctor said it was very fast. Massive, he said. Poppa was gone in seconds."

Terry let the news settle on him. "How's everyone else?"

"Danny's dead, too, son. Died last year—no, two years ago, almost. I'm getting old, son, losing track of time and things."

"Danny? How?"

"Car wreck. A big truck hit him head-on, in the rain, just outside of town."

"Vera?" Despite the situation, his confused feelings, Terry could not help but think of Vera, and those nights and days so long ago, so many years past. The memories shamed him.

"She's gone to Chattanooga. Works in a big department store." She looked at her son closely. "Stay away from her, Terry."

He met her level gaze. "Vera talked?"

"Oh, Terry! Don't you think your Poppa and me knew what was going on? We're not—weren't—fools!"

Terry shrugged that he had no reply to make.

"Vera's met a nice man, Terry—a gentleman. They're going to get married. Everyone in the family likes him."

The "gentleman" took him back in time, to a bar in St. Louis. Jill. He sighed. "That's nice, Momma. How is Shirley?"

"She's a doctor now, Terry." She spoke the words softly. "In Atlanta. A baby doctor. You've been gone a long time, son."

"Too long, Momma. Too long. Too many . . . things in my past."

To his surprise, she agreed with her youngest son. "Yes, I think so, too, Terry. You've . . . I don't know: changed so. I don't believe you could ever live here in Bishop again."

"I don't plan on living here, Momma. Just be buried here, that's all."

"We still got the plots, son."

He saw his older brother and his family, but Robert did not seem all that pleased to see him. He finally made his feelings known.

"Never thought I'd see the day when a Kovak would be a soldier of fortune. A goddamned mercenary. What a shitty way to make a living, Terry. I think that's what finally killed Poppa. The FBI came around, asking questions about you."

"Does Momma know?"

"She suspects." His tone was cool.

"Brother, if you don't want me to stay, just say the word and I'm gone."

The two brothers stood in the den of the home and looked at one another. The hostility in Robert's eyes was very plain.

"Maybe that's a good idea, Terry. Maybe you'd better just go."

"See you around . . . brother."

He went to his sister's law offices, but the building was locked. A note on the door said she was on vacation.

Terry drove back to his mother's house, but Robert's car was in the drive, so he did not stop. He drove to Atlanta and checked into a motel. The next week he went to work at a small service station on Peachtree Street. Pumping gas.

Brandy

Terry would see her several times a week from where he worked, as he pumped the gas, checked the oil, fixed the flats, and pointed the way to the restrooms. He would see her when she drove by in the mornings, on her way to work, when she walked to lunch at noon, and when she walked back to her car in the evening. Discreetly, he made inquiries.

"Forget it, Kovak," the manager told him. "That's Louis Cooper's daughter, Brandy. You know, the architect. His kid. She's high-class stuff. She wouldn't want to have anything to do with a bum like you. Besides, she's married."

"Right," Terry said, taking no offense at the man's remarks. "A bum like me." Then he pushed any thought of her from his mind.

Terry didn't have to work pumping gas: he could have held out for years with the money he had stuck away in banks around the world, but the work ethic was deeply instilled in him. He could have gone to college, but he had no desire to do so. He was working at a dead-end job, and didn't really give a damn. The work helped to keep him in shape, paid his rent, and bought his groceries. His car was five years old, but it was paid for and ran well. He drew a check from the government each month, for wounds received in Vietnam, and for holding the Medal of Honor. So Terry got by, even saving a few bucks each week. He was vaguely content, not particularly happy, but, more importantly, he was at peace with himself, longing to fight no more wars. He had not had a cross word with any man in months. He avoided bars and people and parties.

Terry Kovak, the highly decorated war hero, was now a gas pumper. A nonentity. A zero man. Anonymous. Alone.

He would occasionally see his sister, Shirley, and her husband, but he sensed the husband did not like him, did not approve of him or what he had been, so Terry stayed away as much as possible.

He knew he was being watched by several people. The government, he was sure, kept an eye on him. But a local private investigator was also watching him, and he couldn't understand that. Terry toyed with the idea of taking the local PI out some night, rattling the truth from him; but he never really seriously considered that, concluding that the man was only trying to make a living, so what the hell?

It was two weeks before Christmas, cold at dusk. Holiday time in the city.

Ho, ho, ho. Jingle Bells.

A depressing time for those who live alone. The Suicide Season.

"Merry Christmas, mister," the red-suited Santa with the bell in his hand called out.

"Put it in your ear," Terry muttered, then smiled at his Scrooge-like gruffness. He dropped a couple of dollars in the huge pot by the man. It was for a good cause.

He walked toward his apartment, several long blocks away. His second Christmas back in the States, and this one was going to be just as bad as the first one. He turned up the collar of his jacket against the cold winds cutting through the streets of Atlanta. He thought about buying a Christmas tree, then rejected the idea. There were only two presents in his apartment, sitting on a table: one from his mother, one from his sister, Shirley. He had not been back to Bishop in over a year.

Passing a parking lot near where he worked, Terry heard the

sounds of a car refusing to crank, the starter grinding the battery down to a thin protest, then nothing.

"Oh, damn!" A woman's voice drifted to him as the sky began to drizzle. A cold Georgia rain.

Terry leaned against the side of a building, waiting in the darkness, curious as to what the woman would do next.

The car door banged shut. The woman walked around the expensive Cadillac, kicking each tire, punishing the rubber for the engine's failure to start. She spotted the bulk of Terry standing in the darkness, her hand moving to her throat in a gesture of surprise.

"My car won't start," she said. She did not yell the words across the distance, but spoke them just loudly enough for Terry to hear.

He recognized her. Brandy.

"What do you want me to do about it?"

At the sound of his voice, the woman laughed, causing Terry to wonder if she was drunk.

"Fix it," she said.

"You ran the battery down, lady. I can't fix that. Call a garage." Terry moved away from the building, closer to her.

They stood in the darkness, letting the cold drizzle wet them. The ex-Merc turned Gas Pumper and the High-Class Stuff.

"I've seen you before," she said.

"Congratulations."

"Are you going to fix my car, or not?"

"I told you, lady: I can't fix your car. Lady, how do you know I'm not a mugger or a mad rapist?"

"You're Terry Kovak."

"How in the hell do you know that?"

"Everybody knows you, Terry. You're a war hero; a famous mercenary."

'Bullshit! This nation lionizes football players, not war heroes. There aren't three people in this city who know who I am."

"Oh, I know lots of things about you, Terry Kovak. And don't draw any conclusions from that knowledge."

"I stopped drawing conclusions years ago, Brandy."

She laughed in the wet night. "It seems we both did a little checking on the other. You know my name. I'm curious to know why."

"It isn't important. I asked someone about you once. I do know you're married."

"A regrettable but not insurmountable problem. We're separated . . . for the moment."

"If you regret it, why did you marry?"

"It seemed the thing to do at the time. All my friends were getting married."

"What a stupid reason."

"Yes, wasn't it."

Terry moved closer to her. Now only a few feet lay between them—along with a few million dollars, ten years in age, and their alien social worlds.

Brandy made no move to back off as this rough-looking man inspected her in the dim light from a corner street lamp. About five-six, and slender. A good figure. Light brown hair worn shoulder length, framing her face. Her breasts, under her jacket, were high and full. Terry could not see her eyes in the dimness.

"Do you like what you see?" she asked, her voice low and throaty.

"Yeah, very much."

She wheeled about and walked away, head high. She called over her shoulder, "I've done enough slumming for one evening, Kovak. Perhaps we'll meet again."

"Only if you want to."

She stopped and slowly turned to face him, a dozen yards separating them. She behaved as if she did not really want to leave.

"Would you like to know my husband's name?"

"Is it going to impress me?"

"I doubt it," she giggled. "I really do."

"So?"

"J. A. Cater," she smiled across the distance.

Terry began to laugh, softly at first, no more than a chuckle, then it rolled from his belly in booming waves, bouncing around the buildings surrounding the parking lot. Infectious, the laughter caught and held Brandy, until she, too, began to laugh. She walked back over to Terry.

They stood just a few feet apart, the rain coming down harder now, drenching them, holding them in its silvery chill, plastering their hair to their skulls.

"J. A.!" Terry wiped his face and flipped the water from his fingertips. "That sorry ass."

"Terry, even after all these years, he's never forgiven you for taking Bess away from him in high school, or for whipping him that night—years ago."

"He told you all that?" Terry had forgotten the fight.

"Terry, I know lots of things about you." Brandy stood in the rain, looking at him, up at him, her eyes serious. "I know about you getting Clarissa pregnant, years ago."

"What?"

"It's true—you have a son. J. A. heard about it and spread it all over the city. He despises you, Terry. He's told all our friends that the big, bad, brave war hero is now pumping gas for a living."

"What's wrong with pumping gas? It's a good, honest living. Well, honest, at least."

She laughed. "But you could do so much better, Terry. I'll be honest with you: I've wondered for months just how to go about meeting you, but this," she waved her hand at her crippled car, "was a pure accident. I mean that."

"I believe you." Terry stepped closer to her, only inches apart. He looked down at the woman, then touched her face. "You're going to catch cold out here."

"Where is your car?"

"At my apartment, about two blocks from here." He thought of his apartment: barren and spartan; and thought, too, of the worlds that stood between this woman and him.

Too far apart, he cautioned his mind. Worlds—eons apart.

"Will you take me home?" she touched his hand, touching her face.

"If that's where you want to go."

"We'll go to your place first, then we'll go to the lodge out on the lake. I want you to see it. I know you'll love it."

"Taking a chance, aren't you?"

"No, Terry. I know you far better than you think."

"We'll pick up some dry clothes at my place. We'll be soaked long before we get there."

"We can if you want to, but for what I have in mind . . ." she completed her sentence with a smile.

Terry had never seen such luxury as this. It seemed to him to be almost a waste. There was too much of everything for his military mind to accept at first glance. The furniture was low and expensive, leather and soft velvet, with subtly matched drapes and thick carpeting. The paintings were original, with impressive signatures. Terry, dressed in worn jeans and denim shirt, wandered from room to room, taking it all in. Suddenly, he recalled his unspoken promise to his mother—years past— that she, too, would someday have a home such as this; although Carolyn Skelton's home could not in any way compare to this opulence. For a moment, guilt lay heavy on his mind. He hadn't been much of a son, and Terry knew that everything that had happened to him had been his own fault. He could place the blame nowhere else.

Brandy followed him on his stroll through the huge and richly furnished lodge, watching his expression. She did not regret her impulsiveness in inviting him. Although they had just met formally this evening, Brandy felt she knew Terry well: from J. A.'s cursing him to the Private Investigator's report on him, paid for by Brandy—on another impulse. She felt no man could be as bad as J. A. claimed.

Terry's past was checkered, she couldn't deny that, and much of it was in shadows; a tight security blanket that even the experienced PI had backed away from. The fact that Terry had been a mercenary intrigued her. Terry was not what she envisioned a mercenary to be. For all of his violent past, he knew about the classics, fine art, good food, and good music. Brandy wondered where he had learned it.

They stood in the hall and she said, "You have a curious

expression on your face. What's wrong? Do you see something you don't like?''

''I was thinking of my mother.''

''Your mother?''

''Yes, and of an unspoken promise I once made. Years and years ago.''

She swept the surroundings with a wave of her hand. ''That you would build her something like this?'' she smiled.

''How did you know that?''

''Don't most sons make promises like that at one time or the other?'' Her eyes were a soft brown as they studied his face.

Terry shrugged. ''I wouldn't know. I guess so. I sure have failed in my promise, though.''

She took his arm as they walked down the hall. ''You haven't run your course, Terry. Not yet.''

His eyes turned strange; almost, it seemed to Brandy, omniscient, as if he could see behind the veil that screened life from the grave. ''Yes, I believe I have, Brandy.''

She did not pursue that. In the den, she fixed them drinks; she was sure Terry was a bourbon and water man, and she was right. She switched on the radio as an old tune was playing: *The Poor Side Of Town.*

Terry smiled. ''That's an appropriate song for this occasion.''

Brandy spun the dial to a classical music station. Tchaikovsky's Piano Concerto No. One, selections from the Nutcracker Suite: *Tonight We Love.*

''Now then.'' she said as she faced him, ''isn't that much better?''

''Why, Brandy?''

''Why? Why what?''

''Why me? At this time? Do you do this often?''

''Pick up men?''

''Yes.''

''I've never done it before. You're the first. Do you believe that?''

''Yes, but that doesn't answer my question.''

She carried the drinks across the room and sat on the couch.

Terry stood over her. "I've been married six years—six of the longest years of my life. I've listened to J. A. curse you all that time. You became an obsession with me, did you know that? Yes, Terry, people know you're in town. Didn't you read the article in the paper about you last year? Famous war hero, turned mercenary, living in Atlanta?"

Terry shook his head. "No."

"Well, that's when I decided I wanted to meet you. I said you were an obsession with me, but you're also an obsession with J. A. He hates you. I wanted to see you, meet you, that's all."

"Now that you have?"

She looked up at his tanned, hard face. "I . . . don't know, Terry, and that's an honest answer. I don't regret inviting you here, if that's what you mean, and it probably isn't. I'm certainly not afraid of you, but I think J. A. is. I know he's jealous of you."

"Jealous?" It was hard to believe.

"Yes. Terry, you've done everything most men only dream of doing. You're a national hero—the real kind—you've fought wars, been a Soldier of Fortune, traveled the world at your leisure."

"And I haven't got much to show for it, except for a lot of scars and a little money and a mind full of memories."

"But you've proven yourself, Terry, in life and death situations, and you've stood firm. In our macho society, that means a great deal to men, whether they'll admit it or not. Are you going to tower over me all night or are you going to sit down?"

Beside her, he sipped his drink, conscious of her watching him. Abruptly, he rose and walked to the huge picture windows and looked out at the lake, which was being pocked by a heavy rain.

"Soft music," Brandy spoke from the couch, "rain, the two of us alone: the perfect setting for romance, and you haven't even tried to kiss me. Should I change my deodorant or am I just not your type?"

Terry faced her, lightning from the storm flashing behind him giving him a much more menacing appearance. He smiled, and his eyes softened. "I'm wondering where all this is going to lead."

"Does it have to lead anywhere?"

"At this point in my life, yes. If it doesn't, then what is the purpose?"

"My God! The man's a philosopher."

Her words carried him back in time, to an African *veldt* and a former man of God turned mercenary, for his real or imagined sins. Charles had once called him a philosopher—just before Abby was killed. Terry wondered where all those men were at this point in time? He wondered if the wild dogs had dug up Abby and eaten her.

"I've lost you again," Brandy said, her voice soft against the drum of rain on the roof.

Terry crossed the room and sat beside her. "You never had me."

She touched his face, leathered by years of harsh sun and hot winds. Her cool fingers touched the scar on his forehead, another on his cheek. "Take me to a bedroom and make love to me, Terry."

There was sadness on his face and in his eyes. "Just like that?"

"Just like that."

The stormy night stretched on toward morning; the rain continued to fall, battering the lodge. Lightning ripped the sky. The bed sheets were damp and rumpled, the lovers just awakening from a sex-induced sleep. Brandy kissed his face, touched his body.

"That's the first time sex has been good for me in a long time. It turned really bad with J. A."

Terry lit cigarettes for them. "How long have you and Cater been separated?"

She glanced at him, humor in her eyes. She blew smoke to cover her smile. "One day."

Terry sat up in bed. *"One day?"*

"Yes. I have to warn you: my parents probably won't like you very much."

"I wasn't aware I was going to meet them," he said.

"Oh, yes, Terry. Certainly, you are. There is a small get-together at the club tomorrow evening. Cocktails from five to seven. Dinner at eight. I'd like you to escort me."

Terry was speechless for a few seconds. When he found his voice he said, "You've been separated for one day and you want me to date you? Have you lost your mind? Take *me* to a Country Club? Brandy, look at my hands—I've got callouses on top of callouses. I'm a working man, for years a professional soldier. Hell, I don't fit in with those people."

"You fit in very well with me," she smiled in the dim light.

"You know what I mean."

"You've made up your mind you won't like my friends. How do you know you won't?"

"I don't like pretension and I don't like candy-ass men. I'll bet seventy-five percent of the men there would be selling pencils on some street corner if it wasn't for their father's money."

"Well," she snuggled closer to him, "you're right about that." Her nakedness was warm against him. "Do you own a suit, Terry?"

Her words threw him back in time, to a Memphis street where another woman had asked him the same question. He thought of Paula and wondered how she was getting along. And how his daughter was doing? She would almost be grown by now, and he had never seen her. Now the news that he had fathered another child: a son. Damn, I'm sure leaving a string of woods' colts around the country.

"No, I don't own a suit, and you're not going to buy me one, either."

"Male pride at work," she laughed, her breath hot on his bare shoulder.

"Perhaps."

"First thing this morning, I'd like you to buy a nice dark-gray pinstriped suit, vested. And all the accessories to go with it. Conservative clothes. Will you do that for me?"

He nodded in the dim light of the bedroom.

"Good. You're the type man who can buy clothes off th rack and look wonderful in them."

"Yes, dear."

She laughed at his words. "You already sound like a marri man. Better get used to it, Terry. I have plans for you—f both of us."

He did not reply. Suddenly he was very tired. He'd bee tiring more easily of late, and it worried him. He'd always bee such a powerful, virile man. If these sudden bursts of fatig continued, he'd have to get a check-up.

BOOK FOUR

Eighteen

The women in the room—most of them—felt drawn to him in a peculiarly sexual manner, both drawn to him and repelled by him. The man with Brandy moved like a big cat, totally sure of himself. His eyes took in all the men in the room and, one by one, checked them off his hidden danger list. In case of conflict, none of the males present would pose any problem, for they were soft, without necessarily being fat—mentally soft. He doubted any of them had ever heard a shot fired in anger. If they had ever fought, it had been the step-over-the-line-and-I'll-punch-you type. None of them, Terry was sure, had ever had to prove himself to the breaking point.

Terry dismissed them all.

The men in the room did not like him. Whether they would admit it or not, Terry made them feel slightly uncomfortable, causing them to move a bit closer to their wives: the mother-longing. Breast-feeding. Security. To many of the men, Terry reminded them of their drill sergeants in the Army, and *he* always made them feel like idiots. No, the men in the room did not like Terry—not at all.

For those who have just a bit of worldliness in them, and know what to look for, professional warriors have a certain aura about them. Women pick up on that aura much more quickly than men, perhaps because women are the more mercenary of the species.

"Who *is* he?" Brandy's mother leaned close to her husband and whispered the question.

"He works at a gas station across from my office building." Louis Cooper said the words flatly, and his wife looked at him with something akin to horror in her eyes.

"My God, Louis!" She touched his arm. "You are joking, aren't you?"

"No. I did a little checking this afternoon, after Brandy dropped the news in my lap. I will admit I was rather stunned for several moments. His name is Terrance Kovak. He was a career soldier—quite a hero—until he was severely wounded in Asia. Then he was a mercenary for a number of years, in Africa. Mr. Kovak does not have to pump gas for a living, and I rather doubt he will after tonight. He has an abnormally high IQ, speaks several languages, and, when aroused, has the disposition of a pit viper. He graduated from high school up in Bishop, Georgia. You may recall, this is the Terry that J. A. hates so."

She looked at Terry. "I doubt Mr. Kovak loses much sleep over that."

"Brace yourself, dear, we're about to be introduced to our daughter's new love. Brandy says she's going to make an honest man of him—whether we like it or not."

Mrs. Cooper studied Terry from across the room. "He does carry himself well, Louis . . . in a tough sort of way, and he is attractive. We may as well make the best of it, don't you think?"

Louis Cooper glanced at his wife and sighed.

Brandy's parents didn't like him. Terry picked up on that immediately and was not at all surprised by it. Hell, why should they like me? he thought. They're big-deal society folks and I'm just an ex-merc turned laborer.

His eyes fascinated Mrs. Cooper. So cold and utterly void

of expression. Such a pale, icy blue. They've seen most of what the world has to offer, she thought, and been disappointed or disillusioned by it. He's out of place here, but conducting himself with grace. She took his offered hand. A hard hand, but gentle with hers.

"Mr. Kovak," Louis said, shaking his hand. "I've heard J. A. speak of you often."

"Yes," Terry smiled. "I'm sure you have."

"Brandy tells me you are . . . ah . . . employed in the gasoline industry?" He was uncomfortable after the question, not because he may have made a socially unacceptable blunder, but because of the hot look shot at him by his daughter. He glanced at his wife and there was anger in her eyes as well.

"You mean, I pump gas at a small service station?" Terry laughed.

The father met him head on. "I won't back away from it, Mr. Kovak. But the point is: you do. The question, at least to my way of thinking is: why?"

"Call me Terry, Mr. Cooper. As to my job, well, it's a living."

"A poor one at best, and my daughter is worth a great deal of money."

Terry's smile was tight. "She looked me up, Mr. Cooper. Not the other way around."

The other guests at the Club stayed away from the tight circle of Mother and Father, Daughter and Interloper, none of them wishing to utter what might later be taken as a social *faux pas*. If there were sudden and hot words among the quartet, then the guests would pick the Interloper apart with arrogance and ostracism. If he was accepted, social codes demanded that they, too, accept him. Terry was standing in the center of a mine field: a perfumed, coiffured, cologned, dinner-jacketed, evening-gowned no man's land.

"I won't have my daughter being seen around town with a common laborer," the father's words were cold, backed by generations of old money.

"Laborers build the structures you design," Terry's gaze

did not waver, and his words were of the same timbre as the older man's: clipped and icy.

"I won't argue that," Cooper's nod of agreement was slight, "but my statement still stands."

"Okay," Terry grinned. "How about an unemployed mercenary?"

"Personally, I feel that is on the bottom of the social scale." The father could not help but feel some admiration for Terry's steady gaze. Louis smiled. "Be at my office at nine in the morning. I'll . . ."

"I will not go to work for you, sir. Period. I think nepotism is the ugliest word in the dictionary."

Male eyes met in half-hostility. Locked. The father said, "Would you object if I merely dropped a word or two on your behalf."

"I guess not."

"Good. Now, let's see about getting you something to drink, Terry. You don't strike me as a scotch man. I believe bourbon and water is your drink."

And while their husbands stood around and silently hated Terry, the wives moved toward him.

For the first time in many years, Terry was truly happy with a woman he was growing to love and to know she loved him. With each passing month his happiness grew until he thought surely it must show on his face, in his step, in his actions. He had enrolled in a small business school, preparatory to filing with the SBA for a loan to start his own business. He knew weapons, and understood the out-of-doors, so he would start there, with a small sporting-goods store. If all went well, he could enlarge later.

Terry was happy. Happy with Brandy; happy with his life; happy with the knowledge that he longed to fight no more wars. His fatigue still bothered him, and, very quietly, without Brandy knowing it, he went to see his sister.

"I'm so happy for you, Terry," Doctor Shirley Preston said, as she took his blood pressure, listened to his heart, and took blood from him to be sent to a lab. "I think you're healthy as a work horse, but I'll send this off—just to be sure."

"When will you have the results?"

"Oh, in three or four days. I'll call you. In the meantime, you and Brandy come out to the house for dinner tonight. I want you and Ken to really get to know each other. You two got off to a bad start at first." She touched his arm. "Give it a try, will you, Terry? Try to like him?"

"Okay," he smiled, kissing her on the cheek.

A week later she called him back for more tests. Just to be on the safe side, she said.

Terry faced his sister in her office. Her face was pale and her hands were trembling. "You better sit down, Terry."

"I'll take it standing up, Sis. Give it to me straight, now. Don't beat around the bush."

Her medical decorum crumbled and she flung herself in his arms, crying. He held her for a moment, patting her shoulder, until she pulled away and put her hands over her face, trying to control her tears. She wiped her eyes with a Kleenex, patted her hair, then faced her brother.

"It's . . . leukemia, Terry. And it's pretty well advanced."

He sat down in an office chair, hands gripping the arms. "Is it treatable?"

"Of course, Terry." But her answer came too quickly for him to believe it.

"I know there's all kinds of leukemia, Sis—some worse than others. What kind is this?"

"Myelogenic."

He forced a grin. "What the hell is that? Sounds like something for gas."

"It's a type produced in, or by, the bone marrow, Terry. I want to refer you to a specialist here in Atlanta. He . . ."

"No!" his reply was flat, final.

"Terry, my God! We're talking about your life."

"My life is over and you know it, Sis. Don't kid me; I'm an old curly wolf who is about to see the varmint, and I know it."

She shook her head; she knew her brother too well to argue. "All right, Terry, whatever you say."

"How long do I have?"

"I don't know, Terry. A year, maybe. Six months, perhaps. We may be able to sustain you longer than that. Won't you let us try?"

"No, Sis. I will not die as a vegetable." He stood up and kissed his sister. "Shirley, I have about twenty-five thousand dollars in banks overseas. I'll make arrangements to have that sent to you. Give it to mother."

"Terry . . ."

"Hush up," he said it gently. "You're certain about this leukemia?"

"Yes," she wiped her eyes as the tears came again. "That's why I called you back for more tests. There is no doubt."

"I'm being destroyed from within?"

"Yes."

"All right, then. I've got things to do." He kissed her cheek. "I won't see you again, Shirley: I hate goodbyes, so you say them to the family for me. I've got a lot of phone calls to make and some things to set up. When my . . . body is shipped back to the States—if it is—I want a very quiet funeral. No big deal. I do not want a military funeral. Bury me in Bishop. I deserve that punishment for all I've done in life."

He pushed his sister from him. "Goodbye, Shirley."

She met his bravery. "Goodbye, Terry."

He walked out the door.

"Goddamnit, Terry!" Brandy yelled at him as he packed a few clothes. "Will you at least tell me what I've done? Why you're leaving?"

"You haven't done anything, Brandy. I love you—I truly do. But I have to go." He could not, would not, tell her of his illness. If he did, he knew she would insist he stay, spending his final days in a hospital bed, wasting away into nothing. He did not want to go out in that manner. He wanted to die among warriors, among men who knew what life was all about, who faced it, met its challenge, and died on their feet, with smoke around them, snarling and biting.

"You *bastard!*" Brandy cursed him. "Father was right all the time. You're no good. You can't face responsibility, can't take it, can you? When the going gets rough, you cut out."

"If that's what you want to believe, Brandy."

She sat down on the bed, then jumped up and walked to the door. "God, I hate you!"

"That's too bad. I love you."

She began to cry. "Love? If you loved me you'd stay, work this thing out—whatever is bothering you."

"You'll hear from me, Brandy. I can promise you that."

"Oh, wonderful. I can hardly wait." She walked out of his spartan apartment, slamming the door.

Nineteen

Not many people attended the funeral.

Terry Kovak had been a loner while alive; now, he was almost alone in death.

It was a cold afternoon in early November, a light rain adding to the misery of the moment.

Inside the small chapel of the funeral home, only a few tears dripped and fell down various cheeks: Terry's mother, his brother, his sisters, their husbands, and a few of their children. Terry's daughter, whom he had never met. Five women without men sat in the rear of the chapel, slightly apart from each other, each grieving for Terry in their own way.

The small children in the chapel sat silently, somewhat in awe of death, but too young to really comprehend the finality of it. They fidgeted inwardly, wishing all this solemn stuff would hurry and get over with, 'cause there was a football game on TV that afternoon. Bad enough we have to go to church and listen to a bunch of stuff about sin, now we have to sit in this spooky place half the afternoon.

One of Terry's nephews walked up to the casket and looked at the picture of his uncle on the closed box. Terry in his Army uniform, beret cocked jauntily, a slight smile on his lips. The young man just barely remembered his uncle.

Outside the chapel, the cold North Georgia rain began falling harder, pounding the roof. This winter was going to be a bad one. Everyone said so.

Terry's brother, Robert, walked to the casket to stand by his son. He put his arms around the young man's shoulders as he looked at the face of his brother in the 8×10.

I never really knew you, Terry, he thought. I'm sorry we quarreled the last time we met.

One of the five women seated in the rear of the chapel, away from the immediate family, rose and walked to the casket. She had thought there were no more tears left in her but, looking at his picture, Brandy began to cry.

Mother Kovak, in her late seventies and bothered with arthritis, painfully pulled herself out of a chair and hobbled to her son's casket. She touched Brandy's arm.

"Terry broke with the Church when he was just a boy. So far as I know, he never went back. I suppose God will forgive him."

"Do you believe God is good and understanding?"

"Yes, of course," the old woman said.

"Terry's alright," Brandy reassured the woman, wanting desperately to believe her own words. According to Terry's letter, he had found God at the end. Or at least had talked to Him, if not with Him.

"Were you in love with Terry?"

"Yes," Brandy turned away from the casket, walked to the rear of the chapel, and took her seat with the other women.

"I can't bear to even look at his picture," one of the women whispered. "Not yet." She held out a gloved hand and Brandy took it. "Jill Slane," she said.

"Terry spoke of you," Brandy said. "And not unkindly."

Brandy introduced herself to Jill and to the other two women and the younger woman. Paula and her daughter, Patsy. And the woman who introduced herself only as Joyce. Somehow Joyce was military in appearance: erect carriage, even when sitting, calm eyes, short hair. She spoke very little.

There, in that somber place, the five women looked at each other while the Kovak family looked at them and wondered what was going on.

"Let's get out of here," Brandy said. "Go somewhere and get a drink."

"I'm staying," Patsy said. "I want to spend as much time as possible with my real father. I'll see you all back at the motel."

"She drove over from Memphis in her own car," Paula explained.

"I only passed one bar in this town," Jill said. "Full of rednecks."

"Let's buy a bottle and go back to the motel," Brandy said. "We have to be staying at the same motel; it's the only one in town."

"Let's go," Jill said. "I've traveled a long way to get here, and I've bawled and blubbered half the way. I'm going to come unglued if I stay here much longer."

"Coming, Joyce?" Paula asked.

The silent woman shook her head. "No."

In Brandy's room, the women looked at the box sitting on a dresser, lid open, a black beret in the box.

"When I got that in the mail," Brandy explained, "I knew he was dead. My father said he'd gone back to Africa, to fight as a mercenary." She looked at the women. "I got a phone call telling me Terry was dead and when he was to be buried, but the caller refused to give his name. How about you-all?"

"Same way," the women replied. "Odd."

In the motel room, on that sleety day in Bishop, Paula said, "A little while ago, you said something about a letter from Terry. Would you read it to us, if you don't mind?"

The fifth of whiskey was almost empty, the room was filled with cigarette smoke, the women's voices husky from smoke, booze, and conversation.

"Of course," Brandy said. "I think Terry would have wanted that."

She took the letter from her purse. All could see that it had been read many times. The paper was creased and lined from use. Brandy read it softly, gently, trying very hard to keep her voice from breaking.

Brandy, my darling,

By now I'm sure you know why I left you the way I did. I didn't mean to run out on you, not at all. But neither did I think it fair to either of us to have you witness my transformation from whole man to someone too weak to feed himself. I believe I spared you a great deal of anguish, and myself an equal amount of humiliation.

I love you, Brandy. I'm quite certain I've never loved anyone or anything more—that includes my God, whether He be great roaring thunderer, or gentle lamb, or, indeed, if He even exists—or, if He does, whether He even knows me after all I've done.

I love you. Always believe that. Or, rather, loved you. Past tense, now.

I believe we could have made it, Brandy. And it is because of that knowledge that I can go out to see the varmint with a certain feeling of happiness.

Don't mourn my passing, Brandy, because the day is ending for men like me. Values are changing in America; warriors are becoming a thing of the past, and that leaves a bitter taste in my mouth. I should have been born a hundred years ago but, had I been, I would not have met you.

Ah, well.

I will never be convinced I did anything wrong in my career in the military. I did what I had to do for my country, and I believe I was true to my level of patriotism, conscience, and to whatever God listens to warriors.

As for my years as a mercenary—there again: no apologies. I fought for freedom: my interpretation of that word, at least, and I see no wrong in that. Brandy, what is a mercenary? Surely one must call Lafayette and Kosci-

usko by the same name, and where would America be if not for those men, and others like them?

This letter is difficult for me, Brandy, because I know, I sense, this will be my last letter. I've always been on the other side of death, now I must accept the fact that death is something we all must face—and face it alone.

I don't believe God cares much for cowards, and, as far as I'm concerned, for me to start calling on Him now, when I'm about to die, would be an act of cowardice. I may be a lot of things, dear, but I'm not a coward. There is much about life I did not understand. Perhaps I will comprehend it in death?

No, for me, Brandy, for men like me, I don't know if the God you worship will have us. I have to believe in Valhalla. I hope that is true; I would prefer Valhalla. Yes, a place where real warriors from the beginnings of time can sit at the feet of Odin and Thor for the next thousand millenniums, talking of true heroism and battles fought. Without the presence of Paper Tigers. I have talked to your God of this place, Brandy. I hope He heard me.

One thought of your Heaven amuses me, Brandy. That is the picture of myself, perched upon a cloud, dressed in a flowing white robe, plucking on a harp, while bands of Angels drift stately by, singing celestial songs, being conducted by someone who looks like Lawrence Welk.

No, my darling, that is not for me. I believe God Himself created Valhalla, for I remember—so many years ago—the Priest saying that God liked his warriors. Yes, and as penance for our earthly sins, we'll probably have PT twice a day—forever.

Now I must go and fight my last battle. Perhaps then I can rest.

Always remember: I did love you so very much.

Terry

Twenty

Lieutenant Joyce Flexner, after making her final report on Terry Kovak to the Under Secretary of State, reported in to General Brasher at the Pentagon.

"You saw the body, Lieutenant?" he asked. "Personally?"

"I saw it, sir. Or what was left of it. He died awfully hard. The Rebels tortured him for hours. It was a closed-casket funeral, but I got to see the body while the mortician worked on it."

"You're certain it was Kovak?"

"Yes, sir."

The General leaned back in his chair. "Well, that's that, then. We can close another file. Kovak killed in Africa while working as a mercenary. Thank God, most of those Dog Team people are dead."

A faint smile crossed the woman's lips, coming and vanishing before the General could see it. On her own desk were the papers approving her volunteering for a new, super-secret group being formed by the combined military. She was due to start her training next week. In Maryland.

She hid her smile. "You're certain the Dog Teams are all through, sir?"

"Not really," he folded his hands across his pot belly. "If the military finds enough of the right people, and the right man to lead those people," he shrugged, "who knows?"

Epilogue

At an Army Fort in the Northwest, a young man reported in to his battalion, was assigned to his barracks, and began to settle in. He had just completed many months of brutal training, earning his black beret. He was a tall young man, with very blond hair and very cold, pale, icy eyes.

His top-secret personality profile read: "as having the mental and physical capabilities to be most dangerous."

His CO read his profile with interest, then looked closely at the accompanying photograph. "Damn," he said, "this kid looks just like a bad dude I used to soldier with. The resemblance is uncanny." He glanced at the Sergeant Major. "Find out where he's from, will you, Van? Knowing Number Five, he must have left some bastards scattered around. Maybe this is one of them? If he is, we've got the makings of an ace special team. You read the directive from Sugar Cube. Every special unit got one: Marine Force Recon, SEALs, Special Forces, Rangers, Air Force Commandoes."

The Sergeant Major's eyes shone with interest. "Yes, sir; I heard rumors about reactivating the old Dog Teams."

"Yes, I forgot, Van, you worked with Perret, didn't you."

"Yes, sir, and with Kovak. Back in the fifties, when I was a young buck. Just like you, Colonel."

"Yeah," the CO leaned back in his chair and his eyes faded just a moment, remembering brave men, hard discipline, gunsmoke, and better days. "I wonder how many of the old bunch is left?"

"How you doing, Corporal?" the Sergeant Major asked the young Ranger.

"Pretty good, Sergeant Major. I've been looking forward to coming out here."

"We're glad to have you. Got some good reports on you. You were supposed to have reported here six months ago, then your orders were changed. Where have you been all that time?"

"Maryland."

The Sergeant Major smiled. "That's interesting. What made you want to be a Ranger?"

"My mother knew an Army Ranger a long time ago. She spoke of him often." He smiled, the ice in his eyes melting for just a moment. "I guess maybe I was born to be a soldier."

"Where's your home, soldier?"

The smile faded and the ice returned. "Well, my mom died three years ago, and my dad said he didn't want me around. Said I wasn't his kid and he'd be damned if he'd spend any more money on me. So I ran off."

"Tough break."

The young Ranger shrugged. "Well, I guess the Army's my home, Sergeant Major, but I was raised in Bishop, Georgia."

WILLIAM W. JOHNSTONE
THE ASHES SERIES

ALSO BY WILLIAM W. JOHNSTONE . . .

DREAMS OF EAGLES   (0-8217-4619-7, $4.99/$5.99)

EYES OF EAGLES   (0-8217-4285-X, $4.99/$5.99)

HUNTED   (0-7860-0194-1, $5.99/$6.99)

TALONS OF EAGLES   (0-7860-0249-2, $5.99/$6.99)